Jane Mendelsohn

Burning Down the House

Jane Mendelsohn is the author of three previous novels,
including *I Was Amelia Earhart*, a *New York Times* best-
seller and a finalist for the Orange Prize; *Innocence*; and
American Music. A graduate of Yale, she lives in New
York City with her husband and children.

www.janemendelsohn.com

Burning Down the House

Burning Down the House

JANE MENDELSOHN

VINTAGE CONTEMPORARIES
Vintage Books
A Division of Penguin Random House LLC
New York

The Library of Congress has cataloged the Knopf edition as follows:
Mendelsohn, Jane.
Burning down the house / by Jane Mendelsohn. — First edition.
pages ; cm
I. Title.
PS3563.E482B87 2016   813'.54—dc23   2015018821

Vintage Books Trade Paperback ISBN: 978-1-101-91119-8
eBook ISBN: 978-1-101-87546-9

Book design by Cassandra J. Pappas

www.vintagebooks.com

Printed in the United States of America
10 9 8 7 6 5 4 3 2 1

To
Ann Close,
editor and friend,
and to
Lily, Grace, and Nick

When I came home to West Egg that night I was afraid for a moment that my house was on fire. Two o'clock and the whole corner of the peninsula was blazing with light, which fell unreal on the shrubbery and made thin elongating glints upon the roadside wires. Turning a corner, I saw that it was Gatsby's house, lit from tower to cellar.

—F. SCOTT FITZGERALD, *The Great Gatsby*

I will write my name in fire red.

—JEAN RHYS, *Wide Sargasso Sea*

And after the fire, a still small voice.

—I KINGS 19:12

Burning Down the House

PROLOGUE

I T BEGINS with a child. She lives far away from any city, high up in the mountains. She sits by a fire. Light turns in crazy pinwheels on her soft young cheeks. Wind blows and the moonlit clouds go wild, an armada of wayward ships. Her mother and her father are close by, talking quietly in a tone that could be ominous or soothing, depending on the words, which she cannot understand. Her father says something and her mother begins to cry. The girl pulls her legs up and rests her chin between her knees.

Her father comes over and sits next to her. I remember the day you were born, he says. I swore then that I would always take care of you. He wraps his arms around the girl and holds her tightly. Life is not very long, he tells her. I want you to have everything.

The recruiter had come by when the child was getting water. She was off by the river, with her laughing friends. He seemed to know the area, the family, the girl. He spoke their language and promised safety and good work. He wore a shining watch

and carried a leather wallet and showed the couple a picture
of a restaurant where the girl could get some work. He pulled
the photo out from between a wad of bills. The man and the
woman were not sure what a restaurant was, but they were
too amazed by the recruiter and the bills and the gleaming
diner in the photograph to ask him any questions other than
when.

When is tomorrow.

At ten years old she is taken away. Never again will she see the
swollen sun rise over the hillside behind the hut. The snowy
ashes in the fire pit, the skinny dog. She is taken in a direction
she has never been, a passenger across the landscape, a wisp of
information traveling through the air. She moves up and over
the mountain range, past reindeer, gnarled trees, through
a fog tinged with a piney scent that she has known all her
life and that she takes for granted as the smell of being alive.
She follows the recruiter down and down and down. The trip
takes days. At the bottom of the mountain the scent is gone.
A car is waiting for them. They glide through the countryside
as if on water. Later a city materializes beyond the window,
silhouettes of buildings against a smoggy sky, a demented network of streets and screeching commerce through which she
tumbles like a coin or a broken bit of code, looking for something to attach herself to, to make some meaning.

On Tverskaya Street the women are called Butterflies. The
recruiter tells the girl not to talk to them, that she will be
going somewhere much better, a special place. He keeps her in

the back room of a liquor store, and he brings her salty sandwiches and candy.

Two days later she is on a boat. At the crowded port cranes rise up like gargantuan metal insects against the glowing sky. The water in the river sloshes green and oily. On Tverskaya Street she realized quickly that the recruiter did not have her interests at heart, even when he took her to buy some clothes, even when he fed her the candy and sandwiches. But it was hard to reconcile that understanding with the knowledge that her parents had sent her off with him for her own benefit. When he says goodbye to her briefly, offhandedly, on the ship in the liquid predawn light, she is not sorry to be rid of him, but when she sees her new handler with his dead eyes and his many piercings from his brows to his nose to his cheeks to his lips, she understands that the recruiter had treated her kindly. This new chaperone does not even speak her language. What he communicates is by gesture and force.

She learns on the crossing that she is not supposed to resist the men who come to her at night. She rises up like some demon from the dead when they try to touch her but although she is tenacious she is not big. She has a strong face, beautiful but not pretty. Her eyes are intelligent and curious and still innocent although less so with each day of the crossing. She tries to fight with her fists, her knees, her nails, her teeth. She becomes a better fighter but is still no match for the parade of men. There is a grunting regularity to their visits. When she is not lost in the mystical elsewhere in her mind that she conjures to escape the daily brutality of this new life, she will occasionally catch a glimpse of their fat hungry faces and feel that, although nature as she has known it is beautiful and pure, the world is ugly and mankind unapologetically vicious.

One night a visitor comes to her with a gun. He wants to enjoy her while pointing the gun to her head the entire time. Thrashing to escape the barrel against her skin she is shot twice: once in the arm and once not far from her heart. The man races out of the cabin with his shirt smeared with blood and his pants in his hand. She lies on a sheet drenched in red, and her thin frame shudders. She feels nothing but an eerie peace.

The chaperone screams at her and finds a doctor who will care for her without asking any questions. The doctor comes often and she looks forward to his visits. He makes sure she is given proper food. Over the course of three weeks, as the ship stops at ports along its way, she recovers steadily and the doctor is pleased with her progress. The chaperone arranges to meet the doctor on the deck of the ship in the early morning to pay him as promised for his services. But the chaperone does not intend to pay. The chaperone greets the doctor with a knife and the doctor sees the steep side of the boat slanting against the rising sun as he bobs in the water before he sinks.

Now the child is no longer a child. She has been turned inside out and has felt her childhood cascade from her like the liquid and seeds of a fruit pouring into the garbage, the pure beginning of life discarded, a useless muck. She is allowed to walk on the deck to assist in her recovery. The passengers eye her skeletal shape and see no meat. She breathes in the ocean air. She looks at the rolling gray. She thinks about jumping overboard but for the moment her physical weakness is her salvation: she is too exhausted to kill herself.

When they pull into the port of their final destination she is presented to a new handler, another entrepreneur in this chain of small businessmen. As soon as they are away from the crowd and unseen he hits her to make absolutely certain she knows that he controls her. You are my property, his fists say. She has nowhere, has never had anywhere, to go.

They drive through the monotonous streets of a new city. She is no longer fascinated by the teeming life or the variety of people. As night falls they cross a bridge strung with lights and each light seems to her like a captured star wishing to return to the sky. Within a week she is living in the back of a spa in a strip mall. Her boss is a woman with an enormous forehead and tiny eyes, a cap of black hair and a slicing voice. Men come to the salon, which in the window advertises STRESS REDUCTION. Sometimes the girls, for the girl is not alone, get driven in a van a few miles away to a large hotel. She moves through her days with a determination not to die that comes from where she has no idea. Maybe the bad music that is always playing. Maybe the computer in the boss's room. Maybe those sounds and machines give her the sense that there is another life, another frequency or signal that if only she could grasp it would pull her through a hole in time or space back to where the stars are not strangled by invisible strings and instead free to move continually, fluidly, up above. She sees girls covered with cuts and others beaten blue and another one hang herself with a pair of jeans.

———

She is used by men from all walks of life and given drugs by the woman with the cap of black hair. A customer who says he loves her gives her extra cash every week. She hides the money and fights more fiercely with the drugs than she fights anymore with the men. She wins. She beats the drugs. She takes an action to change her life. In the year 20— when she is seventeen years old she runs away and rides a bus through the dead fluorescent glow of the Lincoln Tunnel into the mirrored darkness of New York City.

PART ONE

The Necessary Condition

He had told her, the first evening she ever spent at Gardencourt, that if she should live to suffer enough she might some day see the ghost with which the old house was duly provided. She apparently had fulfilled the necessary condition.

—HENRY JAMES, *The Portrait of a Lady*

THEY ALWAYS CELEBRATED important family events out of town, usually in another country. Here they were in a black car as it sped along the highway, now turning onto a side road, disappearing and emerging from under trees like a blinking light on a Global Positioning System screen moving across a continent. The tinted windows flickering with shadows and reflections, sparks dancing against the glass. From the outside, the family riding in the car was difficult to understand, the way the movements of a fire, even when viewed within the safe confines of a fireplace, seem random and uncontrolled. However, inside, from amid the licking flames of its interlocking relationships, the Zane family made its own fantastical sense. All families are complicated, but because they constitute the primary reality in which their members live, some families create a world that is more comprehensible to them than the world itself.

From the point of view of the fire in the fireplace, the living room appears extraordinary, disorienting, and obscure. And the unexpected lashings of the blaze feel comfortable, ordinary, and known.

———

This time Jonathan had flown his driver over, so Vlad was taking Jonathan, Miranda, and Alix from the airstrip to the house in the same car. It was awkward for Alix because she had been conscious of the tension between her brother and his fiancée ever since they had begun their journey and they had been journeying for a long time: from New York to London, and then from London on a smaller plane, and now in this sedan, here, on a road in the British countryside lined with ancient trees whose branches and leaves so loose and careless reminded Alix of one of Jonathan's silk ties, flung casually over his shoulder as it was at this very moment. She sat next to Miranda, while Jonathan had opted to sit up front with Vlad. Alix and Jonathan had two much-younger half brothers, nine-year-old twins, and Miranda had recently discovered that Jonathan was sleeping with their nanny. Miranda had threatened to call off the wedding, was still threatening, convincingly, to leave tomorrow and head to Sardinia where some friends had a place, but Jonathan had talked her into coming this far and now here she was sitting in the backseat being driven to the manor house which Jonathan's family had rented for the occasion. Her eyes were red, but she was in possession of her usual perfect haircut and amused expression. Alix had no idea what Miranda was thinking, but she knew that Miranda was capable of impulsivity—and in this case maybe bolting was the rational thing to do—in spite of her preternaturally still surface. Miranda was like a big cat. Composed, she looked out the window at an angle which almost touched her disembodied yet vivid reflection and which made it appear to Alix as though her brother's betrayed fiancée were in the middle of having a quiet conversation with herself.

———

Alix thinks that it is too late. Too late for her to have any kind of life other than this life dictated by her family circumstances, defined by these people trapped inside their pain. She does not believe as she rides in the car on the way to her brother's wedding that anything can grow other than these old green trees which line the road. She is waiting for Ian, for the friend who knows her, who represents a time when she believed that things might grow. She sits in the car and waits for Ian.

Vlad, said Jonathan, could you pull over for a minute?

Thanks.

The rush of green coming at Alix made her eyes blur. So much beauty outside, so much misery in the car.

Thanks, said Jonathan. And now that we've stopped would you mind getting out for minute? Just to give us some privacy. You've got an umbrella, right?

Vlad nodded and reached down for his umbrella and opened the car door and stepped out and stood by the side of the road. Jonathan swiveled around in the front seat and said: Alix, you too, okay? Miranda and I have to talk before we get there.

No, not okay, said Alix. I don't have an umbrella. It's not like I don't know what's going on anyway so you can speak freely in front of me. Or get out of the car yourselves.

Alix, it's not raining very hard.

You're right. It's more like a mist. So you guys won't get too wet. Or you can huddle under Vlad's umbrella.

Alix . . .

Miranda got out of the car without saying anything and walked several yards along the road beyond where Vlad stood smoking a cigarette.

Thanks, Alix.

You're welcome. The fresh air will probably do you both a world of good.

Alix watched Jonathan follow Miranda down the road. The mist swallowed their outlines and as they met in the distance the image of the two of them through the watery window fused with the raindrops in a hazy, romantic picture. Alix could have imagined that they were very happily in love. They were, in their own way. Some people, thought Alix, are happiest when they are unhappy. Miranda was one of those people. I am too, thought Alix. And in a flash of insight that sped past her like one of the cars on the road, she understood: but some people are not like that, some people are happy when they are happy. A flash and it was gone. She wouldn't have believed it even if you had been able to prove to her that she had had the thought herself. The memory of the idea was somewhere in her mind, but already Jonathan and Miranda were walking back toward the car together and Alix was aware of what their postures meant before her conscious brain had even registered that she had seen them. She didn't know what Jonathan had said or promised or what Miranda had threatened or demanded. But Alix knew: Miranda would stay at least another day.

It's on the way to the wedding that Alix remembers Poppy will be coming too. Alix doesn't always look forward to seeing Poppy, her much-younger half sister who is also her cousin, but now Alix does, she looks forward to all that youthful energy and stupid beauty. Looking forward to seeing Ian and Poppy, Alix is able to bear the rest of the ride. Later she will remember the feeling she had in the car while thinking about Poppy and Ian, the mixture of despair and anticipation, and she will think that she'd had no idea what was coming. How could she have known? Why should she have known that Poppy and Ian would begin a flirtation at Jonathan's wedding that would evolve into a romance and escalate into a tragedy?

That she remembers the moment at all will make her feel as though she must have had some awareness, some information. Information that her mind did not actually know it had. This makes her feel guilty. It is a familiar feeling.

The first time they saw S— they confronted pastoral green lawns and grazing sheep, many louche and unnaturally natural trees, and, after much winding road, a grand and stately stone house. As they pulled up, several men with headsets and strong arms arrived to open doors and whisk away belongings. One of them was the leader of the headset men and he welcomed everyone and gestured to the other men about valises and rooms. Jonathan checked his phone as he made the quick walk from the car to the vast foyer with its enormously high ceiling and checkerboard marble floor. He took a sharp inhalation and then exhaled slowly as he scrolled through his texts. Without looking up, he said to Miranda, and to the assembled in general, that the twins, Felix and Roman, would be arriving later in the day at the airstrip with their mother Patrizia, along with the new nanny, a Slavic girl. As he said "a Slavic girl" Alix saw that he ran his fingers through his hair and looked quickly sideways at Miranda. The last nanny had been Brazilian and Alix could tell that Jonathan hoped the word "Slavic" conjured something pale and unthreatening in Miranda's mind. And his.

2

I T HAD BEEN raining on and off for hours when Ian showed up and then the skies cleared, if only for a little while. Alix had unpacked and tried on her new dress for the wedding and taken it off. She'd put her jeans and sweater back on and looked out the window. It was a gigantic window and you could see the suddenly visible sunlight being thrown down in big fistfuls between the clouds, spilling out onto the extensive and still-wet grounds. She took in the view as if she were draining a glass and then stepped out of the room.

Again, her thoughts turned to Ian. Ian had been Alix's best friend since their first week at college nearly twenty years ago. Ian had helped her home from their first party, the one with the nitrous tanks in the apartment at the Roosevelt. Ian had stayed with her until all hours at the Castle Bar, the ripped leatherette seat of the banquette wet with sweat on her miniskirted thighs. Ian now lives across the lobby from her in the Village in the building her father owns, her family having given Ian a rent-stabilized one-bedroom that had made it possible for him to stick it out in the theater world until he had had a hit. Ian brings her stories and confidences at the end of a hard day, handing them to her like the detritus from a little boy's pocket. She knows Ian keeps secrets from her, but the ones he shares are worth more to her than anything. She knows she is in love with Ian, but she knows that part of why she loves him is that he will never love her back in the same way.

The long hall in the grand house led to a wide staircase, and Alix followed a band of dusty light along the banister toward the portrait-lined gallery. Just then Ian rounded the corner below, entering from the marble-checkerboard-floored foyer into the gallery, and headed up the staircase. They met halfway on the wide, shallow, green-carpeted steps. Ian stood before Alix and swayed slightly. His wet hair dripped onto his shirt collar. His gray eyes were gentle and clear. He held a piece of luggage in one hand. Are you going to give me a hug or should I just get the hell out of your way?

Do I look that bad? said Alix.

Not bad, just distressed. But I'm here now. Ian smiled. You don't believe it yet, do you?

He put down his bag.

Alix looked at his smile. Very familiar, very comforting, an embrace. She tilted her head at him. Really? Do I look okay?

Ian eyed her up and down. Refined. Aware. Authentic in a cool way. No one else would guess you were having a terrible time.

Thank you, I think.

Can you show me to my room?

Where's the guy? The headset?

I told him I'd find it myself.

Which means I will find it for you. Follow me, she said.

As they walked, she said, I'm sorry I asked you to come to this.

Why? I love it! I feel like I'm in a movie.

Miranda is thinking of calling it off.

I don't care. I'm not here for the nuptials. Just to be here for you.

You are a true friend. Really.

They crossed a threshold. Ian looked around the grand bedroom. This'll do, he said.

They sat side by side on the brocade bedspread and gazed though the room's original wavy-paned-glass window together, across undulating gardens and lawns.

Ian remembers sitting so many years ago in college on the lawn outside the library with Alix, the green grass stretching out around them, carpeting their world. The force of that memory sweeps through him for an instant. He feels an ache, a longing to be eighteen. But if I were eighteen I wouldn't be here, he reasons. And for now that is enough.

Patrizia here? asked Ian.

Not yet. Coming soon with the twins and a new nanny.

Steve?

Later. No one knows exactly when.

And where's Poppy?

Not yet materialized, said Alix.

You talk about her as if she were a spirit.

She is, sort of. She seems to float through life. You know what I mean. Anyway, she has a boyfriend whom she was reluctant to leave, so she's taking the last possible plane.

Ian turned to face Alix.

A boyfriend?

She's seventeen. It's still called a boyfriend isn't it?

I thought they just "hooked up."

We're old. We wouldn't know.

Ian took off his jacket.

The ache of a moment ago is gone, his inchoate feelings for Poppy replacing the ache with a drift of desire. He thinks, he wishes, he knows: he is young.

She just finished her junior year, right? He said, Where's she going to apply to college?

College. He remembers: meeting Alix, their instant closeness, her introducing him to new worlds, to her aunt Diana, the surprisingly glamorous grad student who would become his mentor. He can't imagine anything more idyllic than his time at college.

She doesn't want to. Doesn't want to leave the boyfriend. Isn't very into school these days. Steve is annoyed.

So what will happen?

She'll go.

You're sure?

We'll see. How are you? How's the show?

A curl formed on Ian's mouth. His eyes shut and opened a little too slowly.

It's going well. A lot of late nights. Thank God I love the music. The story's good but it needs work.

You're reliving the eighties! Our youth. How fun.

Ian closed and opened his eyes again.

That's why I'm doing it, right?

No. You're doing it to make a lot of money. Your shows always do.

You're wrong. My shows make money, but I don't. And anyway, that's not why I do it.

Oh really? You do it for art?

Don't be an idiot. I mean, yes, for art, but that's not the only reason.

He had gotten up and hung his jacket in the closet. He went to the bathroom and took a plush towel and was rubbing his head with it to dry his hair.

He smiled and they looked at each other for a long time.

I do it so I won't buy a gun and blow my brains out in a gorgeous red mess all over the wall.

Ah, she said. Got it. Would you like to greet the bride and groom?

This family, he thinks. It is amazing how people can be so lucky and so miserable. Alix, with her inability to feel pleasure, how can she go on? But she does and he loves her for it, in spite of it, because of it. Along with her money, she has an unseemly almost-buffoonish sense of gloom. He accepts her, her unhappiness, not only accepts it, likes it.

3

Jonathan stood in his underwear holding his phone. He said Come in when Ian and Alix knocked and then Oh fuck when he looked at his texts. When they walked in, he said: Patrizia and the twins just landed. Who wants to come with me to get them?

You guys have a good time, said Alix. Enjoy.

Ian stood waiting and as Alix walked out he grabbed her hand but she kept walking.

You sending me to the wolves? he called after her. I just got here.

Jonathan ripped the tag off of a sweater with his teeth and let it drop to the floor. He pulled the garment over his head as if he'd just killed an animal and was wearing its skin. He did the same thing with his pants. He left the room a crime scene of bags and clothes and products. He and Ian went out and down the hall. Vlad was waiting in a larger car on the gravel drive.

Has Alix always been such a bitch? Jonathan said. You've known her about as long as I have.

Yes, said Ian. But she's nothing compared to you.

Jonathan smiled out the window. His jaw twitched. You're so right, he said. He tilted his head forward, laughing, and began to slide into a knowingly sexy slouch.

Ian ignored it and looked out his own window into the infinite shades of green. Ian thinks: I must believe that Poppy will be on this plane, otherwise why would I be in the car with Jonathan. This is the only explanation.

At the airstrip, Roman was running down the field waving his arms around and kicking up dirt and laughing maniacally. He looked like a sped-up film of a person from another era, only instead of from the past he had come from the future. His brother Felix was the opposite: slow, graceful, curious, a vision of a boy from a previous century. Behind them the plane was already taxiing and gliding away into the dreamy British afternoon.

Jonathan had pushed the fantasy of his much-younger half brothers' Slavic nanny out of his mind for a few hours and now it arrived before him in the flesh and he seemed to unhinge inside and surrender air. Ian saw this happen as they approached her. The young woman was walking with Patrizia, Jonathan's stepmother, who eventually greeted him in her courtly way. Ian could tell by the way Jonathan closed his eyes when he kissed Patrizia that he was affected by the presence of the new woman.

Now the party can start, Jonathan said breathlessly, although he hadn't been running.

Patrizia kissed him several times on alternating cheeks and introduced him to Neva. They nodded hello. Ian too made his hellos. Now the plane was far away and there were horses grazing in the distance and some wild pheasants prancing around a tree. Ian could see that Neva was in her twenties. He could see Jonathan seeing Neva.

She was beautiful but not pretty.

Roman, she called, come take your jacket. It's raining. She had an appealing accent. She excused herself and walked quickly to catch up with the boys.

Ian thinks about what an asshole Jonathan is and at the same time Ian thinks about Poppy. He is disappointed that she wasn't on the plane, isn't with Patrizia and the kids, even though he was told that she wasn't coming until later. His wishful thinking becomes real in his mind again and again. It is like a play that is always running for him. The longest-running show on earth, in Ian's head. He smiles to himself, but this does nothing to change the reality that he is always dreaming.

4

NEVA MET UP with Roman and handed him his jacket and continued to carry his backpack. She cajoled him into putting on the jacket and playfully wrestled one of his arms into a sleeve while he pulled out the other and it went on this way. She leaned into him with her shoulder and pressed against one sleeve to keep him from extracting his arm, Roman squirming and kicking and pressing his head into her body. She led him toward the car. Roman kept shaking his head as if he were saying a perpetual no to the world.

She maneuvered him into the SUV. As she was about to get in, the other boy, Felix, came up from behind her. He looked right through his brother who was by now playing a video game and got into the car and took out a book. He was carrying his own backpack. Neva swung herself up into the enormous vehicle and crouched into the last row, behind the boys. She watched the two of them, each intently focused on his occupation. They didn't look back.

Patrizia and Jonathan and Ian settled in and Vlad took the wheel and the car rolled off and passed by the runway again where another plane was landing and it was bigger than the first and a few more men were standing around watching it, some just admiring its size. The plane stopped and one man emerged and stood on the steps leading down to the airstrip and this was Steve. Hulking, almost ungainly but not awkward, standing on the edge of the world. Surveying, studying, simultaneously rejecting and engaging. A larger more encompassing version of his son Jonathan, as if sleek, handsome Jonathan had been swollen with thoughts and strategies and bloated with the burdens of running an empire, had been drained of some color as in a faded but important photograph, growing more significant, not less, with age. Steve: Patrizia's husband, Alix and Jonathan's father, Roman and Felix's father, Poppy's uncle and father. Steve: whose fortune made possible this wedding, this plane, these people, this life. As Neva pulled away in the car Steve turned and seemed to notice her from a great distance, seeing right through the tinted window. He turned his head as if he wanted her to be aware that he was watching her. When she looked back at him she thought she could feel his eyes staring directly into hers. She took two energy bars out of the backpack and handed them to Roman and Felix and the SUV went sliding out past the tiny airport along the lovely road back to the house.

Riding in the car Neva is reminded of another car ride, her first car ride, sixteen years ago. She was ten. She remembers gliding through the countryside as if on water. Now she glides through another country, another landscape, and feels as if she herself is the water. A river. The River Neva. She has let life run through her. She has suffered. She has survived. She knows this about herself so completely that this knowledge is simply a part of who she is. She is stoic like a river. She is sensuous like a river. She does not need people, like a river. The river takes everything that is thrown at it, into it, and keeps moving, moves on. She has taken everything and moved on.

She has made a new life, found a place in the world. She takes care of children. She keeps them afloat. There is nothing she cannot carry. She is deep and her inner current is a storm of force in which somebody could sink. She is calm like a river. She is reflective like a river. She is strong. She is incredibly, terrifyingly, unapologetically strong.

Now come hours of solitude, hours of time change. Hours of unpacking for the boys while they eat dinner with the family and she is left alone. She's never been to England before and she notices the way the sun bleeds slowly through layers of colored silk and evening comes on in blue glimmers and a thrilling coolness arrives and blows the leaves and flowers. The night air brings sounds of laughter and debate and bitter tones and honest whispers and the boys fall into bed with their hair swept over their faces.

She keeps to herself to avoid explanations, the complicated exposition that accompanies a new job and always tires her. Her room adjoins the boys' and she listens to them move in their sleep as if they are playing soccer throughout the night.

She recalls a conversation on the plane with Patrizia, their words, mostly Patrizia's words, flying along like birds darting in and out of the clouds beside the plane. Patrizia drank wine and she talked to Neva as if they'd known each other forever and her confidences fell from her mouth like teeth in some dream about losing all of your teeth, clattering and a little bloody.

Over the ocean Patrizia tells Neva that she has been trying to have another child for a long time. In a kind of monologue, half drunk, her eyes half closing, she describes years of needles, years of drugs. All for another baby, she says, wistfully, angry, mocking herself. She doesn't seem to care if the boys can hear her, but they aren't listening.

Neva wonders on the plane if she will ever have children of her own, Children of the River. She once read an article about children born of rape in Rwanda. They were called Children of Bad Memories. Her children if she has them will be Children of Good Memories. Her children if she has them will be loved. She has some long-ago good memories but few recent ones. She will make some good memories. She decides to do that. Yes, she thinks, I will figure out how to do that.

In the middle of the night Neva realizes that she hasn't eaten dinner. She goes downstairs in the dark and finds the kitchen.

Inside, dim light and the gleaming angles of appliances here and there. A gnawing sound vibrating from an old refrigerator and the only food in it bottled water, champagne, and eggs. In the glow from the open fridge she could make out a figure leaning against the counter, through the gloom, his hand locked around the neck of a bottle of champagne. He nodded to a glass on the counter. Neva picked it up and held it out and he filled her glass and she sipped and drank. The liquid was arid, elegant. She sipped again.

I would be happy with water, she said.

The man took a swig and then topped off her glass.

You think you would, he said, but you're mistaken.

Solitary, large but not muscular, his eyes searching as if seeking out some hidden meaning beyond enlightenment, beyond reason or spirit or truth.

Really, said Neva, I'm okay with water.

She finished the little left in her glass and walked several steps to the sink. She could see better now.

At least drink the bottled water, the man said.

Really, this is fine, she said, filling her glass from the tap.

You're the boys' new nanny?

She kept the glass up to her mouth while she thought about how to respond.

I'm Steve, he said. Their father.

I know, she said. I'm Neva.

She turned around and washed her glass and dried it and put it back in a cupboard. She thought that maybe she should leave now but the thought was swept quickly along on a river of thoughts. The more compelling thought was about how different Steve was from the way she had imagined him, how much larger and yet more approachable. She had known that she wouldn't be afraid of him, but she hadn't guessed that she would want to be around him. She had expected to hate him.

How old are you? he asked.

Twenty-six.

Where're you from?

Russia.

How long have you been here?

I came to the States when I was ten years old.

Not much older than the twins, he remarked. He took a long swallow from the bottle.

The boys are very sweet, she said. I'm glad to be taking care of them.

They're not sweet. But maybe you haven't realized that yet.

Well—she smiled—they're very bright.

Felix is. I worry about him. Roman's an operator. He'll be fine. He opened the refrigerator and with his hulking back to her he said, Why the hell isn't there anything to eat around here?

I don't know.

They're probably having it all flown in from someplace. Jonathan and his goddamn expensive palate.

Neva began opening cupboards and said, I'll find something. Do you like eggs? I see some oil, I can cook them with that.

Scrambled, not overcooked.

She had already found a pan and lit the stove.

She has entirely forgotten the thought of leaving and is deeply engaged in the feeling of being around Steve, being present with him, settling in to what seems like a very natural rhythm. If she is a river then he is an ocean, and she feels herself flow naturally in his direction. Already in the car that took her away from home she was gliding, gliding toward this moment.

She finds, much to her surprise, that she does not hate him. Instead, she feels as if she knows him.

I'll find a bowl, she said. She looked around for a bowl and a fork to stir the eggs. She opened drawers, but she found only keys, a screwdriver, duct tape. Far off in the house the plumbing rumbled and drifted off. She opened another cabinet and found a fork sticking out of a teapot.

You can just crack them in the pan, he said. I like them that way.

All right.

Neva stirred the watery eggs and they swirled into one another.

Couldn't sleep in this strange house? he asked her.

She didn't answer him.

Steve nodded his head as if answering the question for himself. You've had a hard life, he said. It's a crazy world, isn't it?

Not crazier than any other, she said.

To other worlds, he said, raising the bottle. You seem like you might've come from another one.

She found a stash of plates in a dirty old dishwasher and cleaned one and put the eggs on the plate and handed him the eggs and fork.

I sometimes feel that way, she said.

He offered her his fork. Have something to eat, he said.

I was only thirsty, she said.

They stood together in silence while he ate. The light outside was bleaching a little bit away from darkness and the objects in the kitchen became slightly more visible, dirtier. It was a fancy house with a filthy kitchen. He handed her the plate and she washed it and the pan and dried everything and put it all away.

You don't have any family, do you?

No, I don't, said Neva.

Didn't think so.

He finished the champagne and left the empty bottle on the counter.

I hope you enjoy your time with us, he said.

I'm sure I will. Thank you for the opportunity.

He watched her for a moment and nodded some more. Go back to bed, he told her.

She did. Crawling back under the heavy covers she squeezed her eyes shut and searched longingly for sleep. When it came she dreamed of a dog, its eyes closed, floating on the water. Not dead but dreaming.

She awoke not long after with the dawn not yet breaking and the thick drapes blocking out any early light. Felix was standing next to the bed, looking down at her.

What is it? she asked him. Are you okay? But he said nothing and slunk off and went back to his own bed and when it was time to get up he didn't seem to remember the incident.

5

ALL THAT NEXT MORNING she watched Patrizia conferring with Miranda and delivering womanly advice. By lunchtime Miranda had been convinced to get over Jonathan's involvement with the former nanny and to go through with the wedding. Neva pieced this together from snatches of conversation and gestures and looks, the two women ranging over the subject as if they were surveying and studying the floors of a luxury store. At lunchtime they were talking about rehearsal dinner details, and Neva was giving the boys their lunch. The food had arrived, along with a chef and kitchen staff. Neva served the boys from large platters arranged on a console near an outdoor table. Roman was trying to eat while playing a game. His device fell into his lunch several times and Neva helped him clean off the herbs and oil.

During the meal Neva tried to get acquainted with Felix, who was not easy to unearth. An inward boy with a delicate, occasionally quizzical expression. They ate side by side in silence, the barely audible clicks of Roman's thumbs on his machine blending in with clinking silverware, spilling food, the twittering country sounds.

Felix was usually found reading a book but at the moment he was concentrating entirely on the present, eating with deliberate poise, chewing his fried fish thoughtfully, dipping pieces into the red swirl of ketchup on the white china with a light, graceful movement. He ate his salad using the fork with his left hand.

He had asked Neva no questions since she'd started working for the family a few days earlier. He seemed to have absorbed everything he needed to know about her from watching her, observing both the way others treated her and the subtleties of mood on her generally inexpressive face. He was like a highly intelligent animal, a dolphin mixed with an exquisite monkey.

I've never had fish-and-chips before, Neva said.

Felix nodded underneath a filigree of shadows from a large tree.

I thought it would be greasier, she continued.

They were both quiet for a while.

This is fancy fish-and-chips, Felix said. It's not the real thing. It's usually pretty disgusting and more delicious.

I thought so.

I have a question.

Go ahead, said Neva.

Why is it harder not to imagine something if someone says to you, Don't think of a black dog, than if someone says: Don't think about the sentence "Are you hungry"?

Because the mind works in images. So if you hear the phrase "a black dog," you cannot not picture it. If someone says a string of words, that's easier to forget.

Okay. Thanks.

You're welcome.

How do they study memory? Do they go into people's

brains? I guess they can. I guess they'll figure it all out. It's like the way there used to be diseases that people don't get sick from anymore. We can cure them now. That will probably happen with death. I mean I can't really imagine that I'm ever going to die.

I haven't heard about a cure for that yet, she said.

I know, but it will come in the future.

If you say so, Felix. You seem to know a lot.

Where in Russia are you from?

The mountains. I'm named after a river near where I was born.

Felix looked at her for an extra beat, as if he could see the vibrant blue River Neva flowing in the sky behind her head.

Poppy is coming today, he said.

Who is Poppy?

My sister. Actually she's my cousin who was adopted by my dad when her mother died. She was six. She's seventeen now. Her mom was my dad's sister. It'll be better when she gets here. She's interesting.

Like you?

For the first time since she'd met him he blushed a little and didn't seem to know whether to laugh or to hide.

No, he said. Not like me. She's cool.

I can't imagine anyone cooler than you.

She has totally white hair. Well, the last time I saw her she did. And her eyes are kind of far apart.

I look forward to meeting her.

Are there any more potatoes?

For a long time Neva has had no friends. Not since she was very small. But Felix, this child, seems like a friend. She is twenty-six and yet this nine-year-old boy makes sense to her. He does not seem to need anything, just like her. Except this girl Poppy, he seems to need this girl Poppy. Neva feels a curiosity about the girl and a pull toward the boy. This is new and different. She is not usually taken in by these families. She doesn't despise them, but she usually feels a great distance, a divide having to do with more than money, more than education, more than privilege. She usually sees them as people with no similarity to her whatsoever, as if they were an entirely different species, even when she likes them, even when they seem to be decent, thoughtful people. But now she feels an unfamiliar kinship, a powerful loneliness that she can comprehend in this family. She could misunderstand it, could think that she and they are very much alike, and that she is one of them. But she is realistic and practical and she understands at least this much: what connects her to this particular family is their loneliness and in the case of Felix his awareness that he is lonely. He accepts it, accepts himself. Jonathan is like many of the other families she has worked for. Jonathan does not even know that he is in pain, inflicting pain, always in the vicinity of pain. Steve is something else. Steve is another matter. Steve is an ocean.

For dessert they ate ice-cream sandwiches made in innovative combinations such as gingersnap with lavender gelato or mint-chocolate-chip cookie with Earl Grey custard. Neva took the boys back to their room and got them changed into their tennis clothes and then accompanied them to the tennis courts where an instructor was waiting. Roman catapulted the ball at the Australian pro, and Felix hobbled around the court like he had someplace else to be.

Neva sat on the sidelines watching them, Roman lunging and Felix flitting, two awkward, unnaturally cultivated birds.

6

POPPY DID NOT let the men who appeared with headsets and strong arms to take her belongings take her belongings, at least not one suitcase in particular, a beat-up purple T. Anthony, which she lugged by herself up some stone steps into a vast foyer with checkerboard marble flooring and, following that, up a green-carpeted staircase. She came upon her room by herself and looked around at the quiet chandelier, the Persian rug, the intricately patterned wallpaper, and huge bed. She took in that this house belonged to real people from another family who were once very rich, perhaps as rich as her family was today, and who now rented out their stately home for lavish events. A slight feeling of discomfort, something like pity, stirred the foliage around the gate of her inner mansion, that world usually cut off from too much feeling. However, here—in the orbit of her family and especially Ian—feelings could not be entirely held at bay. They were blowing in, first signs of a storm.

A rumble of the mattress as she hoisted her purple valise onto it, inciting ripples of dark pink velvet bedspread. A rosy reflected light colored her face as she unzipped the bag and rummaged around for a change of clothes. A slight breeze from the drafty house brushed the bangs of her now-brown hair, her new short cut showing off the line of her long clean neck. Her eyes lay wide and searching in her gently mocking, pretty face. Out the window the sun was just slanting sideways through the tall trees, out of which rose little birds like flying thoughts distracting the world from some great mystery behind the greenery. She pulled on a striped and slouchy dress and slipped her toes into low suede boots and strode coolly out of the room.

Before all of this, shortly before the wedding, Poppy had accepted the persistent attentions of a rich young musician who had been slavishly pursuing her for months. They got together at a party Patrizia and Steve threw for Poppy at that semi-new hotel in Williamsburg. Soon after the party Poppy had announced to Steve that she wouldn't be applying to college in the fall. Steve was in the middle of a complicated multinational negotiation at the time and decided to humor her until her idiotic idea went away and that boy with the ridiculous beard finally bored her. Steve had no awareness that she would take his evasive "we'll see" attitude as an affirmation of her plans. And so it continued with the musician whose privileged life was nothing compared with Poppy's advantageous perch atop the universal elite. He—his name was something offbeat his parents had come up with that was meant to make him extraordinary—looked on in lust and admiration and studied everything about Poppy: her angled face, her knowing naïveté, her sarcastic smile and adorable wit. Her careless, fearless, superbly plain sense of style and ravishing big eyes. In the month of June of the year 20—, the boyfriend looked on as she boarded a plane bound for the wedding of her half brother Jonathan, flying away from him, the boyfriend, and away from the sweltering diseased heat of a soot-smeared summer in New York, into the seductive, self-annihilating beauty of time captured in the endlessly rolling, eternally mythic English countryside.

Poppy thinks that she is the heroine of her own life but knows, deeply, that she is not. She feels the calm air around her and senses that nature has some wisdom she does not yet understand, some equanimity, while she herself is all impulse and wonder and fury and bottomless hope. Her hopefulness is so deep that it is almost shallow. It is her desire to understand that keeps it from being shallow. She desperately wants to understand who she is, how she got here, what to do with her life. Her life seems all at once too fragile and insubstantial and the only thing she has, and so this leaves her both willing to destroy it and afraid to risk her entire universe, this not-girl-anymore but not-yet-adult life. Some days she would like to risk everything.

Would she be different if she hadn't lost her mother at so young an age? Would she be different if she had known her father? Would she be different if she hadn't had so many resources? (The fancy school, the low suede boots.) These questions swim absentmindedly around in her consciousness, but she never notices them. If she did they would reveal themselves as impossible to answer, but she might learn something from contemplating them, not the answers but the fact that the questions bother her, worry her, distract her like small invisible insects in the air.

She doesn't know yet that the questions themselves are her biggest problem, that they are keeping her from deciding what to become. Instead she throws all of her love at the world, swatting at the insects, smacking them with love, without knowing that this is what she is doing. This makes her brave but not strong, intense but not knowing. This makes her heartbreaking to anyone who can see her for who she is.

She left the house and walked the grounds. There was nobody around. Eventually she followed a path and in the distance she could hear splashing and a man's voice. At the end of the path there was more grass and, beyond that, gray-stone paving surrounding a swimming pool. Lush plantings bordered the pool and curved and dipped here and there into the water.

There were a couple of tasteful lounge chairs scattered around the pool, and in one of them sat Jonathan. He sat on the edge of the chair, not lounging. Alix was sprawled out on another chair, wearing an oversize man's shirt over her bathing suit, sunglasses, and a hat. Miranda was in the water, doing slow and sinuous laps. Poppy took off her boots before anyone noticed her and walked barefoot on the grass toward her siblings. She crossed the stone paving along the edge of the swaying water and stood at the end of Alix's lounge chair and still holding her boots in her hand said: Hello, Big Sis.

Wide eyed, she continued: I am starving and I cannot believe how beautiful it is here. I've been looking all over for everyone. Where can I get something to eat?

Alix peered over her sunglasses at Jonathan who was scrolling through his texts. Welcome, Poppy, Jonathan said.

Miranda raised her head from the water.

Poppy. How was your flight?

Jonathan looked Poppy up and down and went back to his phone.

Alix pulled her hat brim over her face. She was in a bad mood. Her silence seemed to express the idea that extreme privilege was like extreme deprivation: it could bring people to a savage state. She felt, at the moment, under no obligation to be kind. This was bizarre even to her because she had been looking forward to seeing Poppy, but the presence of a contented Jonathan, the irritating sound of Miranda's lithe figure cutting through the water, and now the appearance of her much-younger, more beautiful cousin/half sister made her want to retreat into a chalet of self-loathing. Perhaps if Ian had been present she would have chosen to offer Poppy her better self, but Alix had no idea where he was and so she was stuck with these shameful feelings and no one to help her manage them, not that she should need anyone. She was thirty-seven years old. She allowed herself to behave badly and this only made her feel worse.

Poppy turned to Jonathan. Do you know how to make her say hello? she said.

Jonathan looked up from his hands. He regarded Poppy without much expression.

Why isn't she saying hello to me?

Jonathan shrugged and made a "who cares" movement with his head.

Poppy stared down at Alix.

Jonathan without looking up said to Alix, I don't know why you're being so rude—can you just say hello?

Alix said: I'm resting. She can see that. And I saw her five days ago in New York. This is not some major reunion.

Jonathan laughed a little breath.

What are you laughing at? said Poppy.

Miranda got out of the water, grabbed a towel, and slid over toward Poppy. I won't hug, she said, because I'm all wet, but we're so glad you're here.

Thanks for saying so but it doesn't really seem like it.

Miranda slipped her sandals on and headed back to the house.

Poppy stared down at Alix again. Poppy's eyes were very blue and narrowed.

Alix readjusted her position.

Poppy made big dramatic pinwheel motions in the air around her head, an act of mime that left Jonathan breath-laughing again. Hello, she said, waving broadly at Alix.

I'm tired. It's been stressful around here. Don't push it, said Alix.

Push it? Push it? Poppy said. What is wrong with you? Can't you be civil?

Hello, Poppy, Alix said, from underneath the hat.

Why am I the only mature one around here? said Poppy.

A languid wind brushed through the trees making them heave and sigh. Poppy dropped her boots on the grass and took her dress off over her head. She let the loose fabric fall to the ground. She bent her thin arms around her back and unclasped her bra. Her rib cage rippled like the inside of a piano. She stepped out of her boy-shorts underwear and dropped all of her sheer decorative lingerie on top of her dress. She swept past the pile of clothes and when she reached the edge of the pool she straightened up and turned her head over her shoulder to look at Alix and Jonathan. Neither of them looked at her.

The wind had stopped, no stirring leaves. Under the water, intersecting wavering ovals of light surrounded her in an electrified net. The bottom of the pool was painted a chalky white. She swam to one end and back and hauled herself out and made footprints like the shadows of faraway birds. Then she came to the pile of clothes and stood there.

Alix and Jonathan ignored her.

Poppy stood naked and dripping.

Jonathan gazed upward and then back to his phone.

How about showing a person a little love? said Poppy.

Jonathan stood up.

Poppy started shivering and Jonathan pointed to a stack of neatly folded towels on a weathered wooden table.

Go, cover yourself up, he said. He made a shooing motion with the hand that held the phone.

Poppy's face clouded. You assholes, she said. She stood over Alix and dripped on her. Jonathan's expression did not change. He just brought up his hand with the phone in it and held it above her as if he were going to strike. A great show of force in the silence. A clicking into place of the unnatural natural order. Then Alix lifting herself up onto her elbows, the rustle of her hat falling off her head.

Poppy stood her ground. You guys are so old, she said.

Alix and Jonathan didn't respond. There was a swooning of air through the trees. Poppy found Jonathan's eyes with hers.

And you are an infant, he said.

I feel sorry for your future children if this is how you treat an infant.

Alix said something about how she was getting soaked and this was ridiculous and Jonathan put your arm down. Then Poppy bent over and picked up her clothes. Then she walked to the edge of the pool. Then she threw her clothes into the water.

Jonathan's face drained. Poppy, don't do that. Look I'm sorry, he said, unemotionally.

She walked back over toward him and Jonathan pulled away from her like a man avoiding a drunk on the sidewalk.

He stepped farther back as she lunged at him with her wet

arms. Then he stepped back again. Poppy leaped lightly onto the lounge chair and pulled the phone out of his hand. Jonathan froze. She scrolled through his texts and read a couple of them out loud. They were meaningless. Then she selected a number from his contacts and made a call as she walked quickly to the other end of the pool.

Jonathan followed her. He was breathing heavily and he cursed and pointed at her, following her around the pool. Poppy turned back quickly and feinted and then threw the phone over Jonathan's shoulder onto the stone paving. The guts and innards of the mechanism sprayed and Jonathan's knees bent and his Oh fuck echoed. Poppy had already run over to collect the parts and she pitched each piece into the water before Jonathan had even picked up the splintered walnut cover and she skipped the little battery across the surface of the pool and yelled a Goodbye you expensive made-in-China piece-of-shit toy into the air as the bits of metal and plastic sank.

Poppy surveyed the scene. Alix looked exhausted and spent and Jonathan was leaning over with his hands on his knees. Neither of them moved. Poppy strode over to the table with the towels on it and wrapped one around her body and secured it in between her breasts and headed away down the path. The birds were gone. The breeze was entirely gone too. She tucked her wet hair behind her ears and walked back to the house.

7

S HE WOKE FROM a long nap on top of the velvet bedspread, one foot touching the purple T. Anthony suitcase that was still open and unpacked and spilling with clothes from her earlier rummaging. The ceiling of the room was painted with tiny gold starlike shapes and she blinked up at them as if she'd landed on the moon. The towel had unwound from her body into a twisted, discarded bandage and her naked limbs splayed out on the bed as if she had fallen from a great height to land here.

She barely remembers what happened at the pool, has dreamed it away. What she remembers she writes off as dysfunctional family dynamics, a phrase she had learned by the time she was ten. She is still half dreaming, half happy, half alive.

Her head felt tight around her skull and the muscles behind her eyes pulled taut in knots. She sat up and looked around. She'd stashed some pills in the suitcase—the reason she hadn't wanted anyone else to carry it—and she sat up and dug her hands into the inner side pocket of the bag and retrieved a bottle. She unscrewed the top, fished out a pale peach-colored pellet with her finger and put it in her mouth. She sat up a little straighter and closed her eyes and made some spit and swallowed. Then she opened her eyes and swallowed the last powdery bitter spit. The tiny stars on the ceiling retreated into their distant galaxy and spun away into a painted heaven. After a while she rose and dressed and went out to look for the rest of her family.

Her family. She always tells people that her family is like the House of Agamemnon or something out of Faulkner because everyone in it can be so mean. She has no idea how appropriate the references are, or how much more there really is to tragedy. She does not realize the wide discrepancies between what she thinks of these people, how she feels about them, and the images she has of them in her mind. She carries with her an image of Steve that is benevolent, magnanimous, and generous, although she also knows him to be controlling, manipulative, and cruel, and her feelings, her feelings about him are entirely different from her thoughts and images. Her feelings for him are radical and gigantic and too much for one brain or heart to bear. They dwarf her. Next to them she is the smallest blade of grass. They walk all over her. They trample her. It is only possible to see these feelings as enormous masked figures enacting a drama in an amphitheater. The moonlight casting long shadows so that the people in the audience are alternately lit up and obscured. And she, she is that blade of grass, watching the play from between two stones where the slightest growth of green has been bestowed by a fortunate accident of sun.

They were nowhere in sight. The house was quietly bustling with staff. There were maids making beds and men filling vases with flowers and assistants of one sort or another placing bottled water in every room. Some of the headset men were moving pieces of furniture around. In the portrait gallery on the second floor, which ran practically the entire length of the house, long tables were being arranged and set for the rehearsal dinner tonight. It was the first event of the wedding weekend at which real guests, nonfamily members, would be in attendance. Miranda and Jonathan had invited at least a hundred and fifty people to the intimate affair and three hundred were expected tomorrow for the ceremony. A tent was being set up outside, not for the wedding but for the babysitters and young children. Inside, it housed a trampoline, video games, many televisions, sports equipment, a refrigerator, and several playpens filled with baby toys. Poppy wandered around, drifting unreal through a circus of childhood, a museum of distraction. Eventually she left the tent out an opening on the far side and found herself in a small garden with a wrought-iron bench. She fished out a second pill from her pocket and let the acrid fire burn its way down the length of her throat.

There was a fountain in the middle of the garden with a bronze fish jumping and drooling and the stone basin had been occupied by the debris of visiting tourists trying their luck, pennies and other foreign coins lay drowned at the bottom of the gray water with bits of lichen and oxidized green upon the surface of the metals. Huge trees hung around the perimeter of the garden and threw a cool darkness over the fountain and on closer inspection the fish held several rusty coins in its mouth, diverting the flow of water and creating a drool as opposed to a spout. Poppy stood blinking in the very early evening stillness. Then she saw the outline of a boy. It was just a subtle disturbance in the distance and it led her toward a path that branched off of the garden. She swiped a cold nickel from the fountain and set out after Felix.

She took the path down toward a fork and realized at the fork that one of the paths led to the pool. She was still following a hint of boy way up ahead of her. She entered a stretch of the path which reminded her uncomfortably of her earlier escapade with Jonathan and then made her way up a rise in the road which swerved her mind around to more uplifting thoughts or perhaps it was the little pill kicking in now and here she was at the pool again. Her clothes had been fished out of the water and laid on the wooden table. The pile of towels had been set up on one of the lounge chairs. Next to the drying clothes some helpful groundskeeper had placed a neat array of all the dead pieces from Jonathan's broken phone. Felix was picking them up one at a time, investigating, seeing if he could fit them back together.

He was fingering the dead bits when he looked up and saw Poppy. He stood there very still but for his radiant smile.

Poppy! he called out.

I see you found my mess.

Mess?

I believe I am responsible for this mess, she said. All that junk on the table.

Felix ran to her as she approached him and he clasped her around the waist. This isn't a mess: these are specimens, he said into her T-shirt. The remains of a visit from aliens who came down and took a swim and left some of their robot parts behind. You could never make a mess, he said.

Poppy grabbed him close. She kissed the top of his head. You are a genius and my best friend and the only grown-up around here, she whispered into his hair.

Felix is her little mystic. When she is with him she feels understood and the world seems understandable. His compassionate expression, his sensitive remarks. His laugh is the chuckle of a philosopher. He has an X-ray vision that sees that she is a good person. She holds on to his vision of her, grasps it, whenever she can. Sometimes he puts his hand on her shoulder as if he is Aristotle pondering the secrets of the ages and she feels so much gratitude that she melts from his touch.

They sat down next to each other at the edge of the pool with their legs dangling in the water. Felix was wearing a bathing suit and an SPF long-sleeved shirt although by now it was approaching dusk. Long days in June that graze on time and fade never completely into night. After a while Felix slid into the pool and swam funny, short width-wise laps. He made his way back and forth and back and forth enjoying the simple pushing of his feet and touching of his fingers on the rough side of the structure. He liked knowing and feeling the boundaries of this domain. Then he propelled himself underwater and circled the perimeter like some baby shark of a thought testing the outer limits of a wholly wretchedly limited but endlessly shifting and renewable consciousness.

8

THE DINNER WAS in the past now, the long tables in the portrait gallery disassembled and put back into storage, the dark red linens waiting to be laundered. The flowers dying. Poppy was lying naked under the covers with her clothes spread all over the room and on the bed around her when a knock came at the door and the door opened.

She opened her eyes. Through the late-night haze she could make out the slim silhouette of Patrizia. Poppy rolled over onto her stomach.

Patrizia entered the room and sat on the bed beside her.

She reached down and with a long finger pushed Poppy's bangs to the side.

Hello there, said Patrizia.

What do you want?

To talk. We didn't get to talk at the dinner. So many people.

Poppy was rolling over and sitting up with the covers held to her collarbone. They drooped slightly from her light grasp and she sat there practically exposed.

What the hell? It's the middle of the night.

I just wanted to chat. I didn't mean to upset you.

You are upsetting me. Because you are waking me up.

Is it true that you told people last night that you are not going to apply to college? I won't get angry, I'd just like to know.

Why? Who cares about this?

Steve. He wants to discuss your future.

My future?

Yes.

What future?

The future that comes after today. Tomorrow, et cetera.

I can't think about that.

He says that you must. You know what that means?

Now?

Poppy groaned and pulled some clothes from various points on the bed and hauled them over her head and legs. She pulled on the low boots and put two pills wrapped in Kleenex in her right bootleg and stood up next to the bed pulling on a long cardigan sweater over her T-shirt.

Patrizia was still sitting on the side of the bed in her silk bathrobe. Her legs were crossed. She had a large ring on one of her fingers, which she examined while Poppy got dressed. When she saw what emerged once Poppy had scrambled into clothes she shook her head.

Did you have too much to drink tonight? she said.

I don't drink, said Poppy. I only take prescription drugs.

Patrizia ignored this.

College is a big party. Why wouldn't you go?

I don't want a big party. I want to begin my life.

Please, Poppy. Don't be so melodramatic. No one ever "begins" their life. And anyway, you'll get so many perks if you go to school: an apartment, an allowance, new people.

I'm sick of school. And people.

Patrizia eyed her. She slid the big ring up and down her finger. What do you want to do? she said.

Work.

Work, said Patrizia. That would be a novel experience.

Poppy looked plaintively at Patrizia. She looked at her hair. Patrizia's shoulder-length hair was brown, the color and sheen of high-quality leather or very expensive chocolate. Sometimes Poppy could make out tiny strands of gray mingling amid the rich gloss. Didn't you work? asked Poppy.

I came from Italy when I was twenty-two, right after university. I worked as a business reporter. Working all hours, slaving in the system. It was fun and interesting for a while, but it couldn't contain me. If I hadn't met Steve I don't know where I'd be today. I was unfulfilled. He set me on a path to salvation. I would be sitting in a small apartment by myself drinking rosé in front of costume dramas or worse if he hadn't found me. He saw something in me worth investing in and he sees something in you.

Now who's being melodramatic?

Just come with me and talk to him.

They walked down the dark hallway with Patrizia glamorous and ghostly in her pale silk rippling and Poppy sullen and slouching behind her like something being taken into captivity. They passed by many closed rooms where the draft wailed under the doors and by paintings on the walls that hung patient and speechless in the night.

Steve was occupying a suite of rooms at the farthest end of the house. Patrizia opened the door to a passageway that led into the central living area. The walls were covered in an oversize toile print that in the dim lighting made it seem as if tiny people frolicking in boats and swings all over the room were being thrown into larger shadows on the walls. Patrizia strode in her wafting robe to the opposite side of the room where Steve was wearing headphones and sitting at a desk.

He was staring at a laptop, with his tablet out on the table and a book open on his lap and papers and two phones atop the desk. Patrizia tapped him on the shoulder and waited. Steve typed away and listened and read and did not look up. Poppy could hear a faint whistling and clanking from some antique faraway pipes. Other than that there was only the sound of Steve's tapping fingers.

When he was finished he took off the headphones and turned around. He looked at Patrizia and then he looked at Poppy and then turned back to his laptop and he read over what he had written on the screen. He nodded and shut the computer and stood up letting the book fall to the floor and paying no attention to it. He kicked it slightly as he maneuvered from between the chair and the desk. The book ended up open and askew on the floor, pages side down, flat and praying that it would not be kicked again.

Steve took large steps over to Poppy and gave her a kiss on the cheek. Then he motioned to two upholstered chairs at one end of the room facing a fireplace and led the way in that direction. Patrizia headed out of the room and closed a door behind her. Sit down, Steve said.

Poppy sat in one chair and Steve remained standing, leaning against the fireplace. He had a commanding presence, but he was not in good shape. He wheezed very slightly as he arranged his body against the mantel. So you have essentially completed your studies, he said.

What studies? said Poppy.

Your schooling. Your education.

Poppy looked up at Steve. She sat cross-legged on the wide seat of the chair and pushed a strand of hair behind her ear. I want to work, she said.

Work, he said.

Yes. Be out in the world. Begin my life.

You have a life. It began seventeen years ago.

I mean my real life.

What do you think your real life is?

I don't know. I have to go out and find it.

Where do you think it will be found?

If I knew that I wouldn't have to look for it.

What kind of work do you want to do?

What you do.

What I do?

Yes. I want to work in real estate.

He stared at her.

Isn't that what you do? she said.

I suppose that is what they call it.

Steve squinted at her. Do you have any idea what I really do?

Make deals, build buildings, move money around. I don't know. That's what I have to learn. It seems practical to just get started soon.

Steve sighed and nodded. He walked over to the other chair and fitted himself into the seat with his legs stretched out far ahead of him like oars off the side of a boat. He was float-ing, for a moment, preparing to change direction. Holding the oars in the current to shift the vessel. In taking a new tack he would be playing a different role. It was as if he had been sailing in a fierce regatta and now he had decided to gently glide in a canoe.

He tilted his big chin downward and nodded his head. He appeared to be changing his mind.

I admire your spunk, sweet Poppy, I really do, he said in a mellow voice. But there's no reason to rush. Why don't you want to go to college first: get an education, have fun, then you can come work for me?

Poppy looked at Steve. He had his eyes shut. Poppy pushed her hair back behind her ear again. She licked her lips and looked over at the corner of the ceiling. I'm sick of people my own age.

I'm afraid you're stuck with them, for now. But they will get older. Whom would you prefer to spend time with?

You.

Steve leaned his head back and smiled. Ah, he said. Flattery will get you everywhere.

I'm not flattering you. It's true.

He slowly rearranged his body and twisted and leaned forward in his chair so that his face was suddenly enormous to her. He looked very deeply into her eyes.

Bravest little girl I have ever known. No one in this family has endured as much as you have. Your mother sick, then dying when you were so young. Ever since the day you were born I have considered myself your father. Did you know that?

Yes.

And it's what your mother wanted. She fought and died in that hospital room and you were the most valiant little soldier. Through the tubes and machinery she told me to take care of you and I promised that I would. Forever.

Steve leaned forward even more. I fought for you. That nanny wanted you. Then that imbecile sister of mine in the Midwest can you imagine? Friends gossiped, said Patrizia didn't love you. My God we kicked the shit out of them giving you everything. And those barbarians who ran your school, they did not always understand the difficulties you had and how you needed to be treated with special under-standing. What a bunch of savages some of those kids were—remember that viral video three years ago—I had to pay a lot to get that taken down from the Internet. Did you know that? You are exceptional and eccentric and I have always protected you. Steve shook his head. He seemed reluctant to say what evidently he felt he was required to say to her. A moral obligation.

I didn't know that, said Poppy. Thank you. But I still don't want to go to college.

Steve leaned back. He inhaled and exhaled deeply.

He appeared to be changing his mind yet again, but he was simply changing his tactics.

What we are confronted with in today's world are cruel degene-rate people with no sensitivity or psychological awareness. Savages with no feelings. Maybe it's always been this way, but it's worse now. They are in charge. We are talking about people who are so numb to their fellow human beings that they think they know better how everybody should live. And do you know what happens to people who know what's best for everybody? They destroy the world. That's what they do. They dismember and disembowel the individual and boil her flesh and entrails down in a stew with everybody else.

It is bad enough in the universities but it is far more dangerous in the so-called real world. In the real world people will sell the idea of security but what they are really doing is stealing the most important thing you have: your freedom. This is true. I may be a crony capitalist myself but that is only because there is nothing left to be, do you see what I'm saying? The government, the elites, the billionaires, the trillionaires: what they don't already own they are in the process of taking, under the guise of being caring and helpful, magnanimous and just. I don't want to send you out to the front lines at the tender age of seventeen. How could I do that to the memory of your mother?

He paused. And then:

I don't think there's any question that higher education is a scam to indenture the middle class with the inflated price of tuition and an inside track for the children of the plutocracy to acquire ever more privilege or spread the gospel of globalization or both. But this is what we are left with. This is reality.

He was watching Poppy. She looked uncomfortable.

My princess, said Steve. I want you to be safe and I think the safest place right now for you to be is in school. I am being honest with you, sharing the ways of the world. I am not sugar-coating this with platitudes about the liberal arts or the life of the mind or the skills necessary for being a global citizen or what a long rave of pleasure and extended adolescence you will be missing out on if you do not attend college. I am speaking to you as an adult.

He leaned even farther forward and put his hands on his knees. And I promise I will let you work for me when you have finished school. We will conquer the world. There will be an office waiting for you with a big desk and two assistants. Teams working under you. You will ride up seventy stories on a construction site wearing a hardhat and high heels. But you're still young. There is time. Am I wrong? Can't this wait? Do you have to run before you can walk?

Steve's voice had become mellow and intense at the same time. He inclined his head to one side and looked at Poppy with a sovereign benevolence, another swerve in strategy. Poppy pursed her lips and they twisted to the side and curled as if a balloonist were finishing off a birthday party poodle. She hugged her knees. She widened her eyes at him.

Why can't I just come work for you when I finish high school?

Poppy, you're breaking my heart.

Steve was beginning to look tired.

You don't really care about school, she said.

I know but I care about you.

If you care about me you'll let me live my life now.

I'll think about it.

That means yes!

I'll think about it.

Oh thank you, she said, leaping up from the chair and embracing him.

I love you so much, she said.

I know you do.

9

DURING THE CEREMONY Poppy experienced a flooding of inexplicable happiness. She was a member of the wedding party and the small visual, sensory, and communal joys of getting ready with Miranda's friends, the first viewing of the bride in her impeccably elegant custom silk-and-chiffon gown with its simple lines, graceful profile, and radiating sense of purity and hope, the slow procession before the assembled guests, complete with adorably shy ring bearers and sassy flower girls, the vows and their declaration of dreams upheld, all of these elements came together to produce in Poppy a giddy tingling joy, a momentary mystical oneness that lifted her perspective high above the proceedings and enabled her to gaze upon the event with a tenderness that she rarely allowed herself. She felt warmth toward everyone. She felt that they would all take care of her and love her back. Oh, why don't I always feel this way? she thought, floating far in her mind to observe the rows and rows of guests. We're all just people. Why don't we all always feel this way?

Already the wedding ceremony is over and it is time for the reception. Hundreds of colorful hats swim over the grounds and circle like exotic fish. The air is filled with the smell of cooking foods coming from a kitchen area hidden from view. Children, released from the children's tent, run through the gardens and pluck flower petals and throw them and climb in the fruit trees until babysitters see them and call them down. Band music drifts across the lawns and people dance on the grand patio in staccato movements like figures on an old town clock. Poppy passes by a group of kids attempting to organize a game with the help of one adult, Neva, the new nanny. Neva directs the movements of her troops with a singular and beautiful authority that belies her position at the wedding.

Poppy had met Neva briefly but now she stops at a short distance and observes her: her black hair, her acute angles, her green eyes, her sharp shoulders. A punk-rock Russian strength to her unsmiling expression and asymmetrical demeanor. Neva is like a tree with no leaves, no embellishment, no distractions. Spiky branches and rigorous purity. Poppy feels sloppy and silly in her silky dress, however modern and edgy it claims to be. She sees that the children recognize a natural charm and command in Neva and they swarm around her and bump into her on purpose and call out to attract her attention. Poppy finds herself fascinated, intrigued, oddly envious, and somewhat in love with this poised slightly older woman, who is now laughing without smiling, the faintest most self-aware curl of her lip indicating pleasure, as she points and gives directions, surrounded by a little army of screaming and happy children.

Poppy arrives at the grand patio and steps around a lone dancing couple as she nears the back doors of the great house. The doors are open and guests are mingling inside and out but mostly out and she enters into a long library where all seems hushed and empty. She strolls around in her large-brimmed wedding hat with its silk bow past the book-lined walls with their elegant proportions and thin, carved Grecian columns and the low couches and chairs and tables where small porcelain lamps sit in the daylight waiting like contented Buddhas for somebody to realize that they are needed. She walks to the far end of the room toward a corner where a chair is positioned near the window.

There is a solitary attractively disheveled man in this chair and he lifts his gaze from his book to look at her. It is Ian in his wedding suit, with a drink, a book. There are three guests who wander in at the far end of the room and glance at Ian and Poppy briefly before leaving. Poppy stands at an angle facing some leather-bound volumes with her champagne flute at her lips and her bare foot slipping in and out of her high-heeled shoe. She sips and doesn't notice him and Ian shakes a rueful head at her and closes his book and takes a swallow of his drink.

You're not dancing, he says.

Poppy looks around at him from under her brim. Are you talking to me?

I thought you'd be dancing.

That stuff? On the patio? She tilts her chin toward the windows.

Yes, the band, he says.

She looks back at the bookshelves.

The real dancing is later, she says.

I see.

They're having a DJ. Somebody big, she says to the bookshelves.

He stares at her. He gets out of the chair and walks over toward her. So you'll be dancing for real later?

If I feel like it.

Do you think you'll feel like it?

Why do you ask?

Poppy watches the shadowy glints of light and dark which play before her on the rows of books, red burning leather with gold etching. She feels the enormous effort of trying to appear as if she is not paying much attention to Ian. Still managing to act disinterested, she turns to him. His eyes are soft and gray. There is a fine engraved pattern around them, a network of very thin lines that looks like writing. If she could read that language it would explain so much. But she cannot.

He speaks slowly: I hear that you don't want to apply to college. I had a blast in college but admire you for wanting to get on with life, he says.

There is a long but surprisingly not awkward silence between them. Neither of them can quite tell if it is erotic or dull. Ian lifts his eyebrows and continues.

If you're interested, there's plenty to do in the theater. After graduation you could be my assistant, or something like that, learn about the electric world of Broadway, he says with an expression that conveys mockery and sincerity at the same time. He lifts his hands, one holding a drink, one splayed out Bob Fosse–style. You know, "All That Jazz," he says. Think about it. It's not the worst way to start a career. He looks at her with the tiniest smolder, not enough to make him seem lecherous, but just enough so that she is too scared to look at him anymore.

But she couldn't be his assistant because she was going to work for Steve as soon as she finished high school, she explained, and anyway she had outgrown her interest in the theater—she was over that—and she moved away along the books and books and books waving her champagne flute in Ian's direction, and of course he accepted it without following her because she was much too young for him anyway and what else could be done?

But he knows then that he will be communicating with her soon. On the dance floor, during their separate return travels to New York, and back in the city as he crosses paths with her because of his close association with Alix. He knows now as he watches her walk away that somehow she will come to him. He thinks this is an intuition of fate, or a form of hope, but it isn't. It is simply a decision on his part that he is going to get what he wants and do whatever he can, however stealthily, to make this to-him-at-the-moment-minor-dream come true. He is his own gullible mark and a con artist at the same time. This doesn't make him an evil person. He is not one kind of person; like all of us, he has many aspects. But his narcissism is a part of him that he has not yet had to examine or tackle or renounce and so in his personal life he is very often destructive. He is not, at least, as destructive as some people. He knows that, takes some remote comfort in it.

———

Poppy is self-destructive. The last thing she attempts to do is to hurt deeply anyone other than herself. As she walks away Ian sees her, for an instant, in all her fierce, stunningly pretty, self-destructive glory. He sees her and for a brief flickering moment comprehends her in a way that he does not comprehend himself.

On the dance floor he keeps his eyes on her even when they are not dancing together. She gets dipped by one of Miranda's dashing financier friends. Poppy's short hair practically touching the floor, her bare legs long and angled and stuck to the ground in her pointy-toed silver sling-backed shoes. Her face rapturous, shining, like a very good, very old diamond so clear and colorless that it looks like nothing but is everything, contains and refracts every color. He keeps his eyes on her.

The way these parties end: in intoxication and mistakes and sex and sometimes blood. They drank on and on and ate and danced under another tent and the fireworks fell all over themselves and the wind violated everybody's hair and people walked off into the shadows with one another and couples argued and things were said that could never be unsaid and as the dawn was bleeding faintly over the proceedings Jonathan was kneeling above Miranda in bed and she whispered something to him but he didn't say anything back. He was in his own element, something like fire but not as pure, one of those chemical fires that glows blue and green and orange. Afterward, he lay on his side, burnt wood. The next day by lunchtime most of the guests were gone. The tents came down. Men with headsets removed the party. Ian woke up late and missed the farewell brunch. He stood on the front steps of the house overlooking the wide pale gravel driveway scattered with the remaining revelers just in time to watch the bride and groom drive off in an Aston Martin. It was beginning to drizzle again. There was a silvery sky behind the tall trees.

Watch out, he muttered under his breath to the newly-weds. You might get what you're after.

He had been holding a cup of coffee and now he took a sip from it and turned around and headed back up the green-carpeted staircase to pack his bag.

10

I N LONDON tall men stood in attendance at the hotel entrance and regarded the new arrivals dispassionately. Steve, Patrizia, Neva, the twins, Ian, Alix, and Poppy swept past like some well-appointed band of itinerant jugglers or magicians, circus performers impersonating aristocrats. An understatedly luxurious scarf of ostrich feathers trailed behind Poppy, a plume of smoke from her neck.

Spending a few days in London after the wedding before returning to New York, the family had settled into a routine of meeting for dinner and spending their days separately, the twins taken to parks or attractions by Neva, or Patrizia when she wasn't consuming, Ian and Alix off to neighborhoods and galleries, Poppy left mostly on her own to wander. Steve worked in his London office or at the hotel.

At dinner Ian asked Poppy, How do you like London?

I love it, of course, but I'm a bit lonely this time.

I'd have to say the same.

They both watched Alix covertly as she sat at the far end of the table, her eyes piercing the menu, her expression puzzled, angry, hopeful, and irritated all at once. Poppy unfurled her napkin.

She's deeply depressed, said Poppy.

Who?

You know who. The saintly nun. Sister Alix.

Ian looked down the long table at Alix's judging, critical squint.

How did you two become such enemies?

Whatever do you mean? My biggest worry is that something will happen to her. I pray to God every day that she doesn't injure herself, said Poppy drily, ripping a piece of bread.

No really, how did it happen?

I always looked up to her. And she can't stand that. She prefers to be pitied, or despised.

Are you always so smart?

Only sometimes. Mostly I'm a spoiled brat.

He didn't think she was. He never would. But he would hear her call herself that again on the floor of his apartment as she cried into his arms and she would use that phrase later to describe him when he found her with her lip bleeding and her cheek bruised yellowish blue.

After the main course the waiter returned for the millionth time and brushed the crumbs from the table into a silver scoop. Another waiter carried a fan of dessert menus at the ready like giant playing cards, as if there might be some fabled game of high-stakes poker among these groomed and shining outlaws. When the meal was entirely finished they grabbed their satchels and donned their light outerwear and moved back into the night. The waiters stood side by side. They waited in their uniforms, buttons gleaming, watching the party of eight drift effortlessly through the dining room. All glowing in the rosy-amber chandeliered lighting, these wondrous lucky humans, like science-fictional royalty. Replicas of some species that roamed the earth millennia ago, long before anyone could remember.

Neva saw upscale tourists from around the world and spiffy locals with their children navigating the parks throughout the day. The Blessed. Former nomads and hunter-gatherers celebrating the cultivation of nature into paths and borders, little rivers and charming gardens. They nodded to her, and their children ran up and tried to engage the twins and sometimes balls were tossed or words exchanged.

She saw young women with clotted mascara so thick it looked like caterpillars were growing from their eyelids. They were smoking cigarettes, walking arm in tattooed arm, eyeing the world suspiciously. She saw the elect themselves rolling prams big as small cars, the future lucky ones snuggled tenderly inside, and she saw herds of consumers carrying glossy shopping bags like weaponry and shields, armed with crests and titles of every description, their logos twisted from humble images of leaves or fruit or clouds into distorted symbols, brightly colored fragments of life as reduced and severed from nature as if they were cutoff human ears or human teeth or human limbs and the carriers themselves at first seemingly benign but on closer inspection crazed looking and wild in their anxious eyes and raw laughter. Neva did not know whether to love all of these people or hate them or forgive them or denounce them or accept them for what they were: a visitation from some alien planet that had entirely taken over this one.

Back at the hotel, foremost among these visitors, unreal in

dimension and disarming with his benevolent gaze, awaited Steve. His office was too crowded and he preferred to do business today in his hotel suite. The enormity of his skeleton especially when he rose from a chair and unfolded himself was disorienting, an optical illusion. He was not muscular or fat or even broad, but of another scale entirely from everybody else. He was alone in the room and when Neva entered with the twins earlier than expected she was surprised to see him in a chair, his legs outstretched, a device in his hands, his reading glasses perched on his nose like a bird on a branch of a gigantic wind-twisted tree.

It's fine, he said, without looking up from his reading. The boys can stay in their room. I have some business to do here.

Neva settled the boys, who were tired from a day at the Tower of London imagining beheadings and the vomit of gore that would spew from lopped heads of naughty kings and upstarts, in front of an even-more-gruesome video game for Roman and the annotated Sherlock Holmes for Felix.

Then she closed the door behind her and walked through the central living area toward her own small room and saw Steve engaged in conversation with another man. He must have entered quietly. Neva stood in the corner of the vast yellow-fabric wallpapered room and watched them. When Steve's eyes quickly glanced at her he gave her a silent nod. Or he seemed to nod. She felt that he had indicated that she should stay. Then he continued speaking to the man.

His name was Grant. He was a young distant cousin of Steve's but one whom Steve took seriously, perhaps because of a long history with Grant's parents. He was in his early thirties and he was a chef. He had big plans for a restaurant empire. He needed a permit to build on a genius location in

Laos, on the water. But there was a problem getting the permits. The local officials were being difficult.

Steve had no contacts there.

Grant knew that. He said he'd find the contacts but he needed help persuading the officials. He said he knew that Steve was brilliant at this sort of negotiation. He said Steve must have people who could help.

Three weeks later Ian traveled with Jonathan and Grant to Vang Vieng. Steve had suggested that Jonathan bring someone along to babysit and as it turned out Ian had time off from the show while some construction work was being done in the theater. Ian was there to keep Grant out of trouble while Jonathan conducted business. Ian did not have any real idea what the business was but he was happy to take a few days in Laos with the lovely girls who threw flowers from the hillsides and swam slick and topless in the water and the Bob Marley music pouring like tequila into the river and Grant introducing him to new pleasures. One day they went on flying fox swings over the Nam Song while tripping on hallucinogenic cocktails from beachfront bars. A few days later amid the seasonal rushing of the river two Australian men were killed while tubing without life jackets and drifted back downriver bloated and naked, their skin the blue-pink ombré of iridescent fish. Then it was time to go home.

11

O N THE JET from London back to New York there were two pilots, two flight attendants, superb food, cashmere blankets. There were no rules about not using electronics. Poppy surfed fashion sites for a while until Patrizia got up from her generous leather seat next to Steve, and Poppy assumed her place in it. She wrapped her thin self up in a thick blanket. Steve ignored her for some time and then removed his reading glasses and fell into conversing with her. He spoke warmly to her and with a studied expansiveness of spirit. From time to time Roman and Felix looked up from their devices and noticed, expressionless, Steve speaking to Poppy in a way that he rarely spoke to them. It wasn't merely because of the difference in age that he used an unusual tone with her; it was because she aroused an intensity in everyone.

Why does she always get what she wants? said Roman under his breath.

Felix shot him a look. She doesn't, he said, and kept reading.

Steve was already leaning in and lowering his voice to Poppy.

He studied her face with a deep understanding that wetted his eyes. He sketched for her the problematic nature of her desire to work for him instead of going to college, his hands holding his glasses and sculpting in the air with an architectural clarity invisible diagrams of the obstacles before her. He presented for her consideration the complexities of land-use transactions, references to obscure tax codes, the psychological difficulties of people in their twenties who lose their way, certain passages from Shakespeare that related to her ambition and impatience, speculations on what might become of her future if she were to isolate herself from her peers in a way that constituted practically an anthropological experiment. Poppy listened to him with great attention and before he was done she had started crying.

Patrizia returned from the restroom and her fifteen minutes of moving her legs. She looked down at Steve.

What did you say to her?

I was just talking to her about her plans.

Why is she crying?

Steve's face was blank. A blinding blankness like an overcast sky on a March day in the Northeast when there is no sun and no birds and a dead stillness that crushes all hope. Poppy was still crying.

What did you say to her, Steve?

I don't know what upset her. I have no idea.

What did you say to her that is making her cry?

Steve smiled. It is disappointing, he said, when something you wish for and convince yourself is possible is not possible. These are the lessons of youth. I had assumed Poppy knew that I was in some sense humoring her when I suggested I would think about her coming to work for me directly after high school. But it is consistent with my thinking that that course of action would not make sense. I think she must understand that it is her turn to humor me and to consider going to college. At the very least, she has to accept that she cannot work for my company until she is older. Words are words. Poppy, I'm sorry if you misunderstood what I said the other day.

She was still crying. Her nose was cherry red and the whites of her eyes were a pale rose against the strong azure of her irises. She had listened to Steve in silence. Roman chuckled softly as he tortured insurgents on the screen. Poppy stood up and walked with her head down to the restroom. Then Steve rose up and spoke quietly to Patrizia, holding his glasses in his hand and listening to her with his head bent forward, exhibiting great concentration and patience. Felix turned in his seat to look at Poppy as she walked back to her seat, her face washed and an impassive look in her eyes. In the car on the way home Steve gave Poppy several thousand dollars in cash and hugged her tightly on the sidewalk before she and the twins and Neva went upstairs.

Poppy feels hollow taking the money. She feels like the white-and-pink ceramic piggy bank that lived on her dresser when she was little, the coins clinking against the inside when they fell. She knows the money means something but she doesn't know what, cannot decode those clinks. Does it mean that she works for Steve or that he is taking care of her as he should? Does it mean that she is independent or that she is a slave to these bills? Does it make her different from anyone else or the same or better or worse or does it not mean anything at all? These questions about money are never talked about with her, around her. Is the money something natural like food or sex or is it manufactured, a construct, another thing among this crowded universe of things? Poppy pushes the money into the bottom of her bag and throws her bag on the linen-upholstered chair in the corner of her room. At her desk she watches one of her favorite music videos on YouTube, the one about the couple where he enlists in the war and she gets mad and then they show her sitting alone on some bleachers at the end. Poppy watches it over and over and over.

After that Steve and Patrizia got back into the car and rode downtown each of them silent in the leathery dark and they met friends in Tribeca for dinner.

12

THAT NIGHT Neva unpacked and settled into the room in which she had spent only one day before leaving for England. This new job had been a trial by fire. But she would last. She could handle Roman and was beginning to understand Felix. Patrizia liked her. Poppy was heartbreaking, tragic, difficult to love and impossible not to. Alix and Ian would barely be around, the same for Jonathan and Miranda. Steve. Steve shook her and left her hollowed and awed, as if she had been granted a glimpse into the underworld. Gleaming, ghostly, but every inch alive, he seemed to be rising and falling at every moment, a catastrophic wave. That night she would listen to him berate Patrizia when they thought that no one could hear them, and his voice was like a great godlike hand sifting through the coals of a fire, unafraid to touch the hottest most scalding embers of another person.

She saw him sometimes very early in the morning, before he left for work. She never got used to how big he was, how raw looking, and the way his eyelids sagged as if the tiny muscles in them had been cut with a blade. He wore tailored expensive clothes but he was often unwashed, staying up late working in the toxic firelight of his computers, stewing in the rancid overripeness of unquenchable ambition.

You're getting along okay? he asked her.

Yes, thank you.

You find the boys manageable?

I enjoy them.

Steve smiled. I've watched you with them. You're a good worker. Smart. I have my eye on you, he said, very directly, into her eyes.

Neva was afraid that something would snap within her from the excessive tension. It was not a sexual tension, or a romantic tension, but something she experienced as profound and frightening. She realized instinctively that this momentary interaction had brought them fearfully close, as if they were soldiers together in combat, or had witnessed a crime. She felt exhilarated and at the same time uncertain whether she was interpreting the moment correctly. She felt a disintegration of her senses, a delirium that she tried to prevent. There was a siren wailing out on the street that seemed to be coming from a vase of pink flowers on a hall table and a smell of smoke that appeared to be wafting from the bronze chevron-patterned wallpaper.

Neva's glance moved quickly up from the vase of flowers to Steve's slightly sagging, philosophical face, his sculpted nose, his head an ancient marble bust. He smiled and began to tie his tie, which he had been holding in one hand and was now wrapping around his neck. Before he buttoned the top button of his shirt she could see the slightest fur of gray hair on his chest. It was the only place he had gray hair: his chest. He did not often swim or go shirtless so she rarely saw his chest although she would see it sometime later on the floor of the apartment when the medics unbuttoned his shirt and again when she would be the only one to notice the malfunctioning machinery in his hospital room as his torso lay panting and shuddering beneath the pale green gown which fell open as he suffered.

I am impressed by you, he said.

She stood silent. She felt an exquisite conflict, a confusion as to whether or not to believe or accept these words, which she realized her soul or something like her soul had been longing to hear.

Who are you? he said. What is your secret?

She thought for a moment about how to answer him.

My secret is that I don't have any secrets, she said.

His tie was tied by now and he laughed silently. He bent down the better to see her.

I admire your dishonesty, he said.

At that moment one of his phones rang. He took it from his pocket. Like a great ponderous mastodon he lumbered down the hallway toward the vast kitchen and took the call. He wrapped his big hand around the phone. He seemed to step into the conversation as if he were casually walking into a bonfire, entering a native element, himself a piece with the licking flames of talk and trades and complex transactions. Someone had misunderstood his instructions and his voice roared low like a thing alive and Neva watched and heard how his power fled out from him like fire catching and racing in chains along a wooden fence, propelled by the wind. She was aware that he was at the center of some tented military encampment, a demented circus lit up by torches in the middle of the howling desert, and beyond him stretched maelstroms, a vortex, a void which he controlled.

Three hours later when she and the boys left with Patrizia for the beach it was a hot morning with the sun shattering against the East River into a million glinting shards. The helicopter rose high above the water and flew away from the FDR Drive, the gray buildings, the jagged city. For once the boys looked out the window, and they flew through the sky like little gods, and the shards of glass on the water melted into puddles of white and the boys rode on together and for a few minutes their faces were lit up and warm and newly open to the natural world.

13

A LONG WIDE ROAD that cut through the city like an absence of city, cars swerving all over the dirt, no lanes, small buildings, almost too small for people, stretching out from either side of the road. This was Laos and Ian felt uncharacteristically free as he and Jonathan and Grant sped out of Vientiane toward the riverside town in which Grant wanted to build a restaurant.

They rode in the direction of green misty mountains that huddled behind one another like children's heads forming a crowd around something of interest. In this case it was just wide brown road, fewer cars now, some bicyclists, backpackers here and there walking in twos and threes. The air felt light and floral and as if there were nothing separating Ian from his vacation. He was one with the easy sweetness and lazy freedom. That he was here on some mission, to be useful in some way, escaped him and lifted like a kite into the sky. Eventually, gone.

At the tourist town twenty-somethings had overtaken the local culture: tubing, zip-lining, mushroom shakes, everyone half naked, the village children dealing drugs, the bars open all night, the idea of civilization floating down the river like a used condom. Grant and Ian headed to get a drink while Jonathan met with two officials in a back room. They sat at a wooden table, discussing.

Jonathan listened to their reasons for declining a permit. The town was overrun. These tourists had no respect for the Laotians. It was time to crack down on the partying, not encourage it. Music was blowing into the dim room from riverside beaches. Jonathan sipped a Coke and sniffed as he listened to the two men make their case.

Thing is, he said when they finished, my cousin really believes in this restaurant. He thinks it will be good for the town. He'll keep it clean.

That's what they all say, the men said.

Jonathan looked down at the table and smiled with his jaw. Well, this time it's true.

The officials sat silently.

He looked back up at the men.

You know, it could all disappear in a minute. You might think that would be good but all the money coming in: poof, gone, that wouldn't be so good. You're lucky all these kids like coming here.

One of the men closed his eyes. The other lit a cigarette.

Might not be so great for you if the kids moved on someplace else. Like, if it got dangerous around here and they decided to find a new party town.

What do you mean, dangerous?

I don't know. Like for example if a few too many of these drunk kids got in the tubes or on the zip lines and fell in the water during the rapid season. That kind of thing. The area could get a bad reputation.

It's the law that they have to wear life jackets.

Jonathan laughed. Some of them look a little too—a lot too—stoned to pay attention to that.

What are you saying?

I'm not saying anything. Just you might want to think about how important this commerce is to you. The American way is to welcome business, not discourage it.

This is not America.

Jonathan finished his Coke.

Yeah, I get that, he said putting down the bottle. Just think about it. I'll be here for a couple of days.

He found Ian and Grant and the three of them hiked several miles to some caves. The hike was hot and the bugs flew in and out of Ian's eyes and mouth. In the damp cave Jonathan handed over money to a man who nodded and translated to his friends while Grant kept a lookout into the blindingly white sunny entrance bounded by leaves. Ian waited outside, as Jonathan had asked him to. The bugs were a little better at the mouth of the cave.

The next day, a few of the men from the cave help two tourists locate some exceptionally strong cocktails. Now, in the afternoon, the tourists are guided to a flying fox, a zip line that runs above the water. The two muscular men get strapped, without life jackets, into their harnesses.

On an opposite hill the man who had taken the money in the cave takes out a gun. The two tourists swing along the line. Neither courage nor fear in their faces, just an expression of astonished pleasure. The man on the hillside lifts his black gun and he pulls the trigger and the shot hits the place where the harnesses attach to the line.

The explosion is muffled by the sound of the rushing river. Just a shudder of foliage that not even nearby hikers would notice. Two strong athletic bodies drop down in a sudden plummet of flesh and the expressions on their faces smear from excitement to terror in a blur like a face in a Francis Bacon painting. There was one in Steve's office. Jonathan had always admired it.

Holy shit, Grant says later when he hears about the accident.

Oh my God, Ian says.

Drunken idiots, Jonathan says.

Jonathan knows that he has gone too far, that Steve would be upset with him if he were to find out, but he figures that Steve will never find out. That no one will.

And he is usually correct in these matters.

The bodies of the two Australians were found later that day. Local officials announced that new laws would be enacted to prevent zip-lining during the rapid season. Life jackets are mandatory, tourists were reminded. Flyers went up on the doors of the bars. Before they left, Jonathan and Ian and Grant stopped off at an office in a neighboring town and picked up a permit for Grant's restaurant. Jonathan took them out for a last drink that night and held the permit up to the torch-light and turned it this way and that and said: We could have just forged this thing. It's like a handwritten receipt. Just one stamp on it that could be anything.

Ian's face looked somber and confused. I keep thinking about those two guys whipping around in the water like underwear in a washing machine, he said.

Poor assholes, said Jonathan.

Taste this, Grant said.

They each had a forkful of the sauce-covered fish that he

was eating. He said he was going to put something like it on his menu, but with more of a citrusy flavor. It would be his signature dish. Ian and Jonathan closed their eyes while they savored the food and made odd moaning sounds. Strange, pained manifestations of delight came over their shadowy faces, under the flare of the flickering torches.

14

P OPPY PAUSED outside the door to the psychiatrist's office
and looked quickly down Park Avenue where the buildings
extended endlessly in a long façade of brownish-grayish brick
and stone, emotionless and without affect. The east façade
looked at the west façade in some kind of schizoid staring con-
test that had been going on for almost a century. Poppy looked
at the door. She buzzed and was buzzed back at and entered
an empty waiting room, decorated in 1966, a room that time
had passed by and then caught up with again. The midcentury discomfort—which had looked sexy and original at one
point in history—now seemed both antique and familiar and
not unfashionable but decidedly unsexy. Poppy attempted to
shrink her lanky self into the sleekly shaped well-worn couch
with no side arms. Her knees bumped against a low, sad, dark
wood coffee table. In a few moments a slender older woman
appeared before her and gestured for Poppy to follow her into
another room.

Poppy arranged herself again, this time in a slightly more
comfortable chair facing the doctor.

Poppy shimmied out of her coat and released the straps of
her bag, letting them fall like loose reins onto the floor. She
pushed her hair behind her ear.

She dove right in.

So what I was wondering is what can you give me that would go with the other stuff I'm taking? Some cocktail but that won't kill me.

The doctor looked at her like one of the Park Avenue buildings.

I mean I understand that you can never be sure how these things will interact and affect you, but I'm okay with that. There are risks with anything, right?

The doctor nodded and began listing the medications Poppy was already taking.

But you told me those were all very low doses?

True, said the doctor.

Poppy pointed her thumb up at the ceiling a few times in a universal gesture of "bump it up a little."

Let's talk first.

About what?

About how you've been doing.

Poppy twisted in the chair and stared at the wooden blinds. They were slightly open, letting in some sour afternoon light. Beyond them, taxis and black cars slid invisibly by, like fish you knew were in the water but couldn't see. The doctor was looking patiently at her through the watery gloom. The doctor had an unattractive face, leathery, loose, her unbearably kind eyes like soft stones in a tide pool on the beach.

How's school?

Unbelievably boring. The only thing anyone talks about is applying to college. You would think applying to college was the highest, most noble aim of human beings. The goal of our existence on this planet.

How are you feeling?

Like an idiot.

Just because you don't want to apply to college?

I thought I'd be able to go work for Steve.

But he didn't go for that.

Poppy looked right at the doctor.

No. He didn't.

What about that other job?

The psychiatrist closed her eyes slightly. Her eyelids were crepey and nearly translucent. Perhaps she was going to take a nap or perhaps she was threatening to or perhaps she merely wanted to concentrate on Poppy, her silences as well as her words. The doctor wore practical, quietly elegant clothes and very good shoes. She moved her foot just barely in the silence.

Didn't you tell me that you had another prospect? In the theater world?

Poppy widened her eyes and looked like some fucked-up celebrity besieged by the paparazzi.

The doctor jolted awake and widened her eyes, for her, and made a fake, slightly mocking gasp. She looked at Poppy.

You had an offer, yes? Some kind of internship? In the afternoons, after school, this year?

Poppy stared. You want me to take the thing with Ian? she said. That's sick.

The doctor didn't say anything.

I don't mean sick as in cool. I mean sick as in messed up, said Poppy.

I understood, said the doctor.

Poppy pushed her hair behind her ear.

What was the job? asked the doctor.

No one spoke.

Poppy made a low groan.

Didn't he say you could work for him on his show?

Yes.

A musical, correct? Based on the songs of that rock group from the 1990s?

Eighties.

Well, that sounds promising.

Look. First of all, it's a jukebox musical, totally contrived. It's Jane Eyre set to the music of the Talking Heads, which is a genius idea commercially but seems pretty artistically bankrupt if you ask me. And second: Ian is twice my age. At least. I think.

What does that have to do with anything? He's the director. It makes sense that he's older than you.

Poppy rolled her eyes. I told you: he has a huge crush on me. Hair pushed behind ear again. What? You don't believe me?

I didn't say that.

The psychiatrist inhaled deeply. She exhaled. She was quiet while the taxis whooshed past outside.

Narcissism, she said.

She gestured toward the window, to the great world of Park Avenue and beyond. The world of buildings and highways and forests and oceans all somehow tainted by corruption and stained with blood. She took a deep breath and reached for a water bottle on the table beside her and took a sip and screwed the top back on the bottle—she was a careful person—and swallowed.

Poppy stared at her. She gazed as the doctor twisted on the plastic bottle cap. When the doctor spoke again it was not directly into Poppy's eyes but to the blinds on the windows, and she seemed to be speaking to the universe.

I pray. I'm not a religious person, but I pray. To whom, I have no idea. But I pray for this world and for you.

She leaned forward in her chair and put her elbows on her knees and clasped her hands and looked intently into Poppy's eyes. She looked down for a moment and then up to Poppy and lowered her voice. You are a fine young woman, Poppy, if only you would believe that. You truly are. But there will always be selfish people, people who try to take advantage of you. You cannot hide from the world. You will have to be very strong. They talk about post-apocalyptic movies? We are living post-apocalypse already. You will have to be strong to survive. It's up to you to not let the world take advantage of you. I'm not saying it's easy.

She unclasped her hands and reached for the bottle and unscrewed the cap again and took another sip.

So . . . what are you saying?

The doctor leaned back in her chair and did that thing of almost going to sleep again, but she seemed, in some still way, more awake than ever.

I mean, she said, that you are not such a little girl. You can set limits. Draw a line! So what if he has a crush on you! That's his problem. Not yours.

Isn't it sort of my problem?

What, is he going to attack you? The doctor was sitting upright again, eyes open.

Well, no, but he is the director.

Now the doctor rolled her eyes.

And so you have to flirt with him?

Why are you blaming me? That's blaming the victim.

I'm not blaming you, I'm asking you. And stop thinking like a victim. Nothing's happened anyway. So: do you have to flirt with him?

No. I guess not. I mean of course not. Poppy blushed.

I'm not naïve, said the doctor.

What?

I know you have a crush on him too.

What?

You are going to have to grow up faster than you want to.

Poppy was utterly perplexed by now but she was beginning to feel a little better.

Oh, she said.

Break away from Steve, said the doctor. From that family of yours. Do something different.

Like what?

Go, said the doctor. Live your life.

How? asked Poppy. Where?

How: like a mature young woman. Where: out there.

There? Poppy looked at the light streaming in through the slats of the blinds. It was a brighter shade of sour now.

Really? Poppy said.

Really, said the doctor. Where else are you going to go?

When Poppy left the office she had a slightly higher dose of her preferred Benzodiazepine in her pocket. She made her way down the exceedingly clean Upper East Side sidewalk in the now less sour but chillier afternoon, the sky white the color of a lightbulb when it is not turned on, opaque and flattening so that Poppy felt she needed sunglasses but could find absolutely no real evidence of sun. She turned off Park Avenue and headed toward the Met. She felt better for a little while and then like an idiot again. As she sat on the steps of the museum she thought about the fact that somehow the doctor had known her feelings for Ian, more clearly than even she knew them. Was she, Poppy, just such an obvious mess to everyone but herself? No, she thought, she knew she was a mess. But what kind of mess? That was the question. The doctor seemed to know. Poppy had no idea.

She did not see Alix until Alix's gray pants were right in front of Poppy's face. Alix had made her way up the steps of the museum cocking her head and waving to Poppy without response.

Did you honestly not see me? Alix looked down at Poppy from a great height, bleached sky pasted behind her head.

I guess not. I guess I was thinking.

Wow. Are you okay?

Nice.

Alix sat down next to her on the steps.

No really, are you okay? You seem more out of it than usual.

I was just wondering what kind of a mess I am.

Same kind you've always been.

No, it's getting worse.

How so?

Should I go work for Ian? Do some kind of internship? After school and on the weekends? Maybe start now?

It was my understanding that you had declined that offer.

Poppy's hair blew around her head. She was slumped in a thin tweedy coat. Her legs in tights. Short boots tucked a few steps below her. Her bony knees up near her face.

That was probably stupid of me.

Probably.

Alix regarded her. She detested and adored this kid who right now looked like she might never leave the steps of the museum, who might just stay there, wondering and sad until she fell asleep and rolled into the gutter.

Actually, I'm sure he'd give you another chance.

Poppy stared out over the river of Fifth Avenue. Her delicate symmetrical face made Alix want to hit her. And to cry for her.

Why is it getting so windy? said Poppy, the prettiest little wrinkles like a series of commas across her brow. It's only September.

C'mon, said Alix. Let's go inside.

Once inside the museum they seemed to forget that they had arranged to see the latest show of the Costume Institute and instead began wandering the halls in the same random way that they had when Alix had taken Poppy to the Met as a little girl, Alix babysitting for an hour or so while the nanny was out. The paintings on the walls marched past in a carnival procession of color and feeling and the people shuffling around the galleries seemed to be museum pieces too, as if they had stepped out of the paintings and were now lost.

Poppy and Alix landed eventually on a long polished wooden bench facing a historical painting, *The Sortie Made by the Garrison of Gibraltar*, by John Trumbull, 1789, and the violence that had been imagined on the steps would now take place. Poppy left her bag on the bench, she was always leaving her bag somewhere, and stood up close to the painting and read its accompanying description:

> This painting depicts the events of the night of November 26, 1781, when British troops, long besieged by Spanish forces at Gibraltar, made a sortie, or sudden attack, against the encroaching enemy batteries. The focal point of the painting is the tragic death of the Spanish officer Don José de Barboza. Abandoned by his fleeing troops, he charged the attacking column alone, fell mortally wounded, and, refusing all assistance, died near his post. Trumbull portrays him rejecting the aid of General George Eliott, commander of the British troops.

There were two sides of the painting, the Spanish on the left and the British on the right. The open-necked flowing white clothes of the Spaniards contrasted with the uptight red coats of the British. The sky above them all was a lurid pink and yellow, hideous in its shimmering twilight. On the ground lay the dying Don José de Barboza, rejecting the somewhat coldly outstretched hand of General Eliott. Poppy thought that the painting was stilted and ugly and pretentious and stale, but she was drawn to it. It brought her to a place beyond judgment—beyond herself, beyond itself—even as she recognized the painting's limitations.

Alix stood up from the bench swinging Poppy's vintage Balenciaga bag by its long thin straps, nearly mopping the museum's floor with it.

Eventually someone's going to steal this bag, said Alix.

What do you think of this painting?

It's ugly.

I think maybe that's why I like it. You must understand that, that ugly/beautiful thing, said Poppy.

Alix had stopped swinging the bag by now.

You're sure you want to say that to me? said Alix.

Why not? said Poppy.

You're sure?

Why wouldn't I be?

How will you ever have a real friend? said Alix.

Poppy had no idea what she had done to offend Alix, no idea that Alix had assumed Poppy was referring to Alix's appearance as opposed to her aesthetic appreciation of an object, and so Poppy had no recourse but to hear Alix's remark as an insult, which, of course, it was. But under other circumstances she might have been conscious of the pain that was behind it.

I guess I won't have a real friend, said Poppy. Ever. So I can grow up to be just like you.

Two thick blobs of salty water welled in Poppy's eyes. Through the blur of them she could make out Don José de Barboza rejecting General George Eliott's offer of help. The don was turned away from him, looking at a dead soldier, and holding a glinting silver knife. Poppy could almost understand that she and Alix had just enacted a scene very like the one in the painting, one of rejection, wounding, and pride, but this awareness was more of a feeling than a consciousness and it had the effect of making her that much more hurt. How could people be so stupid as to act out what they saw in a painting just because it was staring at them? How out of control were human beings? And were they so out of control? Or had she and Alix landed in front of this painting because it was a depiction of their own private warfare? This was impossible, this trying to understand anything, this trying to communicate with anyone. It was getting too crowded in the museum. It felt as if all of the murdered soldiers in all of the paintings had risen from the canvases and were wandering around the halls: headless, steaming, ashen, stumped. Aghast, blackened, smoky. Alix and Poppy wound their way toward the exit.

15

A LIX AND POPPY didn't notice when they left the museum,
Alix scurrying, Poppy rambling, down the broad steps
toward the sidewalk, that Neva was walking along the other
side of Fifth Avenue—beyond the food carts and waiting taxis
and the rush of black SUVs and colorful pedestrians—with
Roman and Felix. She escorted the two blazered boys through
the gorge of buildings on a shadowed side street, turning onto
the avenue toward the late-afternoon majesty of the museum
and then curving around to stay on the east side of Fifth to
deposit Roman at a friend's apartment for a visit of video warfare and interpersonal victimization, an activity Roman was
looking forward to after having been beaten at After-School
Chess Club by Felix. Neva and Felix rode up with him in the
wood-paneled elevator and left him in the hands of the other
boy's meek nanny and a spiffy male house manager rushing
with a vase of flowers from the kitchen into a library. From the
far reaches of the foyer you could see the expansive kitchen, at
work in which were two cooks, its floor a neon-green laminate.
Investment art in shades of orange and electric pink loomed
on the walls and a cartoonish, contemporary Japanese sculpture beckoned toward the living room, but Felix and Neva
stayed near the front door, bade a brief goodbye to Roman,

and lingered just long enough to see him knock off his shoes and join the other boy in a sports jersey (he had changed out of his school uniform already, not having been enrolled in Chess Club), and with sweaty hair happily race down a hallway to where the electronics awaited.

Neva and Felix now enter the museum. Felix takes a drawing class there once a week and Neva usually wanders the galleries while waiting for him. She and the boys have already settled into a routine only a few weeks into the school year. Patrizia is efficient about signing the children up for activities and arranging a full schedule for Neva to execute. But today instead of looking at paintings or pottery or jewel-encrusted headpieces Neva realizes that she has forgotten some of Felix's art supplies at home and so she rushes back to the apartment to get them for him. She walks briskly up the avenue, the apartment is only a few blocks away, and she enjoys staying on the park side of the street, the full green trees making a canopy above her as if deftly sketched for her to walk beneath.

Under the trees she feels memories dart through her without stopping. Trees, smoke, a dog. She picks up glints of such images all around her and they flash in her brain making sudden connections too brief to comprehend but rushing through her with feeling after feeling. She has the sense of a wild place far back in her past, a welcoming wilderness to which a part of her wishes to return. At the same time she is attuned to the movement of her life speeding forward, onward, under this canopy of trees, toward some goal, gliding, gliding among a million possibilities toward one singular event. She knows that she cannot stop for either one, not the backward past or the uncertain future, knows that she has to keep going, keep soldiering in the present, under these leaves, marching through her memories, bearing her own witness.

She is not going to stop, she will not let anything stop her, and this makes her, underneath the shifting shadows on the sidewalk where nobody is watching her, curl her lips in such a way that she almost appears to be smiling.

That afternoon Steve is home unexpectedly when she enters the apartment. Patrizia is out. Everyone else is out, shopping for the household, doing errands for the household. Even the housekeeper is out purchasing cleaning supplies. Steve is home walking the ruins of the apartment, the new ruins freshly decorated, beautifully appointed, as quiet as the museum, contemporary ruins. Steve and Neva run into each other in a hallway lined with family photographs, all framed in the same kind of frame, an entire wall of witnesses to this encounter. He doesn't fully explain to her why he is home and she doesn't explain to him why she has returned alone. He says something about a doctor's appointment and that he couldn't go straight back to the office. In the carpeted quiet of the hallway it seems as if Steve is on the verge of doing several things: tracing his fingers along her face, confessing some long-ago sin, asking for forgiveness, telling her that he is dying. But he doesn't do any of these things. Instead he says: Come, let's talk for a while in my study. I think I may have some work for you. It might be interesting.

She notices then that she desires him. But she is not attracted to him. They are both suffering, and she is drawn to him. It's impossible to resist, this current.

16

THEY WERE RUNNING through the opening number when Jonathan entered the theater. He slid in by the front door past the empty ticket windows and made his way into the audience where a few assistant producers and investors sat toward the back behind various crew people, stage managers, and assistants who flanked Ian at the fifth row center. The houselights were on and the velvet seats spread out smooth but naked looking in the daytime and the dancers and actors in their rehearsal clothes stood onstage in a silvery-gray void like beings on another planet.

An old college friend of Ian's, who was a British theater critic, and his wife, a playwright, sat in the last row and gazed upon the proceedings among the other scattered audience members. Their faces registered nothing outwardly but Jonathan could read the billions of impressions of rivalry, condescension, misunderstanding, projection, false enthusiasm, shallow judgment, and studied criticism in their posture, blinks, and subtle movements.

The exuberance of the American musical, said the critic.

The hysteria, said the playwright.

Suddenly the young woman playing Jane Eyre and one of the other players spun around and kicked and sang something and the company all turned and shifted and began to move in a line down the stage toward marks drawn in chalk on the floor that denoted a destination. Men in tight sweatpants were leaping onto one another and looping their arms around necks and shoulders. By the time the men had jumped down and thrown themselves onto the floor under the lifted feet of some of the women and with their arms outstretched along the stage, more dancers were beginning to appear from the wings, a moving frieze of arching and bending bodies that trembled and swayed to the rising music. They crossed the stage and vanished back into the wings and reappeared again one by one and by now the lighting designer was at work and so they were silhouetted phantoms with kicking legs that seemed to stir up an unreal shimmering smoke as they wove together and separated and divided into angles and rows and then coalesced and in the lightening aura around them there began to appear what seemed to be a second company of dancers behind them but which were their shadows cast elongated and precise, lurid and howling against a scrim at the back of the stage. Their immense voices and wild screams filled up the theater like a ghostly orchestra heard through some faulty transmission from the underworld normally unheard.

Okay, now let's have you murmuring, engaging the audience as you crisscross downstage, called Ian, and as he spoke they did what he described, extending their faces and arms out to the phantom audience. The footlights came on and colored rays glazed their skin and made them into garish psycho killers who called out to the empty seats from the distant decade of the 1980s. The first chorus began.

The Jane Eyre character was standing in one corner of the stage on her own holding a giant torch which would be lit during production and which she used to fend off the oncoming killers as if in a dream. The dancers passed close by her, one by one, turning, twisting, spinning, and drew close to her and then crumbled away as she defended herself with the invisible flame.

The company now lay on the ground as the number ended. Some of the dancers breathed more heavily than the rest and others sat up impatient for the notes and next routine. Jane Eyre stood at ease now, adjusting her cropped dance sweater. Others chatted quietly to one another.

They walked up onstage, Ian, the stage manager, and the choreographer. They each picked different people to talk to and began gesturing and enacting various movements. Ian looked for a moment offstage to where the killer dancers had fled. He instructed Jane Eyre not to look at them as they danced off and to concentrate on the forces propelling toward her. He conferred with the stage manager and jumped off the stage.

The theater critic and the playwright sat in a stupor. They were nakedly uncomfortable and they looked around the bustling theater as if in a nudist colony or a strip club. Jonathan moved elegantly out of his seat along his row, approaching some investors and producers and making conversation. Then he reached the seats of the critic and the writer.

He stood over them—they were still conferring in their seats—like a nightclub owner stopping at a table of tourists. The lighting designer was playing around and now a golden light suffused the theater while the stage sat in a reddish darkness. Jonathan was standing by their seats, looking down at them before they noticed him. They were discussing commedia dell'arte and its influence on musical theater. Jonathan placed a hand on the critic's shoulder.

Angus, long time no see, he said.

What? Angus turned, startled.

Jonathan smiled.

Oh, hello, said the playwright, named Kai. Angus, she said to her husband as if translating, it's Jonathan, Ian's friend, Alix's brother.

What do you think of the show? Jonathan asked.

They critiqued, politely, emphasizing that musical theater was not really their thing. Jonathan towered over them, casual, comfortable, listening with a bemused expression to their hesitations and exaggerated admiration. Jonathan let them know that he was thinking of investing in the production.

From a huddle with his associates and assistants Ian emerged and strolled up the aisle. A few of the performers were left onstage, some had headed backstage and several roamed the aisles collecting bags and heading out for a break. Ian patted them and squeezed their shoulders as he passed them. They accepted his attentions hungrily, happily, some childishly. They stepped aside as he opened his arms to embrace Jonathan.

Entertaining? Ian said to Angus and Kai.

They were nodding enthusiastically with their heads, all the while withholding any real praise with their bodies and tone of voice. They had just come from Warsaw where they'd seen an incredible experimental production of Ibsen, very political, they explained. *A Doll's Horse?* said Ian. *Hedda Hair?* said Jonathan. The playwright looked at them.

What do you make of the concept? said Ian. The Jane Eyre meets Talking Heads idea?

Nothing yet, said Angus. I'd need to see the whole thing first.

What do you think of the staging?

It's hard to tell, said Kai. Without the set, or costumes.

That's good, said Ian, who didn't really care what they thought. Because it's all going to change anyway. This is a work in progress. Early days still.

He gazed down at them and thought about how many years he had known them. At one time, he had considered them friends. But ever since his early success they had treated him resentfully, dismissively. Now he saw them as pompous and pretentious and deeply vain in spite of their bland academic outfits and aggressively aging hair. They'd followed his successful career as if they were bird-watchers and he some common pigeon who had inexplicably been accepted by a flock of rare eagles. They no more believed in his talent than they believed that they themselves might be untalented. Over the years they had won prizes and fellowships and commissions and professorships. They had been invited to lecture and appeared in numerous footnotes. These achievements had been like snakebites on their egos, swelling them out of proportion to the rest of their beings so that their sense of importance bulged and tottered on top of them like extra heads, as if they were monsters in a fable, muzzled, drooling, snouted, skin split to reveal pink bone and yellow ooze. There was a flurry of conversation as Ian tried to swat away their lumbering passive-aggressive attacks and Jonathan enjoyed the performance like a stallion watching smaller animals argue over a rodent.

After Angus and Kai left the theater Jonathan told Ian he'd like to invest in the show. Then he said: So Alix tells me Poppy is starting an internship with you. Interesting.

PART TWO

The Total Dark Sublime

Were all stars to disappear or die,
I should learn to look at an empty sky
And feel its total dark sublime,
Though this might take me a little time.
—W. H. AUDEN, "The More Loving One"

17

Poppy came from a complicated family but this much can be explained: she knew Ian as the best friend of her considerably older half sister Alix. Technically, Alix was Poppy's first cousin, but Alix's father Steve had adopted Poppy at age six, when Poppy's mother, Steve's sister Diana, had died and left Poppy an orphan. There had never been any father in the picture. At least no one that Poppy knew.

It begins with a child.

Poppy does not know much of anything other than that when she is with Ian nature seems inverted: the air between them pulses but her own heart stops beating every few seconds, the outside world falls silent while a siren in her head blares from atomic synthesizers. There is conversation and a dangerous warmth, a raw heat rippling in what seem like visible waves as she and Ian speak, and Poppy, nervous, red cheeked, talks too quickly and ends up regretting half her words.

Ian is unmarried and pushing forty, and his age, combined with the feral attraction he feels for this teenager, has sentenced him to a low-level appointment with his own mortality, a feeling of dread as if an unpleasant yet unavoidable conference call were perpetually looming. He has no idea what to do with this feeling. His career is reaching new heights after his early successes, and he is not in favor of any distractions from work, such as an entanglement or even an emotional connection. He throws himself more feverishly into the Broadway show he is directing, staying up until all hours at workshops, jumping onstage to demonstrate choreography and gestures, in that way that directors do.

Onstage he is a black silhouette, the bright lights blinding behind him, illuminating nothing. He will be burned into her brain, branded on her frontal cortex. She will be able to call up this image and feel her every emotion singularly fixed on this picture. It is as if the rest of her mind ceases to think and each connection points only to him. It is a reflex and it is a meaningful feeling. She is frightened, awoken, awake.

After weeks of flirtation—texts and e-mails and old-fashioned phone calls—that had begun during Poppy and Alix's brother Jonathan's wedding at a rented estate in the English countryside, Ian and Poppy had been reduced to bodies with heads, no sense in their brains. Poppy had lost the ability to think clearly, to formulate coherent arguments, to do her homework. Ian threw himself even more intensely into his show. When she arrived for the unpaid internship that Alix had secured for her at the theater on the wrong afternoon and found Ian alone in the fifth row center, his hands folded over his chest, his feet up on the seat in front of him, she should have gone home. He should have sent her home. The enveloping darkness of the empty house, the feeling of her feet walking ahead of her down the aisle, and then the slow hours during which they sat side by side in velvet seats, talking and later touching: everything that happened should not have happened. He was too old. She was too young. But something, some encoded understanding that they were meant to be together, compelled them to abandon any notion that this was probably not a good idea.

Should I walk you home?

No, that's okay. I'll find a taxi.

I'll get you one.

No, that's okay. I'm okay.

It's late. I'm coming with you. It's dark outside. Let me help you. I mean help you get a cab.

Poppy and Ian had no plan, no vision of how their relationship would unfold, only a chronic twisting in the pits of their stomachs, a nebulous, persistent sense that what they were doing was inevitable and also a mistake, which propelled them forward. For days, then weeks, there were long, amorous walks and secret meetings at the theater and even Ian's apartment. Receipts and napkins and other mementos of their time together filled Poppy's pockets and book bag and the drawer of her bedside table. Poppy waited for someone to find out, until she realized no one would and she told one friend and then forgot to worry. She followed Ian's lead for how to keep their involvement both daring and secret, hiding in the folds of the curtain until all of the actors and tech people had left, sleeping for a couple of hours at his place before heading uptown, through the galvanized light of early morning in the city before anyone at home woke up.

The silver light blasts off of windows, bounding across roof-tops, blinding. She squints, trying to find an explanation for her self, her situation, her unfamiliar ecstasy. Is this just a superficial metropolitan gleam or is it more? Does the sun make any sense? Does morning? She is a vessel of questions, with no answers. Are there answers? She leans back and closes her eyes and calls up an image and her mind fires and the questions fade away.

They had spent several months in this state, sharing every feeling that drifted by, stealing tiny moments and burning glances, and suffering through serious conversations about whether they had any future, until one night, in the grip of a new degree of passion, Poppy came across a letter. Rummaging through Ian's desk while he was in the shower, she had found the bloated white envelope filled with photographs, and for the first time in her life she threw a bottle at a mirror and it broke. It was clumsy and impulsive. She burst into the bathroom and smashed the glass into the medicine cabinet, and Ian, without even stopping the rinsing of his hair, finished his bathing and then calmly explained, with a towel wrapped around his waist, that he had been looking through photos of old girl-friends from the eighties as part of his research for the show.

The corner of the towel drooping, careless, nonchalant. She wants to pull it, rip it out, like ripping out his tongue.

Poppy did not succeed in getting a rise out of Ian at that moment, but her jealousy was duly noted, and it changed things.

She had never known her father and been orphaned at six, but there wasn't much for which she had had to fight: she had grown up with marble foyers and private chefs, attentive teachers and other perks of being rich that seemed, from very far away, to make up for a grossly dysfunctional family. Now, for the first time, the instinct that had made her clench her fists while she slept, the impulse that had led her to be fiercely independent and appear aloof and eccentric to her peers, was manifesting itself with a purpose. Possessiveness matured her and gave her definition. It brought out her true nature, her terrible longing and submerged rage. It heightened everything about Poppy: her angled face, her knowing naïveté, her sarcastic smile and adorable wit. Her careless, fearless, superbly plain sense of style and ravishing big eyes. And the womanliness it graced her with caught Ian's attention and made him, finally, begin to love her.

Where are we going? she asked.

To a movie, he said.

To a movie? In a movie theater? Really?

What? Is that so crazy?

Can't we just watch something at your place?

No, we're seeing an old movie. A real film. And it would be sacrilegious not to see it in a theater.

Okay, if you say so, Grandpa.

Look, I'm proud that I was formed by the twentieth century. No Internet, no texting, no cyberbullies. We had art. We had live, communal experiences.

People tweet while they watch TV, you know, Poppy said, knowing this would drive him crazy.

Oh Jesus, he said, smiling wildly, and took her by the hand.

They were running across Houston Street. The Saturday

after Thanksgiving and the day ending so early it felt like what she imagined it might feel like in Sweden. A blue, crisp holiday air and a vibration of excitement, the intersection of urban consumerist buzz and genuine social well-being, people looking one another in the face if not the eyes along the sidewalks, bustling families and children in parkas that left their arms puffed out at an angle as if they were ginger-cookie people, little happy robots breathing in the brisk New York City climate that changed block to block, but that was on this evening maintaining a steady supply of wintertime cheer, fellow feeling, camaraderie among strangers, something akin to joy.

He took her to see *L'Atalante*, by Jean Vigo, at the Film Forum. Ian held Poppy in the darkness and she thought it was the most beautiful movie, the most beautiful day of her life. When the skipper dove underwater and imagined that he saw his wife circling, circling with one arm curved loosely above her head, her white dress shimmering, Poppy felt a wave of pleasure wash over her as if she herself were underwater, circling, circling. It was warm and cool under the water, fast and slow. Temperature and time floated away, melted, disappeared. Only being was left, being and circling in the water.

The love they share is an attempt to express the inexpressible. There is no word for what they have, who they become when they are together. It is theirs and they belong to it.

Alix invited Ian, as usual, to the family's holiday party at Steve and Patrizia's apartment and of course Poppy was there, bantering with Steve's business associates, flirting with the bartender, swiping canapés from silver trays with a sophisticated, practiced touch. The tables bulged with arrangements of fruit and ornaments, pale green grapes and pears and orbs made of glass, and burnished, dusky-gold garlands running the lengths of the tablecloths and slipping their thick dark leaves and glinting metallic beads in between plates of smoked salmon, sliced steak, bowls of brioche rolls, sourdough rolls with olives and rosemary, and wheat rolls with raisins and hazelnuts. Who spent time thinking up so many different kinds of rolls?

Poppy was sitting now on a long, low oyster velvet-covered couch and Ian watched from a careful distance as she talked to Felix. Felix stood by the couch, neither comfortable nor uncomfortable, at peace in his trousers and leather shoes and jacket and the bow tie that he had insisted on wearing in spite of Patrizia and Roman's objections. Ian could see the way Poppy treated Felix with graceful kindness, a reverence that she reserved for very few people. She looked at him thoughtfully, patiently, recognizing his complex inner life and dignifying what others might have deemed his eccentricities by listening to him, answering his questions, allowing his truthful eyes to rest on her.

Later, when Felix had gone to sleep and Poppy and Ian were seated on a different couch, this one a chesterfield upholstered in sovereign blue, having been unable to avoid each other for an entire evening, the two of them balanced dessert plates on their laps amid a large group engaged in conversation about sports, politics, technology, and television. At first, Ian had thought of offering his opinion on a recent political scandal but the actual idea dissolved in his brain and he found himself unable to understand why anyone would care about the incident. Similarly, Poppy considered proffering her thoughts on the latest hot movie star and whether he was hotter or less hot than another hot actor but as she was opening her mouth it occurred to her that she was completely uninterested in the subject. In keeping the nature of their relationship a secret, she and Ian were carrying on their own private conversation, not spoken but some internal communication that heightened the energy connecting them and kept them close. Joyful, afraid, joyfully afraid, they sat at either end of the long sofa, smiling at other people, pretending to listen, nibbling at their ganache, falling more and more in love.

SO IT REALLY WAS a tragedy when the housekeeper told Jonathan about the receipts and souvenirs and Jonathan told Steve about Poppy's affair with Ian and Steve told Ian that he, Ian, was Poppy's biological father. Steve was a ferociously intelligent self-made mogul who had scaled the sheer-glass mountainsides of the international real estate community to become a member of the planetary elite. He was sixty-two, and he was wearing a bespoke suit on his large, unmuscular frame. He stood up and took his jacket off, hanging it carefully on the back of his chrome-and-leather chair, and walked around his desk to position himself, as he rolled up his shirtsleeves, to sit, just barely, on the front of the desk, looking down at Ian. After explaining to him how he knew that Ian was Poppy's father and that he wanted Ian to never tell Poppy of this relationship, because, of course, as Ian would agree, such knowledge would be devastating to her, Steve insisted, effectively, that Ian sign a confidentiality agreement. Therefore, in spite of Ian's feelings for Poppy, in spite of his stunned recognition that he was facing, for the first time in his life, a moral dilemma—the kind of thing that in his mind only occurred in screenplays and nineteenth-century novels—in spite of his idea of himself as a good and relatively speaking noble person, when Ian broke up with Poppy and hurt her more than she could possibly understand, he was not legally permitted to tell her why.

18

IAN HAD FIRST met Steve over twenty years ago, when Ian and Alix were freshmen in college, but he had never in all those years received a phone call from him. Who knows how long Steve had been waiting to make the call, but on that particular day Ian answered his cell, arrived shortly thereafter on a high floor of a building in Rockefeller Center, and, after walking down the gleaming corridor lined with modern art as violently and visibly expensive as if it had been painted in blood brushed on with thousand-dollar bills, learned from Steve that he, Ian, was Poppy's biological father.

Ian did not believe it, not even when Steve, sitting behind his gargantuan desk in his spotless office, explained coolly that his sister Diana, Ian's former writing teacher, had told Steve so, shortly before she died. Ian did not believe it when Steve described how Diana had known from her intimate, perhaps drunken, conversations with Ian that he had been making extra money to pay for his off-campus apartment by donating sperm at the local sperm bank. Ian did not believe it—because he could not bear to believe it—when Steve told him that Diana had been able to get Ian's sperm because she had known that he had lied on the medical intake form, Ian having told her, laughing over vodka and tonics at the Castle Bar, that he had claimed on the questionnaire that his mother was in perfect health, that he had been captain of his high-school basketball team, and, just for fun, that he knew French, Italian, Swahili, and ancient Greek. It was easy, Diana had told Steve drily from her hospital bed, tubes worming their way from her nose and arms, to look for the basketball captain who spoke Swahili. There were only two.

Ian's equanimity, whatever was left of it, slid to the floor as if he were shedding a skin. He felt naked, cold, exposed. Being told his own secret was a new kind of humiliation, and one he quickly rejected. That he had possessed a mystery previously unknown to him could have stirred his lively sense of drama, but it did not. Instead, he struggled to regain his self-control in the face of knowledge about himself which was too painful to comprehend. In an instinctive gasp of emotion, his love for Poppy rushed through him, a sudden warmth, a radiating orange glow, and then dissipated, like the fading blink of a firefly's pulsing brightness. Now he felt naked and dark. This was shock. He had never really experienced shock.

Ian would have been more prepared to respond to the news that it was Steve who was his, Ian's, biological father, and that he was leaving Ian his vast real estate empire, its tentacles extending and gripping tightly around the globe, to inherit and oversee, effective immediately. But that could not have been further from Steve's intent.

———

Steve walked around his desk to position himself, as he rolled up his shirtsleeves, to sit, just barely, on the front of the desk, looking down at Ian.

Ian hoped that the glow from a moment before would return to warm him, but it had been extinguished. Or, rather, he had extinguished it in an act of self-protection. But he waited, waited for it to return.

Ian was saying: I don't know what to say. I'm stunned. I need some time to process this information.

To Steve, the word "information" meant many things. Information was the currency that greased the wheels of commerce, and which you hoarded and then revealed with care—let it slip from your grasp too easily and you would never succeed. Information was knowledge, the means by which people learned about one another, obtained access to their inner machinery, and then manipulated them. Sometimes, information was fatal, something that chased you until it caught up with you and struck you down in the thriving prime of consciousness. But as Steve watched Ian, who had gone pale except for a bright redness around his eyes, it became evident to him that information was not, not in any universe that he was master of at least, something that you needed to "process."

Steve had wondered for years when Ian would become aware of his relationship to Poppy and step forward to make some claim. To begin with, everyone always suspected that Poppy's father must be someone whom Diana knew—she wasn't the type to just let anyone share her child's DNA. She was an intellectual, an artist, and very, very picky. All three traits had combined to keep her unmarried, according to her mother and brother. Was she too intimidating—slender Diana with the ferocious blue eyes and patrician nose? People surmised for years that the father must be Diana's first boyfriend from graduate school, the genius one who went on to found an Internet company in the nineties and then killed himself in the dot-com bust. Others guessed that it was Diana's editor, the one who convinced her to write lush, political, historical fiction and who made her semifamous, the one with the fluffy hair and the decisive cheekbones. But no one, not even Alix, had ever made the connection that Ian was the father, in spite of the fact that Diana obviously adored him—he was her favorite student—and he had remained close with the family for all this time. Perhaps it was because he was several years younger than Diana and seemed so eternally boyish, even well into his thirties. Or perhaps it was because no one wanted to see, thought Steve, because from his point of view the physical resemblance between Ian and Poppy was clear, if not uncanny. It had seemed strange and tragic to everyone when Diana died that there was no one to come forward and claim paternity. Who was this hidden man, this secret father, who would let his own child be orphaned? Who was this Arthur Dimmesdale character who would not accept his responsibility and shoulder his moral obligation? The tragedy was mitigated somewhat by the Victorian-novel good fortune of Steve's being a billionaire and raising his niece in plutocratic splendor. But the questions and guesses and rumors persisted. Now Steve had finally, for Ian only, cleared up the confusion.

Don't you want to know why I'm telling you now? Steve asked, somewhat like a villain in a thriller.

Obviously I have a lot of questions, Ian replied.

Disappointingly, Steve thought.

I'm telling you because it has come to my attention that you have been spending a lot of time with Poppy, now that she is working on your—and here he hesitated as if having a hard time saying the silly word—musical. And I am uncomfortable with the idea that you might misinterpret any, shall I say, unconscious forces that might draw her to you. I had hoped not to have to share this with you, not only because it was not something my sister wanted me to divulge to anyone, even yourself, but also because you do not impress me as a person who would be a good father . . . figure. Here Steve paused to see if his insult had fully registered, but he received no indication if it had. He continued: I have given great consideration to telling you, and I am only doing so to keep my Poppy safe. I also want to keep her happy, which means I fully expect and insist that you never say anything to her about this. Obviously, and here he smiled, in a menacing impersonation of empathy, it would be traumatic and possibly devastating information to encounter, particularly for an adolescent.

Just so that they were both completely clear about their understanding, Steve went on, he'd had some papers written up. Due to the sensitive nature of the information therein, he said he'd appreciate it if Ian could look them over now—he could sit down on the couch on the other side of the room if he'd like and make himself more comfortable—and then sign them. It was very straightforward, basically a nondisclosure agreement, which he was sure Ian must have seen before, his line of work being the entertainment business. Then he said he was very pleased that they had had this talk.

———

Steve held out the forms to the shaking figure in the chair. Ian took one cursory look over them and, his hands trembling, asked for a pen and signed. And that was how he found out that he was Poppy's father.

If Ian had been another kind of person, someone less interested in professional success and others' approval and more curious about the whorls and depths of human psychology, he probably would have spent more time having wondered about Poppy's parentage. As it was, he had given the question very little thought, and had assuaged whatever guilt and soothed whatever sadness he had felt about his beloved late mentor's young child by thinking of himself as an "important grown-up" in her life, someone who appeared from time to time with interesting stories from the world of adults and with excellent wide-eyed listening skills. He had shown enthusiasm for her interests over the years, the play kitchen and sparkly tutus, the books and movies and byzantine social world of girls, and just as he was becoming interested in Poppy as a female he was excited when Alix had suggested to him that he hire her, smart, sophisticated, well-educated Poppy, to be an intern on his show. But the musical—a rollicking exploration of 1980s America seen through the eyes of a group of friends and based on his own drug-addled yet somehow indelible experiences of college, deconstructionism, the Reagan years, and New York nightlife—sent him so far back into the cataracts of his own myopia that he was less inclined than ever to consider from whose sperm his new girlfriend had sprung, divided, evolved, and been spawned.

Every day, he paced back and forth in front of the stage, reliving his debauched, intellectual, and weirdly innocent early adulthood, bewildered by the feeling that his life had changed so much and not at all. A banal revelation, he knew, but it led him to the less-ordinary understanding that in the middle of his life he was becoming aware that there was no such thing as the middle. Either everything was the middle, in which case there was nothing on either side to make it, by definition, the middle, or everything was the beginning, or, of course, everything, and he did not like to think about this, was the end. He had not forgotten his time in college. On the contrary, he remembered it vividly and in detail, but his memory was changed by all that had happened since: his first play, which had been an unexpected hit, his ambivalence about its success, his descent into despair about the politics and pretensions of the artist's life, his subsequent escape into directing, his realization that no world was better than any other, people were people. By now, everything was new again, and this equal parts giddy and depressing sense of the eternal newness of life contributed to his leading himself and Poppy astray. The relationship made him on the surface feel closer to his college days, and underneath reminded him annoyingly of his distance from that time, his hunger for an irretrievable excitement, his disappointment with either praise or criticism of his work, and the many slender, well-read, and hyperarticulate women with whom he had blundered through much of his life. The scent and seduction of Poppy had been very familiar to him, and he felt certain that his scent would become familiar to her, as no doubt she would meet other men like him when she left, in a year, for college, or real life, or whatever.

Then came the day when Poppy had found the letter on his desk. He had experienced it before—the flash of violent anger from a jealous woman, furious with hurt. But this time he saw how the hurt opened other hurts and changed

Poppy, made her tough, and he watched her more closely from that point on, with her round eyes growing elegantly narrower every day, and for the first time in his life, he allowed someone—Poppy—in completely.

Now he feels that orange surge beginning again and at the same time feels himself attempting to extinguish it, like an insect in the process of committing suicide.

The love they have is an attempt to express the inexpressible. There is no word for what they have, who they become when they are together. It is theirs and they belong to it.

Take it away and they feel expelled, afraid, unknown, bereft. Unwanted, unalive, alone.

It is impossible to extinguish this without denying who he is. So he will have to deny who he is, become someone else. He makes the decision—it is not really a decision, he has no real choice—to do that. He decides to do that for her.

After he left Steve's office, Ian went down to the rink at Rockefeller Center and looked at the skaters. Across the ice, past the little kids clinging to the railing and the girls practicing spins, past the older couples holding both hands with crossed arms and pushing expertly forward, skated an actress from the show. There was the escape he craved, just within reach. He did not show up at the theater for the next two days, but when he returned he found Poppy. She had, obviously, been acutely aware of his absence. One of the notebooks that he kept backstage had been ripped apart, and the pages lay scattered around a garbage can, like pieces of a carcass, illustrating her frenzy and despair. He picked up the strewn bits of paper and carried them to the audience, where he sat with them in his lap for a long time. Three nights later, he found a plastic Baggie stuffed in his jacket pocket. It contained hundreds of shredded slices of a photograph. It took him a while, but he eventually puzzled together that they were fragments of a picture of Poppy. Some nights later he finally called her, breaking the tense silence that existed between them at the theater, and she came over to his apartment. He broke down when he saw her, his face twisting in a series of awkward expressions. He promised he would stop seeing the actress from the show, acted as if that were the only problem, and they fell asleep side by side, fully clothed, after nothing more than an embrace.

Poppy can still see the ceiling of that room, will always be able to see it. The blank expanse onto which she had projected romance, passion, real love, and now hurt, betrayal, confusion, pure pain. Each one of the feelings has been thrown up onto the ceiling above Ian's bed like shadows in *The Allegory of the Cave*, the cave she had learned about last year in eleventh grade Social and Political Philosophy with Mr. Newman. She had liked reading Plato, but even now could not reconcile her awareness that each of those fleeting feelings had felt so real, each one with its own distinct shape against the wall: plantlike, animal-like fringed clouds, Rorschach tests of her emotional development as it passed by, shadowy, across the Benjamin Moore Linen White–painted ceiling, with the sense that they were unreal, illusions, reflections of bodily sensations that while hers and hers alone still may or may not have depended on some truth outside the reality of herself. Was that truth Ian? Real Love? Some Platonic sunlight burning beyond human vision, above University Place, above Greenwich Village, New York City, all the cities on the planet, the world? Did such a sun exist? Did it matter? Did it make any difference at all if her interpretation of events was real or unreal as long as her feelings had felt real to her? Whenever she remembers that ceiling she will feel a sharp acute pain, as if her heart muscle tears a little bit. She will always feel a sadness when she remembers those feelings, those shadows, that color, that ceiling.

The following night she rode up in the elevator and rang the doorbell to Ian's apartment and he greeted her without a smile for the first time. She could sense his hesitation as he stood on the threshold, one foot holding the door ajar, as if he were frightened by her presence. Her head, a riot of confusion, throbbed painfully. He let her in: the rooms looked the same as before, but she breathed in a different scent, not of another woman but of a cleanliness that admitted no earth, no skin, no dirt, and she could tell that he had scrubbed the apartment clean of their passion, of her, and she could see him now, sitting in a chair, his elbows on his knees and his head in his hands.

19

I AN LEFT POPPY sitting in the corner of the couch with her face in her hands while he stood up to walk to the kitchen to get her a glass of water.

I'm so sorry, he said, heading back toward her. His voice had the flat unreverberating sound emitted by someone who knows that the only words available to him are useless clichés, however true they might be. His face was pale and strained, nervous and determined. He could not believe that he was in this situation, and his amazement at the circumstances made him seem robotic and unconvincing.

I know this seems crazy and completely out of the blue, but I promise you it's the best thing for both of us. I love you. I know you don't believe me right now, but it's true. Please, can you please let me see your face? Poppy? Poppy. The last thing in the world I would ever want to do is hurt you. Please, Poppy. Please believe me.

———

He sat down on the couch and with the water in one hand he tried to touch her arm or stroke her hair. She batted him away. He was putting the glass very gently on the coffee table when Poppy lifted her head and pulled one elbow back as if she were stretching a bow. It wasn't something she'd ever done before except perhaps in a nightmare and now it surprised her with its ease. She furled her fingers into a fist and raised her arm up high and put her weight behind her shoulder and slammed her naked anger against his back and hit him and then she did it again.

They fell onto the couch. Ian was trying to restrain her, but he could not. Poppy knelt above him with her forearms grasped in his hands and her face reddened with fury, her eyes vivid blue. Her wide eyes, usually searching, now glared. Her expression not its typical, gently mocking self. She shook her head and the brown bangs of her short haircut flew to the side. The line of her long clean neck straightened. She began to kick. She pressed her full weight into his hands and kicked into his shins, into the couch, sending a pillow onto the floor. She bent her bony knee into his thigh and tried to knee him with her other leg in his groin. She was flailing like an enormous bird. Ian only held on more tightly. She writhed until his arm buckled and he let go of her for a moment. She fell onto his chest. They jerked on top of each other. Then his breathing slowed and they stopped moving. Ian wrapped his arms around her while she cried. When she pulled away and got off of him and stood up she knocked over the glass and swept her hair out of her eyes and went to the bathroom.

She splashed her face with icy water until she could not feel her hands. She sat on the toilet with the lid down and took a number of deep breaths, studying the pattern of small black and white hexagonal tiles on the floor. When she had calmed down she went into the living room and scooped up her bag and her jacket and fished around in her pocket for some keys and dropped them on the rug. Then she slipped her feet into her low suede boots and told Ian what she thought of him and left the apartment and didn't wait for the elevator but instead ran down the eleven flights of stairs.

On the sidewalk Poppy marched with a steady step and the wind ruffled her hair and she moved her lips the tiniest bit while she talked in her head. It was going dark outside, violet bands of light sliding between the buildings. Shapes massing in shadows like old twentieth-century film negatives thrown on top of one another. Weaving red taillights drawing quickly disappearing arcs and lines between the otherwise disconnected people. Night didn't fall in New York so much as rise, the saturation deepening, the volume lifting, the energy elevating and heightening people's consciousness of themselves, their sensations or their thoughts, depending on who they were.

What were you thinking? she thought.

You were thinking that he was cruel and that this was the worst thing that had ever happened to you.

That was smart, have a temper tantrum and behave like the teenager you are which is probably why he wanted to end it to begin with.

Would you just forget about him? He's pushing forty. Well, he should pick on someone his own age.

———

Poppy stopped at a corner and waited for the light. She could feel the doubts accumulating and dispersing through her mind and body, and beneath them, a deeper river of pain like a second nervous system, an even-more-hidden network of hurt. The idea that this was the worst thing that had ever happened to her was ludicrous. She had lost her mother when she was six. This was just a reminder. So why the searing heat in her solar plexus like a sword being slowly pulled out? This had to stop. In her mind she stood with Ian on a high rock, and miles below them pooled a glassy ancient lake. There was no sound at this altitude, on this craggy cliff of sublime remove. A glowing white sky behind his head. She looked at his face, the fine tracings of lines around his gray eyes like hieroglyphics, letters of another alphabet. If only she could read them she would understand so much. But she couldn't. They didn't mean anything. That's what I must seem like to him, she thought, meaningless. Then she raised her arm and put her hand on his chest and pushed him. He fell soundlessly down and that was it.

20

STEVE HAD TAKEN to holding some meetings in the apartment. He liked to have people brought to his study directly. He would be reading or writing when they arrived and they would be seated beside the large low round gleaming marble table, asked what they would like to drink, brought the drink with a square linen cocktail napkin, and be made to wait for Steve until he finished his work. He had an enormous office and several conference rooms at his headquarters in Rockefeller Center, but he preferred to speak to certain business associates in the privacy of his own home. Since these meetings were always held during the day when the boys and Poppy were in school and Patrizia out and about in the city, Steve knew that Neva would be free on occasion to greet these guests and accompany them to his library. He had several assistants at the office and there was a secretary at home too, but she had her own little room, and as Steve explained, as if he even needed to, to Neva, the secretary was handling household matters, scheduling, event planning, returning deliveries, making appointments, and so on, but he did not involve her in his business affairs. He trusted Neva, he said, enough to give her this important task. And, speaking to her in a low whisper, as he made notations in a notebook, he expressed his interest in having her stay in the room during the meetings.

Neva asked him what his purpose was in all this.

Steve adjusted his glasses and kept writing. He stopped for a moment as if he were going to answer her but then kept writing while she stood there, in his study, her spine aching from standing so still.

Steve shut his notebook and checked his computers and then closed a few screens and took off his glasses. He breathed deeply and wiped his huge hand over his face. It looked like a massive tarantula grappling with its prey. When he was finished with the gesture he breathed deeply again.

There is no one else in my employ I can trust in this matter. Anyone I bring into this from my team will try to persuade me to act against my conscience.

He looked about the room. He nodded toward bookshelves and maps, glass-covered model ships, photographs of natural grandeur taken by the great American landscape photographers, mesas and cliffs, canyons and boulders, waterfalls spilling and tangling down, framed and matted, hung at ideal viewing height.

These business associates of mine, he said, they may seem harmless or as though they want to collaborate with me for our mutual benefit. They may appear to bring useful suggestions or valuable opportunities. Yet they would devour me. Any ground I give them will be despoiled. This country was built by raping the land and these people would take it to the furthest extreme, pioneers of depravity. This is what they don't understand: nature conquers all. And by nature I don't mean man's nature or wildness I mean the endless timeless force of nature. Nature will bring them down in the roughest way but I do not want to be brought down and so I am forced to fend them off, hold something sacred. These are vicious people and I am going up against them naked.

Naked?

Unprotected, outside the law. I could bring the law into it but then they would have me killed. There are too many of them, everywhere, and I would expose myself by bringing in the law. No, I have to stand up to them myself.

Why me? Why do you need me?

A witness. I need a witness, someone strong who will not send me the message to cave to them and who will show no fear.

How do you know I won't?

I don't. I'm trusting my instinct.

Neva stood before him. She had elevated her style of clothing after having worked for the family for a few months and now she wore a neutral-colored blouse, a black skirt, and black leather boots. They were not expensive but the effect was elegant.

If nature conquers all, then why bother to fight these people? she asked. Eventually, they will lose.

Steve angled his large head. His chin jutted out and his eyelids drooped. He spoke slowly: Eventually is too long. What they want to do is too terrible.

Why is it your responsibility to stop them?

I can't stop them. But I can keep them off my property. I don't have to give them a place to violate.

They will find someplace else.

Steve looked at her with a menacing, rocklike determination. Yes, he said. But not my place.

She thinks he looks like one of those heads on Mount Rushmore but thousands of years from now, when the wind has worn them down, not to the bone, not to dust, but softened them and in so doing made them more ferocious because they have lasted, their softer edges expressing their endurance. She looks at him and it is like the Sphinx staring at Mount Rushmore, two monuments, two ruins, sand blowing, no people, stone and clay.

A few days later Neva greeted two men at the door and escorted them to Steve's study. She seated them on the couch and brought them bottled water. Steve kept working at his desk. His fingers tapped rhythmically. Eventually he took off his reading glasses, sighed, and stood up. He looked at the two men sitting on his couch. One was slender and tall, the other of average height and very broad. Steve's face was furrowed, sagging, thoughtful. He breathed deeply and nodded for Neva to close the door. She did so and stayed in the room.

The slender man was named Warren. He was some kind of sinister professional. He had a briefcase on his lap. His long arms dangled at his sides. He spoke first.

Did you have a chance to think about our proposal?

I did, Steve said.

Warren looked at the broad man. Excellent, Warren said. He began opening his briefcase as he said: We were concerned you would dismiss the idea outright.

That's not your problem, Steve said.

Warren stopped. He spoke without lifting his head from looking down at his briefcase.

Do we have a problem?

Yes, Steve said. We do. But it isn't that I didn't think about your proposal.

Warren looked again at the broad man and then back at Steve, who was by now leaning against his desk, towering.

We have a mission to get this thing done, Warren said.

Steve didn't answer.

You know this will happen with or without you.

Steve unscrewed the top of a water bottle with his articulate fingers. I'm aware that this is the direction our world is going, he said.

So you want to be a part of it, we assume.

Don't assume.

You'll go out of business without us.

Maybe. Eventually.

And that's okay with you?

That's not your concern. You do what you want.

Warren rose and looked beyond Steve out through the large windows that contained a view of the park. The apartment was on a high floor on a side street between Madison and Fifth. It was late February and the waves of bare trees rippled from the East Side to the West. Warren had no idea that Patrizia had assumed they would take the full-floor apartment with a treetop view of the park up the block, but that Steve had preferred this more stealth penthouse off of Madison. Warren shrugged his shoulders at the vast expanse of distantly writhing branches. Real estate, he said. It doesn't mean anything to me. It's just property. He walked toward the door and asked Neva where the restroom was located. He looked back at Steve, who was wheezing the slightest bit, the water bottle held to his lips. I'm not coming back, he said. You know our offer. Warren took a moment to look at the broad man who was still seated calmly and then he opened the door with his skinny hand and was gone.

Steve had by now seated himself in a club chair facing the couch. The broad man had a wide face. His name was Wolf. That was his first name and he used it with everyone. He sat very still looking across the apricot marble table shot through with gray and white veins, back at Steve. Wolf came from

Eastern Europe and had arrived in the United States when he was fourteen. He lived in Brooklyn, near the water. He couldn't remember how exactly he'd gotten into the business he was in, but it seemed inevitable, like the tides. This was the way the universe was tilting, toward hotels, strip malls, and the women who worked there. He was just making business possible. He watched Steve and he watched the enormous sky out the window white and foamy like the ocean on a foggy day.

Mr. Zane, what don't you like about our proposal?

Steve stared at him.

You understand what I don't like. You don't need me to explain it to you.

You are a man of high morals, is that what you're telling me? Wolf asked.

You flatter me, Steve said.

But isn't that what it is? You think you are above this kind of thing?

Steve stood up and walked around his desk. Some pigeons had risen and were winging toward the clouds, moving like dark gray letters across the blank page of white sky.

If that's how you want to think about it, Steve said.

Wolf said nothing.

Steve walked back toward the couch. As he sat down again in the club chair he said, offhandedly, I think of it as a question of being human or not.

Wolf's entire body tensed.

You are saying we are inhuman?

I didn't say that. I don't know what you are.

But you think you're better than us?

I'm not thinking about myself in terms of you. I am merely acting on my own principles.

What if we destroy your business?

How exactly can you do that?

We use other malls, other hotels, and we make those developers and landlords more successful than you.

So they'll make more money. That doesn't mean I'll be unsuccessful.

Eventually.

Eventually I'll be dead. So will you.

This is a terrible position you're putting me in.

What would be a good position? I let you do illegal, immoral, inhuman things on my property? That's a good position?

This is going to happen someplace.

Not my place.

My boss is going to be disappointed.

That's not my problem.

He is willing to pay you a tremendous cut of the profits. Almost fifty percent.

Steve looked like he might pound his fist into the chair, or into Wolf, but he did not do it. He leaned in very close toward Wolf, and Wolf's head instinctively moved away. Then Wolf gathered his strength and stood up. Without standing Steve seized his arm. Wolf looked at Steve's hand on his arm and Steve removed it. Steve stood up and the two men stared hard at each other high above the low marble table, Steve's head reaching up toward the ceiling while his eyes gazed through Wolf. Wolf's legs solidly planted on the ground.

I won't sell people, Steve said.

You wouldn't be doing the selling.

I would be giving my permission, enabling it, and then taking a portion of the proceeds. That's close enough.

Isn't that what you do in all your properties?

You misunderstand completely. That's what's wrong with you and your boss.

It's all the same, Wolf said.

If I had a gun I might kill you, Steve said.

Neva watches them from the corner of the room. Her heart is pounding. She is somewhat afraid but more than fear she feels ashamed that she has ever doubted Steve or that at one time she had expected to despise him. She is confused, alarmed, feels stupid and amazed. Impressed by Steve's refusal, his fearsome and tragic determination. She is afraid of him again, but in a new way. She respects him.

Wolf's face was red. The veins in his neck stretched. He stuck out his hand.

Well, I'll be going then, he said.

Steve looked at Wolf and his wide-set nearly black eyes. He was staring not at Steve but out the windows. A darker shade of white had covered the sky, as if the brightness had been turned down. Another handful of birds appeared to be thrown into the view, this flock rising as one and breaking up into words and sentences. Steve took Wolf's hand and shook it briskly. He nodded for Neva to open the door. She did and Wolf pressed his hand against his tie and made his way around the low table and slid out of the room. He was gone.

21

THEY WERE STANDING in the study not speaking when first Steve and then Neva moved toward the couch and sat down with perhaps ten inches between them. She couldn't tell what he was thinking as he was leaning back into the leather, breathing heavily. After a while she saw that he was sweating slightly and next she noticed a translucent cast to the skin around his eyes and she felt that he was not okay.

He was spent. Neva got up and left the room and came back in with a damp hand towel. She pressed it to his forehead. She patted it a few times and then moved it down to his neck. She left the towel resting against his neck as she unbuttoned his shirt. Then she patted the towel across the top of his chest, against his mingling black and white chest hairs. His breathing settled.

Can you talk? she asked.

He started coughing.

He sat up and leaned forward and rested his elbows on his knees. He coughed and spat and she held the towel up to his mouth, and his spit was a little bloody. He finished coughing and the white glow from the sky cast his face in light and shadow as if he were made of marble. He looked at Neva.

They won't stop.

I know.

And they will retaliate.

I know.

Were you afraid? he asked.

Yes—but not that much.

I had a feeling they wouldn't frighten you.

They seemed small.

They have bigger guys behind them.

What are you going to do?

The only thing I can do.

Which is?

Protect myself. Make sure they're not on my property.

How?

He breathed out a long slow stream of air. He closed his eyes. It was as if there were a tornado spiraling and strengthening inside him and he was controlling the pressure by allowing a small stream to seep out. He fell back onto the couch, his shirt open, the damp towel crumpled in his lap, its monogram sz illegible. His eyes heavy lidded, hooded, the slightest bit open.

I'm going to ask you to help me.

Why? What can I possibly do?

Neva picked up the towel again and began pressing it against his forehead. Strands of her black hair fell in front of her face. Her skin was pale, and her dark eyes questioning, receptive, concerned.

Reconnaissance, he said.

Neva stopped patting.

I don't know this word.

Check things out. See what's going on.

She held the towel in her hand. She gazed at him but he had closed his eyes again. She fell back into the couch herself and looked out the window. It was beginning to snow. She could picture it sticking to the long branches of the trees, like snowflakes on the eyelashes of a horse. She closed her eyes too. She could see the city as pure as she had ever seen it. Everything white but not blank, instead a radiance, gentle, spilling over the acres of park, floating over the buildings, the quieted cars, the trudging citizens. She felt as though she were inhabiting a headquarters of safety and from here something good was being attempted, some measure to stop the worst from blowing in, bearing down, taking over. She felt herself getting carried away and saw the snow falling like the softest ashes accumulating in a fire pit, a dog sniffing through them, and the ashes disintegrating into powder, the whitest dust. Her thoughts were disintegrating, floating randomly in her head. She was trying to sweep the ashes into a pile, sweep them away, when she heard herself saying:

You mean a kind of spying.

Not really. Just watching. Following up.

Don't you have people who would be much better at that? Trained? Smarter than I am.

He turned to look at her without lifting his head from resting against the couch. Their faces were nearly touching.

I don't know anyone smarter than you.

She looked back into his eyes for a long time.

Is it dangerous what you're asking me to do?

I will have someone nearby, looking out for you.

Why do you think these people won't notice me? Won't figure it out? Isn't it safer to send a man, a customer?

They expect that. That's the obvious thing to do.

So you want me to just go looking? See if they are there? In one of your buildings?

A hotel.

She shook her head: No. I've done that. Years ago. She looked at him. She altered the truth: I was a chambermaid. I won't do that again.

You don't have to do anything. You can just inquire. Pretend you are looking for work.

Her eyes were starting to well up.

People don't go looking for that kind of work.

Yes, they do. When they need it.

There was a tear sliding down the side of her face.

Just ask. Just find out if it exists.

Why would you want me to do something like this?

Because you can do something very few people can do, something good. I want to get these people off of my property if they are there, and I think they are. They are trying to make a deal with me so that I will look the other way, but I want to get rid of them. And I trust you.

Why? Why do you have all these ideas about me?

There were more tears now, drawing lines down her face.

I just do, he said.

We'll be in danger, both of us, she said.

Cut off from everyone else, he said.

Already, now, she said, we're cut off.

They continued to talk, to plan. Outside the snow was blowing in billowy smoky gusts, the aftermath of some mythic cannon fire, its thunderous discharge silenced by the enormous soundproof windows. In the vast apartment nobody could hear anything going on in the room, nor see the gleams of reflected metallic-orange lamplight shooting like arrows from the faceted corners of the glass boxes in which the model ships waited out the storm.

When Patrizia came home Neva was sitting with Roman at his desk, helping him with his homework. He needed to get up from his chair every five minutes to throw a ball or check sports scores or go to the gun store in a video game. He was permitted these breaks and while he was taking them Neva would gaze out the window and make note of the progress of the snow, which was piled high now on the roofs of the townhouses across the street. Roman's room did not have a park view. It did have a climbing wall, a basketball hoop, built-in bookshelves, this desk with a globe that Roman never examined, a video-game console, a bed with embroidered linens, and many other objects strewn by Roman and rearranged by the housekeeper daily. The room was connected to Felix's bedroom by a shared bathroom, and the doors to the shared bathroom were open on either side and Neva could see Patrizia come into Felix's room and sit on his bed for a moment while he told her about the book he was reading. Neva could view part of Patrizia's figure through the doorways, her midheel mahogany-leather boots with their fashionable detailing, her understatedly luxurious skirt and sweater, her solar system of rings and bracelets and necklaces glinting in orbit around her.

Patrizia was listening as intently as she could, intelligently, animatedly, enjoying Felix's unexpected observations and arrestingly mature remarks, yet there was an anxiety that permeated her every expression, which gave her listening the quality of talking, as if she herself were the one reading the book and commenting on it, not Felix. The very enthusiasm of her reactions to him, her overeager responsiveness, her head-nodding appreciations, became less a reflection of him than a magnification of herself, although this was the last thing she consciously wanted to do. She wanted to love him in the way he needed to be loved, but always an unnatural eagerness to please him, or to please some invisible spectator, animated her face when she spoke to him. Was it his preternatural wisdom that intimidated her? Or his unself-conscious intellect? The unfortunate effect was one of isolation, mother

and son separated by a distance neither one of them understood. It was easier for Patrizia to relate to Roman. When
she entered his room through the bathroom she swept him
into her arms and he wriggled away and she laughed and said
something about her little savage and he smiled and the air
was easy between them.

Patrizia and Neva chatted while Roman took one of his
breaks. Patrizia mentioned Angel, the family's driver, and
how he had told her just now in the car that he wanted to be
a crane operator. He'd been learning how to do it.

Imagine that, dangling hundreds of feet above the sidewalk! said Patrizia. I'd be much happier driving a car.

Some people like to be high up, said Neva, looking out at
the snow. Isn't he from Quito? Maybe it reminds him of the
mountains.

I suppose so, said Patrizia. Anyway, I'm going to say something to Steve, see if he can find something for Angel.

Steve loves Angel. He loves to talk to him in the car.

I know. He'll miss him, said Patrizia.

Patrizia watched the snow out the window and lost herself for
a moment in the churning wave of white, mesmerized by the
way the flakes appeared to regenerate themselves in midair. In
the middle of her life she seemed to be having not a crisis but
an awakening. Things she had always ignored, blocked out,
now rushed to the forefront of her mind like the spinning snow,
like planets in the credit sequence of one of those blockbuster
movies which her sons, or perhaps only Roman, enjoyed. She
found herself noticing things, some beautiful, some ugly—
the dreariest stores on the streets, ones with limp, frayed
awnings; a dirty plastic spoon convulsing in a trash can; the
grime washing up the reptilian sides of the white brick buildings on Third Avenue—that she had previously edited away.

But now she did not have either the energy to look away or the desire. She wished she could say she wanted to take it all in, could proclaim that with age she had matured into a saintly sage with a compassionate approach to every sentient and nonsentient being. But she knew what was more likely: that time had depleted the urgent will to organize and edit her world. And so, the silver lining: she noticed more, took in a wider and deeper spectrum of experience.

Of course this had its pitfalls. What had been perfectly acceptable if somewhat dull swaths of life suddenly burst forth with vigor in a violently colorful manner, the way a puddle in the gutter can look at one moment blank and metallic and the next brilliantly aswirl with oily ribbons of pink and green and blue and orange, a pool of photo-filtered blood to jump over as you cross the street. These puddles were the blind spots that in her forties now bloomed with detail and discovery. She had never considered herself naïve, but people whom she had known for years and taken for trustworthy or at least mildly empathetic had turned out to be neither honest nor even decent. Individuals she had assumed were well meaning were not even nice. This wasn't paranoia on her part, more a belated understanding of human nature, something that others had known much earlier, while she had been, presumably, learning things that they hadn't. However, at times she suspected this might not have been the case. She might have just been naïve. Her ambition had convinced her and others that she had understood the world, but now she saw that she had only understood a tiny part of it. Now she saw more variety, more color, and more ugliness.

So she was not unaware that her husband had fallen deeply for Neva, that he was engaging in a romance with her, if not of the body, then of the mind, or of the heart, that is insofar as he had one, she thought, her foot kicking an invisible soccer ball as she bounced her ankle while she pondered the snow and her marriage. She was upset, jealous, angry, but at the same time unconcerned. This duality was made possible by her ability to compartmentalize and her extreme possessiveness. If he was a monster, at least he was her monster. She had no doubt of that. Whatever his feelings for Neva they were not the same as his feelings for his wife, Patrizia was sure of this. In her awakening she was discovering that nothing was black and white. It was all silvery gray, glinting, iridescent, like the puddles that held a multitude of color. If he was sleeping with Neva, who cared? If he was in love with her, who cared? Was he Neva's husband? No. He was hers. And he was not about to leave her because quite simply he appreciated what she had to offer, even if it was not a meeting of souls. He appreciated her proprietary confidence, her aristocratic entitlement. He actually admired it and felt affection for it. He never ceased to be amused by what she had thought was her sophistication but which he had always realized was her superficial materialism and charm, like a flouncing girl in a fairy tale. She was a prize to him, a possession. And in this way Patrizia possessed him too, more inextricably than the way she owned the boots on her feet and the jewelry at her neck. Or at least she owned a part of him.

This is what Patrizia saw, understood, accepted, and found solace in: that Neva could never be owned by Steve. And so therefore Neva could never own him.

Roman was thrusting and spinning around in the middle of the room, in between the two women, playing Wii.

Oh well, sighed Patrizia, he'll get over it. Angel's been driving that car for a long time. If he wants to do something else, Steve should let him.

Yes, said Neva, I'm sure he will.

So, Patrizia said, turning her gaze to Roman who was now

kneeling and sliding and twisting, how is it going with the homework?

That night Neva had a series of dreams. In one of them she was running, in another drowning, in another she had entirely forgotten who she was and someone was expecting her to explain herself. When she woke up, tormented, sweaty, twitching, she had the feeling that there was something urgent she was required to do, but she did not know what it was and she had a deadline. Gradually, as her heart slowed and her mind settled and she returned to her bedroom, she began to piece together the events of the day and to recall what had transpired between her and Steve and to understand why she was in this state of panic and dread.

She could not still herself completely. No matter how deeply she breathed or how many times she told herself that she was safe at this moment and that in any future moment Steve would be looking out for her, she could not untangle the terrible, writhing, screaming pain that lived behind her heart and slightly toward the middle of her back, between her shoulder blades, like one of those tumors that grows nails and teeth, screeching and clawing and insisting that it be allowed to survive, to live, and even to burst through her skin in some grotesque hatching. One instant she pictured it as a deformed squirming creature and the next she felt unbearable pity for this desperate helpless thing. Her pain. She held it. It quieted. The shrieking subsided. It did not go away, but it quieted.

The idea that she was going to return, if only as an observer, to the world that she had so narrowly escaped seemed unreal and impossible at first but slowly formed a kind of sense in her mind and she was able to encompass the thought without it entirely overwhelming her. She felt herself at some inaccessible height, above everyday occurrences, viewing her life from a tremendous distance, seeing patterns and repetitions, variations on a theme, and she felt an enormous tenderness for her tiny being, hiking up and down the mountain ranges of her experiences, tracing the shape of a steep and jagged EKG, not unlike the beating of her own irregular heart. She felt no happiness or peace or torment or anger, just an awareness that the fear she had felt on behalf of this being, herself, was a part of her life. It would never go away, she realized. No matter what she did she would carry this fear with her, so she might as well do something with it, use it, take some action. She would do what he asked. She felt a release from the lingering suffering of her nightmares and was able to fall back to sleep.

A few days later Angel drove Neva across the George Washington Bridge to New Jersey. He dropped her off a few blocks from a large midscale hotel and handed her an envelope that contained a small map with directions, the name of a woman she was supposed to ask for at the front desk, and his, Angel's, cell-phone number. She knew his number by heart from calling him so many times to arrange pickups and drop-offs for the boys, but he had written it down for her just in case. Angel was originally from Ecuador, in his early thirties, and had a wife and a young son. He had worked for Steve for nearly ten years driving and maintaining Steve's cars. But he liked big machinery, and being outside, and thought that working as a crane operator would be more interesting, exciting even, and possibly enable him to work his way up in construction, maybe to become a site manager. There was nowhere for him to go as a driver. He appreciated the work, was grateful for it, but he was tired of sitting in traffic, and his young body was getting restless. He was also concerned that being a driver would lead to too many gigs like this one, taking the nanny out to who the hell knew where and dropping her off in a sketchy neighborhood to walk alone. No one had told him what any of this was about, but he didn't like the looks of it. He was supposed to drive several blocks away and wait for an hour until he got a text from Neva to return to the pickup spot. He would listen to the radio. And worry about her. She was always reserved, but she looked especially tense now. Her jaw even more sharply angled than usual, her eyes more narrowed. Her clothes today seemed a little revealing to him, down-market for her, he thought, almost a bit trashy, which was not a word he would have ever used to describe her. He leaned against the car and watched her as she walked away from him past a strip mall toward the hotel. In the extremely high-heeled boots she was wearing, she looked like a colt learning to walk. Cars whizzing past, the faded primary colors of store signs smearing in the background. Her strong body suddenly appearing fragile to him. The sound of the highway was deafening. If he called out to her she wouldn't hear him. He got back in the car and turned on the radio.

22

POPPY WAS LYING backward on Felix's bed, her feet on his pillow. This is kind of like an old-time psychiatrist's couch, she said, and you're the doctor.

Felix was spinning in a swivel chair at his desk.

How can I help? he asked, midspin.

I'm beyond help at this point, but you could make me feel better by telling me that I'm not crazy for not wanting to go to college.

You're not crazy. You're following your own path.

Right.

I mean it. You want to experience life.

Tell that to Steve. And to everyone at school who's waiting to hear where they got in. What a bunch of fakes. Half of them had tutors write their essays.

What kind of tutors?

People with PhDs. Geniuses who can't make enough money to live in this city without writing application essays for teenagers. There's this one philosophy professor at Columbia who helped a ton of kids, a totally brilliant scholar who charges like a million dollars an hour.

What kind of essay can a philosophy professor help them write?

Felix was tapping away at his computer, looking up Wiki-pedia entries on philosophers.

Poppy pointed one long leg up toward the ceiling. I don't know, she said. "Wittgenstein's Treatise on Community Service in South America."

Felix giggled.

Who are some other philosophers? she asked, twisting her head around to see him.

Here are some, he said. Kant, Spinoza . . .

Okay, Poppy said, I got another: "Kant, Spinoza, and How I Made My First Billion by Creating a Website That Teaches Underprivileged Kids to Sell Handcrafted Things on Etsy."

Poppy, you're going to make me pee. What's Etsy?

You don't need to know. What's some philosophy vocabulary?

Felix Googled the words: "Glossary of Philosophical Terms." Cartesian, dialectic, hermeneutics . . .

"Towards a Hermeneutics of Field Hockey," said Poppy.

Felix fell off his chair in a fit of laughing.

I don't even totally get it, he said, but that's really funny.

Maybe I should do comedy. Stand-up.

Stand-up? Like Louis C.K.?

How do you know Louis C.K.? That's terrifying. You're too young to know Louis C.K.

Felix was back at the computer already, showing her You-Tube clips of Louis C.K.

He's really good, Poppy said, but it's too depressing to do stand-up. I couldn't handle it. The humiliation. What if nobody laughs?

Oh, everybody would laugh at you, said Felix.

Thanks, I think.

Felix smiled. I meant with you. Not at you.

No, you didn't, but I forgive you.

Felix became absorbed in some entry online. Poppy circled her ankles in the air.

This guy seems smart, said Felix.

Who? Plato? We read *The Allegory of the Cave* in history. That was cool.

No, his name is M-A-I-M-O-N-I-D-E-S.

Never heard of him.

Poppy rolled onto her stomach. Her hair had grown since the summer and swung below her chin, with straight short bangs that she had cut across her forehead. Her wide eyes sparkled when she spoke to Felix, but at any lull in the conversation the sparkles wavered and faded and went dim.

He wrote a book called *The Guide for the Perplexed*, said Felix.

I could use that.

He says that evil isn't real. It is a lack. It's the nonpresence of good.

It doesn't feel that way, said Poppy.

He's right though. Listen to this:

"Yet every fool imagines that the world exists only for his sake, as though no other being existed outside of him. But if he meets with the opposite of what he wanted, he decides that all Being is bad. However, if he were to contemplate and understand all Being and recognize the insignificance of his share in it, then the truth would become obvious to him."

Okaaay . . . , said Poppy, so you're saying if I'm upset I'm just being self-absorbed.

Basically. Listen:

"The right way of looking at things consists in seeing the totality of existing mankind . . . as of no importance to the interdependence of all Being."

I think what he's saying is that I'm a spoiled brat.

He's saying that most of us are.

Gee that makes me feel better.

It should.

Maybe it should but it doesn't.

Maybe it will. Eventually.

Poppy felt a bright sharp pang behind her eyes and then the tears came falling. Maybe, she said, hiding her face in another pillow. In a muffled voice she said, How did you get to be so smart? And why I am I so stupid? The thing about evil is it doesn't feel like a lack it feels like pain. Her wet red eyes stared at Felix. It doesn't feel like something I can just think out of existence.

Felix was kneeling by the bed now, his small hand on her arm.

What is it? he asked. Is this just about college?

No, it's more than that. It's something a lot worse and I don't want to talk about it. She sobbed, gulping, desperate, desolate sobs. He kept his hand on her arm.

Maybe you need a life goal, he said.

Maybe I need a life.

Poppy, it isn't all that bad.

Well, what's your life goal?

I have a new one, he said, his compassionate expression suddenly changed to a look of secret excitement.

What is it? Poppy sniffled, drying her eyes with the corner of the pillowcase.

I want to invent a new color.

Poppy's pretty brow wrinkled into a series of loving apostrophes. Oh Felix, you're amazing, she said, hugging him. But I'm not like you, she whispered over his shoulder, her lips quivering. I'm just not. I'm not a philosopher or a mystic and it would never occur to me to create a new color. She squeezed her eyes shut. Can you even do that?

Sure, he said pragmatically. First I have to invent a new substance. So light can reflect off of it in a new way.

Poppy sighed. Her face was expressionless, exhausted, but utterly beautiful, even more beautiful because she had no idea how beautiful she was in this moment. Her gigantic blue eyes gazed out through the window, over the townhouses, over the buildings, over the rivers, but saw nothing. She pressed her arms around Felix tightly. I wish I had hope like you do, she said.

He held on to her. His little face was stoic, unwavering.

It's okay, he said.

No it isn't, she said.

Yes it is, he said. It's okay.

In the coming days Felix can tell that something is wrong, that Poppy seems to have slipped out of herself, into an artfully concealed madness that only he notices. He knows nothing about what's been going on with Ian or about what has happened recently between them, but Felix senses some change, suspects something in Poppy's air of strangeness, her manner of weird composure tilting into distraction and then teetering on the edge of performance. She is unusually, animatedly, interested in trivial concerns—what Felix had for breakfast, where Roman has misplaced his hockey stick—and detached from the issues that would normally merit her energetic response, such as an impossible-not-to-overhear argument between Patrizia and Steve vibrating from their bedroom while Poppy and the boys watch television in the entertainment room or the announcement that Jonathan and Miranda are going to have a baby. She's become a spectator of her own life, as if it were an accident unfolding slowly before her eyes. Felix feels a terror taking over, but he can't quite identify it. All he knows is that Poppy is in danger and that he is witnessing a profound unhappiness he has never before encountered. He tries to talk to her but she can't keep up her end of the conversation. She goes off on tangents, non sequiturs, charming free-associative remarks that make him smile but also frighten him. He considers discussing this situation with an adult but is unsure if anyone would believe him. They have often dismissed his obscure ideas. The only person who seems a likely candidate for his confession is Neva, and she too is distracted, absorbed, although in a way that appears to him less dangerous than simply distanced. He would tell Neva if the right moment arose, but it hasn't. They are always rushing to school, from school, to activities, from events, and the conversations they used to have are now less confidential, more perfunctory, businesslike. He thinks that being around his family has turned Neva into a businesswoman. And made Poppy go insane.

This is what she did, what it was like. She didn't sleep at all or she slept until two in the afternoon, missing classes and pretending to be sick. She drank. She has never liked liquor but now when the house is empty—it is never entirely empty, there is always someone working, cleaning, rearranging, but when nobody is nearby—she opens the mirrored liquor cabinet and tries different drinks, based on their colors, their semiprecious hues. On the days she does leave the house to go to school she skips classes, takes the subway downtown or to Brooklyn, smokes cigarettes—she has never really enjoyed cigarettes—until they burn not only her fingertips but her lips. She sells quite a few of her most expensive clothes, for the feeling of selling her clothes. She goes out with friends and drinks and smokes cigarettes. At the same time! She thinks: Two things I hate but I am doing anyway! Actually three! She meets boys from other schools, boys she has never met before. And she meets men, the kind of men who are on the lookout for girls her age, or a little older, for she looks older when she gets dressed up to go out. She wears her hair messy, a tank top under some stylish blazer or sequined jacket that she will take off when she sits down before casually, immodestly reaching across the table, or the bar or the sofa if she is in a bar or a lounge or club with a sofa, and revealing her pretty lacy colorful bra beneath her tank top. She puts on sheer black tights or no stockings at all and when she does wear stockings there is usually a discreet rip someplace. She sports a tight skirt or leather pants. Her accessories telegraph that she has money, and her movements explain that she has knowledge. She is affectionate, especially with the girls with whom she travels. She slings her arms around them and they all lunge forward, laughing without really smiling. She rummages in her bag for another cigarette and spills credit cards on the floor and has to bend over to pick them up. She feels ridiculous but continues to behave this way. She thinks that this must be what it feels like to be a true teenager, that she is very successfully impersonating a teenager. She never really felt like one before, always wise beyond her years, or at least sophisticated if not wise, and now she has decided to be stupid, just the way she was supposed to be during high school while instead she was too busy being a snob to really play with the other kids, when she was too caught up in her sophisticated sadness to make a mess with them. Now she puts aside her eccentricities, her interests, her feelings, and chooses to drown with the others in an ultra-premium-vodka puddle, striped with shivering colored lights that make her think of fuel rods at Fukushima, a radioactive rainbow wriggling beneath her feet as she trips out of the restaurant onto the sidewalk into a waiting car. She dances with people who exist somewhere on a spectrum between friends and strangers, but not acquaintances, these nonrelationships feel more intense than that, something like estranged cousins reunited at the end of the world. That is what their revelry is most like, that of a merry band of distant relatives who have put aside their animosities, their petty differences, and even hatred, to join in a frenzied celebration on the last night of the universe or more likely the first night after the end, survivors gathered to remind themselves that they are alive. A writhing necklace of silhouetted figures joined in some macabre gavotte across the rooftops of the burned-out buildings and through the dusty abandoned parks of an uninhabitable, previously unimaginable, city.

When the psychiatrist had told her that they were all living post-apocalypse, Poppy hadn't understood what that meant. Now she gets it. Poppy constructs her world in terms of pre-Ian and during-Ian and post-Ian and post-Ian is the same as post-apocalypse. This isn't, she feels, necessarily a bad thing. It is an organizing principle and a time-management tool. And anyway she can't really remember in her booze-fueled and pill-enhanced brain—yes, she has started to mix the two, an ingenious suggestion made by her latest private-equity semi-boyfriend—what life was like before or even during Ian. The blurry present annihilates all happy memories. But sometimes an image breaks through and she remembers a distant and shimmering good fortune—what must have been an ordinary moment at the time, a walk along the river with her mother that now takes on a pure brilliance. Light falling on the rippling Hudson in a cascade of transparency, a vivid nothingness sparkling silently and moving continuously and reflecting a meaning and mystery beyond naming. Her mother a presence beside her that stood for solace, consolation, the coalescence of everything safe. Poppy understands that this memory may just be a figment, a fantasy. But does it matter?

Where is Ian in her thoughts? He's a figment too, a fantasy, already disintegrating like dissolving ice caps, floating wads of frozen lake separating, drifting apart, their melting patterns revealing memories trapped in memories now sliding into the

sea of the past. This is going to be a slow process. She hears
ice crack, echoing in an isolated valley. The reformation of her
interior world. No sign yet of life in the cold water. No arctic
flower seed fossilized under centuries of frost, waiting to be
reborn. Not yet. Something—her soul?—trudges across the
white landscape, her shadow spanning miles across the snow.
A pale walking stick curved like the horn of a woolly mam-
moth plunges into the crisp powder. Footsteps, the thudding
swish of an animal-skin cape, the walking stick breaking the
surface, the inner warrior traveling through the inner landscape. The arctic flower buried at the icy peak of a distant
mountain.

These figments: her mother, Ian, her self, they shift inside her.
The movement of tectonic plates, continental drift, human
change.

It's one of those long dead streets in Bushwick that's getting
trendy, with a restaurant that has no door and warehouses
covered in spray paint. It's always deserted on this street even
though everyone comes here and the bars are crowded. That
evening, like most evenings, she feels herself about to break
down and so she leaves the restaurant to smoke a cigarette by
herself. An unplanned unpleasantness meant to distract her
from the planned unpleasantness of her social engagement. As
soon as she heads into a doorway she senses that she has made
a mistake. The black paint, the men emerging from the shadows, the scene as if she's dreamed it, someone grabbing her
arms, speaking softly but unkindly. A cold fear that comes
sweeping over her, beyond her strength, beyond her understanding. A feeling that she could enter a place beyond death,
enter fully into the madness she has been circling, narrowly

avoiding, or at least disguising. And suddenly she's hearing another voice, the voice of the private-equity guy whom she would no more have expected to intervene in a dangerous situation than she would have expected her mother to reappear in the dark doorway, dove gray, angelic, wings made of feathers, tubes still dangling from her nose and mouth.

Somehow he talks the men out of it, whatever it was, and gives them some bills and they leave her alone. But the fear hasn't left her and when they go back to his loft in the Financial District she finally accepts the drugs he's been urging on her for weeks. He says they'll be good for her. He calls them by their scientific chemical names as if that makes them medicinal, clinical, FDA approved. She believes that she will know when she has gone too far, when the time has come for her to recognize that enough is enough, that she will be able to change course. But the surprising thing about this situation is, the thing she is most struck by as she sits slumped in a matte-velvet-upholstered original midcentury French chair staring at the quarter-sawn oak floorboards in a herringbone pattern is that it is actually extremely difficult to change. Once on a highway it is remarkably difficult for a person to exit. If she had said this aloud in English class she would have felt like an idiot, it was such an obvious idea. But she was not herself, she was now that foolish girl who said foolish things, and so who was she to judge? That no one has noticed what she has become lends this experience its darkest terror. That no one would realize she had lost her mind, that some substitution had taken place and her identity had been plucked away and that she was powerless to replace it, this must be worse than insanity. The worst, she thinks, is when you go crazy but you are completely aware of what has happened.

23

ALIX MET IAN at an exquisitely appointed bistro in the West Village. All rustic industrial and so tasteful that she felt as if she had slipped into a design blog. The furniture and objects glowed with a fanatic essentialism that attempted to wordlessly explain why they were so expensive. Ian had arrived first. He was at a table by the window, nursing a hot beverage and looking more unkempt than usual. He seemed to be having a private moment, and Alix almost didn't want to intrude, privacy being so scarce, practically illegal these days. What was troubling him? she wondered. What would she find if she could undertake surveillance of his brain, his thoughts, his mind? Of course, what she really wanted to know was what was in his heart. However, even entry into his neural synapses could not have told her that.

Could she see how his heart ached and his head hurt? He groped for thoughts but they were pulled under by waves of disturbance, guilt, regret. He was riding wave after wave and yet from the outside he appeared only slightly messier, some-what tired, preoccupied, stressed, overworked, distracted. Not like a drowning man.

She sat and it took him a moment to notice that she was there.

Hey, said Alix. Hello.

He didn't say anything for a long time.

Then, quietly, his head tilted: So this is middle age, he said.

I'm skipping middle age, she said, picking up the menu and squinting at it. I'm going straight to aged.

Ian's forehead rippled and twisted in eddies of understanding.

I know what you mean, he said. Aged is more dignified.

Exactly.

But the thing about middle age is—he leaned forward—it is undignified. It just is. And you can't skip it. I thought you could too, by not even getting to full-grown adult, but—

What? Ian are you crying? Have I ever seen you cry?

But you really don't have a choice. We don't. Trying to skip middle age is like trying to go straight from child to adult and not stopping at teenager.

That's exactly what I did!

He was letting his eyes well up, not fighting it.

And how did that work out for you?

Oh, she said, sighing. You know how.

She reached her hand across the table for his.

Listen, best friend, you can tell me anything.

His whole face contorted and his eyes shut as if blocking out an image beyond horror, beyond death, something that should never have been seen. He gripped her hand. He covered his face with his other hand. This went on for a while.

Pretty undignified, huh? he said, when he had finished.

That's okay, she said. It's totally okay.

Thank you, he said. I really don't deserve any of this.

Any of what?

You, your friendship, listening to me.

Don't be ridiculous. I'm not even listening to you. That's because you're barely saying anything.

The waitress had hovered in their orbit for a while and by now had given up.

I can't, he said.

The contortion again, rivers and mountains of a textured globe furrowing his brow, like the world being born.

Did you kill someone?

No.

Then I think you can tell me.

The mountains rolling into hills, then prairies. His face relaxing. His gray eyes staring into hers.

For him the whole room, the whole city, the whole world is inhabited by Poppy. She's laughing, mocking. She's crying, brooding. Her wide eyes. His heart a mess, a raw organ laid out on a chopping board. He can see it quiver. This is the ache of actually loving her. Not knowing how she is, if she is okay. How long can he keep this secret? He thinks about telling Alix, about showing her his heart, taking a bite out of it right in front of her. But for the same reason he doesn't tell Poppy who he is he doesn't tell Alix: he is afraid to hurt them. Afraid for whom?

Finally he said, I really can't. But you've been very helpful. I feel better, or at least a little stronger.

Okay, I'm puzzled, but that's okay.

Thank you.

What has gotten into you that you are so polite all of a sudden? You don't have to thank me. I'm offended that you would thank me.

I'm sorry—

No, don't apologize I don't like that either. You do look better though. Hungry?

No, he said. I'm not sure I even deserve food. But you eat.

Thank you. See, your manners are contagious. Yes, well, I think I'll order now that you've decreed that I am worthy of sustenance.

He smiled a little and laughed.

Good, she said. You're laughing at me.

His eyes were tilting downward at the edges, sorrowful, handsome, helpless, but showing the tiniest signs of strength in the steadiness with which they held her gaze.

You really have been able to get away with a lot with those eyes, she said.

He nodded.

She continued: Being immature, an asshole, not growing up, acting helpless, feeling sorry for yourself, being passive-aggressive, playing dumb, not taking responsibility.

Oh go on, he said, drily.

I love you, pal, but you're too old for it, she said as she buttered a sourdough roll. And you're also too old for this bullshit crying. Whatever you've done, and I'm sure it's pretty bad, don't kid yourself that these tears are real. Unless, that is, you actually plan to do something about whatever the hell it is you've done. But of course I'm not asking what that is.

Thanks.

Miss Manners again. Does she even exist anymore? Alix held the piece of bread aloft, midbite. I feel really old this week. I keep getting ads on my computer regarding different diseases: multiple sclerosis, cancer, fibromyalgia. It must be because I'm searching for things that a person with those ailments would search for, don't you think? What else could it be? It's like the Internet—and by Internet I mean of course whoever or whatever is following my whereabouts on the

Internet—it knows on the basis of what shoes I'm lusting over and what gossip I'm scarfing, which out-of-print authors I'm hunting down and what esoteric journals I'm pretending to read, it's as if it knows what is going on in my body, what I'll get sick from, when I'll die.

When?

Well, from what. And the next thing you know it's when.

You're more morbid than I am.

That's always been the case.

Thank you for trying to cheer me up.

Will you stop with the thank-yous?

I'm sorry.

That too. Enough apologizing. I don't want polite from you.

But I am sorry.

But it isn't helpful.

I'm sorry anyway.

24

JONATHAN STOOD at the top of the Spanish Steps and thought: Europe is Disneyland now. He surveyed the exquisitely rendered panorama of elegant proportions and found it lovely, but too familiar, too charming, precious. He remembered coming as a kid when the Continent still felt foreign, exotic, when products in every country announced themselves with different logos, packaging, typography. Today the streets were lined with the same global citizens swinging the same shopping bags from the same luxury brands. He could just as easily have been in New York as Rome. But it was a cliché to complain about such things, and the truth was he didn't much care. He made a note of it, that was all. Nostalgia, yearning, these feelings didn't penetrate him. He experienced them as observations only, information which he might use, or more accurately misuse, in order to further his plans, objectives, desires. At the moment he desired a macchiato before his next business meeting. Mission in mind, he scampered down the long flight of stone steps, shiny new shoes striking the stairs like black keys on a piano slipping between the ivories.

He decided to take the scenic route, or rather his favorite route, since every route was the scenic route in Rome. All roads led to Rome, and all roads in Rome led to beauty, pleasure, an opera set around every corner, a quiet narrow snaking *via* opening suddenly onto a stage lit with the softest colors, a solemnly beautiful church, an empty restaurant, each piazza a new location for delight, a fresh setting for a dream, as if dancers in chiffony skirts and dolce vita bodices might unfurl from the church door and spin on the trattoria tables, or a line of clergymen in jewel-toned robes might march through from stage right, incense swinging, or ancient philosophers might walk out of the Forum, or step out of the paintings in the Vatican, and find themselves facing the perplexing question of how they had arrived in the Renaissance. These ideas manifest themselves in Jonathan's mind as a backdrop, as a pleasing scrim against which more-urgent matters stretched themselves out, his mental exercises needing a comfortable setting, a kind of hotel-bar environment—artificially costumed, a mélange of periods—in which to lounge and strategize, display themselves, and size up the competition.

His upcoming meeting was not exactly authorized and therefore required a fair amount of mental preparation. It wasn't exactly his first unauthorized activity, but now he was aggressively taking his career into his own hands, to the next level. He hoped to do something to impress his father, benefit the organization in an unexpected manner, and thereby overcome the boringly predictable control Steve exercised over him, the rigid, manipulative, domineering behavior which Jonathan both raged against and interpreted as love. He had begun his secret campaign in Laos, when he'd taken it upon himself to have the zip liners assassinated. It was bold. Beyond the call of duty. And unknown to Steve. Jonathan had wanted to get the job done right, eliminate the obstacles completely, so that Grant could get his permit, build his restaurant, and the profits, a large percentage of which went to Steve, could begin rolling in. If he had left the job half done, leaving room for the local authorities to doubt him, to think he might bend to their pressures or submit to their customs, he would have opened himself up to potential failure. Had he overdone it? Sure, but in his mind that had been necessary. Did Steve have to know? No. Did Jonathan accomplish his mission? Yes. He had returned home proud and arrogant, expecting to be praised and, in Steve's eyes, elevated. Instead, he returned home to discover that Steve had developed a vigorous fascination with and unexpected closeness to Neva. This came as more than a surprise to Jonathan. It was an affront and marked the onset of a rivalrous anger and childish shame, a feeling of rejection, humiliation, and narcissistic mortification. Jonathan was no more prepared to manage these feelings than he was prepared to actually run the family business, but in squelching his emotions, in strangling, suffocating, decapitating, and disemboweling them, he found himself plagued with a thirst for revenge that admitted no reason. He would have to take over. This was his only redemption. So when two men named Warren and Wolf approached him with a financial opportunity, he seized it. Fortune favors the bold. Jonathan had heard as much.

He turned a corner and emerged in Piazza di Sant'Eustachio, his destination. He drank his macchiato, and then walked to the Pantheon, where, ambling in circles around the perimeter of the building, the light from the perfect hole at the top streaming in milky-white rays of liquid cloud—weightless, angelic, fresco light—he and the man with whom a meeting had been arranged by Warren and Wolf's people detailed for him the intricacies of transit through Italy. The country had become a popular way station for women on their journeys from Russia, Moldova, Ukraine, and other locations to the United States and other developed nations. A prime stop on a grand tour, much like the tours of the nineteenth century, only not. On these twenty-first-century tours the passage was involuntary and the sightseeing limited. The gentleman explained to Jonathan how Steve's hotels could be of service, in Italy and elsewhere. He either did not know or did not mention Steve's earlier refusals, about which Jonathan had not been made aware. But there was the understanding between this adviser and Jonathan that their plans would be orchestrated without Steve's approval. It was a matter of efficiency. And discretion.

They celebrated with a drink. It was a new beginning for Jonathan, or so he felt. Yes, there were many more real estate deals to be made, but this was where the smart money was. This was the future. There was no fighting it: the very newspapers that ran editorials condemning such practices and demanding action by the UN carried classified ads for women. Women for sale. The gentleman cupped his hand and lit a cigarette as he explained. Jonathan looked around and imbibed the Roman air, the Roman elegance, the Roman women walking their Jack Russell terriers and the men eternally tan. The buzz of a Vespa as it swerved around a corner, a woman's dagger heel balanced steadily on the runner, her leg the length of the road, her black hair flying out from the back of her helmet in swift, brilliant brushwork. He made no connection in his mind between these women he admired and those women whose exploitation he would be facilitating. His was an inconsistent mind. A mind in which principles gave way to expediency. Actually, a mind which did not recognize principles.

After their drink Jonathan walked and walked, all the way to the Coliseum. As he approached it at dusk he could make out a gray cloud lifting up from the majestic structure, smoky and billowing against a pink sky. Coming closer he realized that the cloud was made of bats, hundreds of bats, rising above the city.

Their jittery view: quick fragments of ruins, sharp sightings of cypress, jagged jump cuts of slow buses and shuffling crowds of tourists, the sloping rise and fall of the hills as seen from the slanted perspective of a winged, nocturnal creature.

He looked at the cloud of bats dispersing into the night. Nothing was pure, thought Jonathan. We are all complicit. This idea was his version of believing that everything is connected. It was almost spiritual. Almost.

25

AS DIFFICULT AS it had been for Neva to carry out Steve's request, as much as she had dreaded it, then prepared for it, and finally accomplished it, she had never expected that seeing traces of a situation similar to the one in which she had been held captive years ago would have so terrible an effect on her. She had not anticipated that finding evidence of the horrible inhuman business that she had escaped would make her feel so removed from herself, so thrown. It should not have been surprising, but so many things in her life should not have been. This was yet another unsurprising surprise.

At the hotel she had asked for the woman whom she was supposed to meet and had been required to sit on a stained microsuede club chair facing an undercleaned wall-length fish tank. She had waited dutifully for a long time until a "manager" had come out to meet her. The manager was a man with a beard. He had taken her to a small office and asked her many questions, about her background, her experiences, her interests, her address, her phone number, her friends' names. She had prepared for these kinds of questions, but still as the interview went on she could tell that her responses were unsatisfactory. She was a good actress, but not a great one.

She could not conceal the traces of sophistication that had marked her in the last few years. Nor could she successfully convey the desperation necessary for someone to believe that she would be seeking out this kind of nightmare. The manager was not naïve. He was not convinced. Neva was persuasive enough not to arouse his suspicions too strongly—she did a compelling drug addict and a passable criminal—but it was clear that he would not take her on, would not even attempt to lure her into his fold. She was not vulnerable enough. Her nervous glances around the room had been too curious, her posture too dignified, her shoes too clean.

After returning to the designated meeting spot, seeing Angel's relieved face, riding in silence across the bridge, and changing clothes discreetly in the backseat before getting out at the apartment building that she now called home, Neva was unable for a long time to understand what she was doing. It's all over now and I'm fine, she kept saying in her head, but she felt more anxious and confused now than she had earlier in the day or even during her expedition. I'm alone. I'm safe. I'm Neva. I have a good job. I take care of children. I'm home. No matter how many times she repeated this mantra in her head she still felt disoriented. It wasn't until she was sitting with Roman helping him with his gladiator project that she realized why.

She had been hoping before today that she would find nothing at the hotel. No trace of the subjugation and slaughtering of will that she had once endured. Now she realized that her former life had been caged inside of her, the memory of it trapped and caught like a wild animal. But on seeing the hotel, the manager, his dirty office, and the tiny hints of that parallel world, her old memories had begun to press against their cage, beating themselves on the gates of consciousness, and then had burst through the bars, ragged and bloody, dumb things, stumbling, again and again, riding along like dead bodies on horses that keep running, blind yet gaping, unable to stop. Looking out the window of Roman's room across the rooftops she felt images and feelings circling madly in her head, exhausting, tragic in their unceasing gallop, a barely contained pandemonium.

I thought gladiators would be cooler, Roman said.

Well, said Neva, you have to do some research. Have you read the books?

Roman rolled his head back and closed his eyes, as if the word "books" had been conceived to torture him.

I looked at them, he said, with his eyes closed.

Out the window, a distant corner of Central Park. A stirring of wind that begins in the clouds. Branches sway. A whole swath of them bends and they brush one another and to Neva it looks like water flowing. Then she remembers: I am a river. And she thinks: I will carry these memories on the current that is my strength. These memories will flow through me like corpses on horses swimming across a river and these horses will drop their burdens, let them fall. These bodies will fall into my waters, float along, and they will sink. These bodies are old memories, gone forever and dead to me now. They cannot hurt me. I will lower them down. I will let them fall to the bottom of the cold and muddy river. They will drift or they will dissolve. These memories will be borne along or they will drown. They will be a part of me but they will not stop me. They will not slow me down. I will carry them, bear them, dissolve them, decompose them, but I will not let them slow me down.

What did the books say? Neva asked Roman.

Nothing, said Roman.

Nothing? Not one word about gladiators? asked Neva.

Roman threw a basketball across the room. It bounced off the corner of the ceiling and landed on his bed, steadied for a moment, and rolled off onto the floor, a rogue idea.

I don't remember, he said.

Neva told Steve what she had seen and heard at the hotel and he arranged for some form of authority—she was not sure if it was the police or a private security firm or his own men—to remove the people who were using his property for illegal purposes. The whole thing ended quickly. Nobody knew. It wasn't in the papers or on the Internet. There were no arrests or sentences. There was no story. The hotels were clean again. The storm held at bay. The darkness, with its roiling current and riderless horses, was gone.

It appeared to Neva that Steve had handled the incident with expert firmness and calm, dispatching his people, displacing the intruders, protecting his kingdom, and restoring order. But she noticed in the following days that he seemed older, less agile in his movements and thoughts, as if a rumor of his aging had spread and shadowed him and had now—perception as they say being reality—come true. His thick wavy hair looked slightly less robust, his tailored jacket hung with the tiniest gap around his neck, a new shrugging looseness through his shoulders. His relationship to age had always been perfectly clear: any businessman or gambler knew that the first one to give a number would lose. So Neva understood that Steve would never go first in this negotiation. He would maintain his poker face, assess risk with equanimity, acknowledge his ignorance, tolerate uncertainty, protect against fragility, and prepare for pain. But he could not abide weakness, disease, or dying. They were unacceptable.

He awoke in the night coughing and he continued to cough until his lungs felt raw. He sat up in bed and Patrizia sat up with him and then went to get him water. When she returned, the coughing had subsided and he was sitting in a chair with a blanket wrapped around his head and shoulders and he drank the water slowly and set the glass on a side table. He looked absurd but no one would have laughed. Out the window the darkness tilted gently toward morning. The buildings across the park on Central Park West twinkled in the charcoal light, a dashboard lit up from within, a control panel waiting to be instructed and manipulated, as if the city itself were a car or an airplane at the ready, keys in the ignition, wanting, begging to be driven.

Am I getting too old for this town? he asked.

No, of course not, she said. Don't be ridiculous.

She was wearing one of her silky robes and it fluttered and fanned out around her as she sat on the arm of his chair.

I used to feel like I could ride this place like a cowboy, like an astronaut.

You still can. You still do.

I felt young until about ten minutes ago, he said.

You are not old, she said.

Maybe I'm having a bad dream right now.

He started coughing again and it lasted a long time. Patrizia hovered beside him, holding the water glass. When he had finished she suggested they call the doctor.

I was right, he said. I am having a bad dream. And he

stayed in the chair until she had gone back to bed and gone to sleep.

The next day he stood in the foyer, about to leave the apartment, when a light-headedness overtook him and his back seized up in pain. Neva was in the next room and heard a quick sound and she rushed to him. As he fell he reached and took hold of her head in his hands and began to explore her face. His eyes moved under heavy lids, darting, as he pulled her downward with him. He had her whole head in his grip as if she were some orb that he was clutching and examining for prophetic purposes.

When his curved back and then his head reached the floor his arms seemed to fall with a heavy weight and he had no choice but to let her go. That's when she loosened his tie and unbuttoned his shirt, saw his gray chest hairs rising and falling as if some wild creature were running over his body, making him shudder up and down, and called out to the housekeeper to phone an ambulance and kept talking to him, saying that everything would be all right.

It seemed inappropriate for her to get into the ambulance with him. She took a taxi and followed. The short trip to the hospital took only a few minutes. By the time they arrived Patrizia had been alerted and a little while later she was there, managing the doctors and speaking calmly into her phone, informing Alix and Jonathan and a few key people in Steve's office. Everyone agreed that Poppy and the twins should not be disturbed while in school. And the whole world didn't need to know. This was private. Neva would pick up the boys as usual and tell them then. In the midst of all the activity, confusion, and emotion, no one thought about who would tell Poppy.

As it turned out, the task fell to Neva. Poppy looked ashen, stricken for a few minutes, and then visibly set the pain aside, relegating it, Neva thought, to that place where images of Diana must live in Poppy's mind. Poppy said she had a ton of homework and was going to a friend's house to study.

Steve stayed in the hospital for several days undergoing numerous tests. After a while the boys expressed a desire to see him and Neva brought them to the hospital after school. Walking down the brightly lit halls Felix thought about whether his father would live or die, what the nurses felt toward various patients, how the doctors never seemed to get tired, whether it made sense for all sick people to be housed together or if it would be more sensible to keep them at home, away from other infectious beings, even if that meant less access to the newest medical equipment. All these questions swirled in his head and made his brain tingle as if each atom had its own thoughts and feelings, and he felt himself glide down the halls as if he were a cloud of spinning electrons, a force of energy moving through space, not one person with a coherent set of beliefs but many thousands of thinking beings magnetically connected, orbiting, intersecting, bouncing off one another and held together with love, fear, some kind of cosmic, invisible glue. Roman appeared to have an entirely different relationship to the present events, as if questioning the circumstances of Steve's hospitalization or the nature of life in the hospital or life itself, for that matter, were not an option or, worse, a waste of time. Felix could tell that Roman viewed any situation as a playing field of power and movement, a landscape in which to make progress but not to dwell. Felix accepted their opposing points of reference and yet he could not help feeling that Roman's way of looking at things was not only more useful but more in keeping with Steve's perspective and therefore made Roman more like Steve and, as a result, closer to Steve.

Although Felix recognized that Roman did not actually feel very close to anyone, Felix could not help the stirrings of jealousy and loneliness brought about by the sensation that his outlook on the world made him essentially another kind of person from Roman and from Steve.

Felix knew that his father appreciated his sensitivity, even, at times, valued it as a type of intelligence that elevated Felix and made him special, but he knew that Steve believed in a world dominated by people who thought the way Roman thought, who looked on life as a game, a battle, a theater of war. Felix admired his father, wondered in awe at his power, sensed in his bones and blood that Steve was the personification of power, neither good nor bad just pure power, a thundering wordless force. This left Felix unsure of how to view himself. What he knew was that his way in the world was all words and sensations and thoughts and feelings. He was not power, but at least he knew that about himself.

So it came as a shock and a nauseating, sickening blow to see Steve in bed, in a hospital gown, hooked up with tubes to machinery and what appeared to be a dangling water balloon, his face drained of color, his hair matted in parts, tufted in others, his big hands immobile on the sheet, his lidded eyes like drawn shades in an empty room. Felix felt the giant weight of his father reduced to a fatty, bony, wispy body, a ragged vehicle for breath. Felix stopped far from the bed, took everything in, and only then slowly approached Steve. Roman ran into the room and went straight for the window, drank in the view of the coursing river, and then picked at a fruit basket on a table, taking a handful of grapes whose purple skins fading to the palest green near the stems were bursting with juice and flesh and a muscular pull when he plucked them from their branch. Dad, can I turn on the TV? were Roman's first words to his father that day and, as far as Felix could remember later, his last.

When Patrizia appeared shortly thereafter she spoke quietly to Steve for a few minutes, conferred with the nurses and a doctor, and took the boys home. Felix placed his hand on Steve's wrist as he said goodbye. Roman grabbed a banana. Neva was asked to stay until Jonathan showed up, which was expected to be sometime in the next hour. Steve was improving, according to all accounts, and Patrizia seemed relieved and ready for life to return to normal. As she left with the boys she pulled on her coat and swung her bag with a quotidian efficiency that conveyed an impression of moving on with things whether or not Steve improved, as if this were the appropriate way to behave. Neva could not tell if this was a false front covering anxiety, a complete denial of how frail Steve seemed, or if Patrizia were simply thinking of other things, if for her, as for Roman, life moved on, today was a game, and sentiment was for lesser creatures. It was impossible for Neva to know. All she could be sure of was that her own feelings were stormy, rough, and just below her own surface calm coursed a charging current of fear flowing into determination. The room was now empty except for Neva and Steve. She sat in the chair by his side. He was breathing, resting, not sleeping, rising, falling, not dead, alive.

She sits upright, watches the day fade, a March light being absorbed into the room, the medical equipment, the paint on the walls, the sheets. It is as if the room is thirsty for light. Steve lies still, breathing loudly. On the other side of the barely open door feet hustle, doors open, conveyances are wheeled, voices lift and lower and laugh, occasionally. Once she turns around in her chair and glances out the window where birds are dipping and gliding over the molten river, a barge slides along, cars race along the veins of highway that line the water, helicopters—she has flown in them—lift off on this gray day.

When she turns back around something about Steve seems changed: he is breathing slightly more heavily. He says: There is no mystery. Or: This is history. Or something that sounds like that. His fingers pat the bed. She stands up and touches his head, which feels the same. She looks over the various pulsing and beeping machines and they make no sense to her but nevertheless she feels that something is amiss. She pushes a button for a nurse. Should she leave the room and go searching? Then if someone comes there will be nobody to explain. Should she wait patiently for a nurse or doctor? Then what if they come too late?

She decides to brave the hallway. Fluorescent air and the feeling that the ceiling is pressing down on her head, that everyone is carrying the ceiling around on their heads. She rushes first to the nurse's station and finds a woman on the phone, a man filling out forms. No one has time for her. Her voice stretches into sounds but she is not entirely sure of what she is saying.

We need help in Mr. Zane's room, pointing.

What for?

Something isn't working.

What?

I'm not sure.

Someone will be there in a minute.

I don't think we have a minute.

Is he breathing?

Yes.

We have a minute.

So she is looking for the doctor. She notices that he usually arrives from one particular elevator and bizarrely she decides to stand in front of the elevator as if he will magically appear. This is unlike her, this reliance on magic. The doors open and out wheels a woman in a chair and an orderly leading what appears to be a parade of people who are not the people she needs. She returns to the nurse's station.

Can someone please come to the room?

Someone came to the room. There was no one there but him.

And how was he?

He was fine.

But he's not fine.

Miss, would you like a pill? Something to calm you down? You've been here a long time.

You're not a doctor.

Yes, I am a doctor.

Really?

Really, says the doctor.

Please come look at him again.

I looked. He's fine.

Did you check all the machines?

Everything is okay. Go back home. Get some sleep, the doctor says and trots off.

She stands alone in the hallway and the activity disperses around her, things pulled away by a tide. She feels like a castaway. She staggers or feels as though she staggers back to his room. On the way she evokes no recognition in the doctors, nurses, patients, whom she passes. She is apparently invisible.

Back in the room he is talking with his eyes closed; his words drifting from phrase to phrase. She could make out:

Anyone who is really serious about this country would fix this carried interest foolishness . . . Of course I didn't vote for a single one of them . . . Poppy, come home this instant and what is that article of nonclothing you have on . . . ? Yes, it's true we really do not know much of anything. Can you believe it? Can you face it? The truth of how little we know? Our ignorance is vast like the ocean and what we understand is so tiny, so meager, it is not even a droplet of spit upon the waves . . .

His hands begin to arc and curve above the sheets, and his voice grows louder.

If I were a . . .

And the coughing starts again. A wrestling in his throat with mucus and saliva, a deep pulmonary argument raging in his chest. Neva scans all the machinery beside the bed, a flickering dashboard, and sees nothing she understands, nothing changed. A glance up the tube attached to the IV, where the clear liquid bobbles in the air, and she sees that it looks about the same as before, but of course there should be less of it, if it is dripping properly, if it is working, and now he is shaking as he coughs, she has pushed the button for the nurse but there is no way she is going to leave his side, and her arm reaches up, turns the bag of hanging water, untwists it from a position it has shifted into, perhaps earlier when the boys were there, moving around, knocking into things, and she gently tugs at the bag and she sees the liquid slide through the tube and the coughing subsides and she doesn't know for sure if she has saved him but he is looking up at her and through the heavy lids there is a gratitude that she has never before witnessed.

Jonathan does not come. A nurse arrives and checks things and sees that they are fine and leaves. The time passes and Neva waits in the chair while Steve sleeps and she gets a text from Jonathan saying to stay there, he is running late. Her heart is still pounding. She has not forgotten the terror, it has not left her body. When Steve is deeply asleep, nearly inert, she stands over him and checks that he is breathing. She puts her hand on his chest. She talks to him. In the darkening room she whispers her story to him and he has no choice but to listen. She says she is telling him now because she is afraid she may never have another chance and he is the only person to whom she can tell her story. It does not take long, the truth. When she is finished she says she thinks that he knew most of it already but the full confession had to come from her—not confession, really, because she knows that she hasn't done anything wrong, but nevertheless it feels like a confession.

When Jonathan finally arrives and releases her she is sitting in the chair again, upright, and nobody would know that she has told Steve anything or, in this case, everything. Steve is breathing; the room is dim; Neva is waiting; the liquid is dripping from the bag. But Jonathan has the feeling that his relationship with his father has changed because of this woman. For the first time, he senses her power. Perhaps it is the sight of his weakened father that hits him not unlike the way it hit Felix, only in this case the blow is followed by a reaction more like Roman's, a reaction based on strategy, shifts of weight, control. Jonathan's jealousy of Neva is not registered but subsumed, repressed and made utterly logical if entirely irrational. Feeling turns to fantasy in his mind and what was jealousy becomes, for him, a real injustice.

I'll take it from here, Jonathan says, taking out his phone and resting it on top of a piece of medical equipment. You go home. I've got this covered.

WITHIN TEN DAYS Steve had returned home, a new man. His jacket hung slightly looser around his shoulders, and his hair had thinned, but otherwise he appeared healthier than before, having paid a visit to Patrizia's dermatologist and been given a chemical peel in order to look refreshed. He went to the office, gave specific instructions, lectured associates, closed deals, came home, had medically unsanctioned sex with his wife, and late at night spoke to Neva in his amber-colored study. He spoke with a strange urgency about his business, his properties, and his holdings around the world. In hushed tones he opened up to her about his office towers, malls, skyscrapers, housing developments, business contacts, political connections, both domestic and foreign, the ministers he knew in Europe, in Asia, the Near East, and beyond. The more he unburdened himself the more he seemed to trust her. The more he told her the more he revealed, his reflections unfolding like a mansion in a dream with rooms leading off of rooms, hallways ending in stairways that cascaded floor after floor after floor.

This was the House of Steve, a mental construct, a dynasty, a place, as much an idea as an enterprise, a vision that appeared in a darkroom on a negative and then burned the paper through, bleeding colors and light so lustrous, vivid, effulgent that a hologram of a house seemed to develop in reality, a 3-D rendering of an estate, a rambling mansion and outbuildings, a bright green glade, a stand of birches, blue meadows, a world of purple leafless trees in winter, bending boughs in summer, a small cemetery in the woods, a single grave, a soulful breathing in the swaying branches, sighing yellow fields and low hills, and, beyond, a ring of silver mountains reaching up to the sky. Shadows fast-forwarding across the steep cliffs. A gathering of clouds. A tremble at the top of the highest peak. Echoed, distantly, imperceptibly, by a shiver in the walls of the house.

I heard everything you said, he told her, leaning close.

What do you mean?

Everything you said to me in the hospital.

She closed her eyes, looked away. I didn't know if you were even conscious, she said.

I was conscious, he said. And I was listening.

So you know. She breathed deeply. I guess I wanted you to know.

The first time I met you I knew that you had been through a lot.

You said I seemed like I'd come from another world.

To other worlds, he said, and held her.

She hadn't realized until then how much she had wanted someone else to know her story. How much she had wanted him to know it.

She couldn't cry. She was so far past crying. But she let herself be held.

Now I know what your secret is, he said. And I will never, never forget it.

Once, when she had been in a desperate situation, she had placed her mind elsewhere and the question had come to her: What would one call a group of angels? A flock? No. A herd? No. A calamity, she'd thought. Because that's what would bring a congregation of angels together and that's what a large group of them would signify. Wings brushing wings. A thunderous rustle. A feathery gathering. Messy, sprawling clouds. She did not believe in angels but she believed that a collection of them would be called a calamity. A calamity of angels.

He talks to her for hours and hours in the middle of the night. He is passing on his wisdom, handing over his knowledge.

Money is a mystery, he tells her.

What does it mean? she asks.

The mystery is that there is no mystery, he says.

I'm not sure I believe that, she says.

Believe it, he says. And you will understand, sadly, practically everything there is that we can know.

But there's so much more, she says to him.

I wish, he says, looking at the golden reflection of the sunrise hitting the buildings across the park. I wish.

You see, he was saying, what I have achieved is the pinnacle of capitalism. An accumulation beyond anyone's wildest dreams. But I stayed away from buying and selling people: not politicians, not women, not anyone. Did other people do that and did I benefit? I suppose so. But now we have crossed a threshold in the world and what was democracy has become a buyer's market. People did not realize that if you let certain principles slide—due process, separation of powers, the rights of individuals—that the very fabric of democracy could wither. We took for granted that the Constitution could withstand practically anything, but it cannot. The mid-twentieth century was a golden age and we squandered it, as humans squander every golden age. People thought our ideals were safe. People thought they could have leeway, impose some positions over others, cut corners, ignore principles in the interests of ideals, skirt around the Constitution. But that is a utopian fantasy. Or a dangerous inconsistency. Or both. And the idea that some opinions matter more than others is the antithesis of democracy. Democracy requires a level of detachment that perhaps we are not capable of anymore. An ability to put reason above emotion, to have great passions but not let them hold sway over the agreed-upon structure. I'm just an old oligarch and I probably sound ridiculous to you but I have never been more serious. Money is not speech but we have declared it to be speech. Tell me, when I speak, do coins fall from my mouth? Money is not speech; it is power, plain and simple. Speech is freedom. They are not the same thing.

Was he the personification of evil or a wise man? Could anyone be all one or the other? Did it save his soul that he had drawn a line in the sand? Did it absolve him of a history of domination? He had his ideals but his history had a life of its own. His history had lit a path that continued to burn in his wake, a degenerate ribbon of fire wriggling across deserts, over mountains, igniting the ocean, easily mistaken for a strand of moonlight strewn in sequins from the shore to the horizon.

You should get some sleep, she said.

I don't need to sleep, he told her.

He nodded off at dawn on the couch, his enormous frame rising and falling with each struggling, risk-taking breath. Rising and falling, like an empire.

———

At the same moment the sun rose, pink and bloody, an ethereal cocktail, in Manhattan, Jonathan's plane landed in Istanbul. Midday and the lines were long at the airport, men in T-shirts and shorts, women in burkas and glittery eye makeup, tourists and children and travelers and the sweating, teeming crowd of pilgrims snaking their way through customs. Jonathan breezed past through the Turkish Air Elite travelers' check-in and arrived at the Four Seasons Bosphorus by three. Horrific traffic meant it took him two hours to get to the hotel, the city out the window an intricate mosaic of disparate images fit together by his brain in starts between texts and phone calls to his local contacts. Women silhouetted against an orangey-white sky, standing by the water like large black birds. A playground where children hung upside down from red and blue climbing bars, an ornate art nouveau façade behind them butting up against a modern apartment house. Crowded narrow streets with no lights, no direction, cars meeting each other face-to-face, backing up, sliding onto the sidewalk, the cursing, affectionately irritated sound of drivers and pedestrians arguing, directing, explaining, forgiving, cursing again. The avenues lined with shops, mosques, trendy restaurants, old cafés, spilling toward the water, everything moving toward the water, where the breezy, contemporary atmosphere intersected with the ancient rolling river. Wide vistas with the Asian side of the city spreading out like a fairy-tale kingdom complete with sultans' palaces and candy-colored wooden houses sound-tracked by the throbbing music of Euro pop competing with the call to prayer.

Jonathan's room had a terrace facing the water, and even he was moved momentarily by the spacious undulating waves above which seemed to hover the gods of Homer—he remembered them from reading the *Odyssey* in school; he had been impressed by Odysseus's cleverness—Poseidon, in his athletic yoga pose holding a spear, poised on the river like a surfer. Now it was late afternoon and jagged gashes of sunlight were ripping through the water, an Olympian fleet of burning torches alighting, and in the distance vessels idled, merchant ships and oil barges waiting to be steered by expert pilots around the Golden Horn. This was where it all began, he thought. And this is where it's happening now. Jonathan pulled a new shirt out of his suitcase and bit off the tag. He had a dinner reservation at the most fashionable restaurant in the city.

An hour in traffic later he arrived at a tall hotel and rode an elevator to the top floor. The restaurant was new and entirely wrapped in windows that seemed to gape at the sprawling metropolis which was just beginning to twinkle at this hour, its fingers of land reaching out into the green sea, its minarets pointing up to smoky-lavender clouds. The businessman whom Jonathan was meeting was already seated at a thick wooden table set for four. Jonathan joined him and they began drinking raki. A waiter leaned forward proffering a menu. The cuisine was Norwegian-Turkish fusion. The food sounded incomprehensible to Jonathan but he did not want to appear unsophisticated. He looked up. The waiter was pausing for him.

I'll have this, Jonathan said. And sliding his finger to point at an item that came on the side with the dish he had ordered, he asked, What is that?

That? That's birdshit. Birdshit paste.

Ah.

The business associate ordered.

As the waiter took the menus he said, It's pistachio. The birdshit is pistachio.

Okay. Jonathan took another sip of raki. Good.

The man was named Suleyman. He helped foreign real estate developers connect with the friendliest people in government for assistance in acquiring contracts, permits, and construction crews. He picked up a large envelope that had been resting on his plate and held it in his hands. He opened the envelope and took out several oversize pages of blueprints and plans. There was an elaborate scheme for two shopping malls connected by gardens. In the drawings the gardens were populated with walnut trees and partridges and landscaped walkways. The figures in the plans were illustrated in purple ink with beautiful clothes, and the exteriors of the malls were hammered steel and decorated with alien-looking animals, and the entryways to the malls consisted of arches designed with colorful and intricate mosaics.

Suleyman examined the pages and looked at Jonathan. He looked again at the plans. The families strolled along past flowering bushes and silvery fountains.

You want to build this? he said.

Yes, it's a spectacular mall. Very elegant. Jonathan pointed to the walnut trees.

You can't build this.

Jonathan looked at him. I can't do it?

No, I'm afraid not.

Jonathan patted his lips with a napkin and looked around the restaurant. Huh, he said. I thought if anything could get built around here it would be a gorgeous property like this.

You're crazy. Why would you want to build this?

What do you mean?

Suleyman spread his hands out across the plans. I just mean that this is so involved, so grand, it will take years to build. Why would you want to make something so complicated?

I can't believe you're asking that. It's modeled on Topkapı Palace, your city's great historical site. It's a magnificent design. You think I'm crazy?

No, I didn't mean it literally. But you could make something simpler.

Are you going to get me the permits to build this or not?

I can't. It has to be modified.

Jonathan looked this way and that.

We have the contracts. What would it take to get the permits and the crew?

I'm not doing it. It's an endless project that will never happen. I have some responsibility to my city. We have to build things that can actually get made. This would cost many, many millions.

I have many, many millions.

I'm sure you do but we don't need unfinished projects all over the place. Half-built buildings. Skeletons of skyscrapers haunting this city.

Suleyman pointed out the window to one teetering structure, all scaffolding, an orange crane moping idly beside it. There were others like it all over Istanbul.

I'm sorry you feel that way, said Jonathan. I need to use the restroom. I'll be back in a minute.

When Jonathan returned another man had arrived, and this was a minister in the current regime. He wore thick glasses. Jonathan sat down and began folding the plans and sliding them back into their envelope. The minister leaned forward and looked closely at Jonathan's face.

Suleyman tells me you have an unrealistic plan.

Depends on what your idea of reality is.

Our idea of reality is the real one, the minister said.

Jonathan continued to put his plans away. You call this meeting real? I was told I could get permits.

I never promised him a permit, Suleyman said. I told him the plans were subject to consideration.

What do you have to say? said the minister. Will you modify the plans?

Why do you care if it takes a long time to build? We are willing to put hundreds of millions into it.

If it doesn't get built we get blamed. The government is cracking down. People are resigning, being fired, going to jail.

So what do you want me to do? Make something cheap and ugly?

The minister laughed. Suleyman laughed.

Of course not, said the minister. We just want you to alter the plans a bit.

You won't give me the permits unless I build something blockish and unattractive? Something inexpensive and expedient?

We didn't say that.

I think you did.

Don't put words in our mouth.

Jonathan looked from one man to the other. I didn't put them there.

Jonathan left the plans half in and half out of the envelope. He reached down with his right hand to his gleaming black leather briefcase and took out a smaller envelope, a very thick one. He placed it in the center of the table. Then he reached into his bag again and took out two boxes wrapped in paper and tied with tags that said PATEK PHILIPPE on them.

Let me see the plans, said the minister.

Jonathan spread them out again on the table. The three men gazed at the exquisite mall.

I suppose we could eliminate this, Jonathan said, taking a pen and striking a line through the hammered steel. And this, he said, rubbing out the mosaic archway. And in the interests of speed and therefore the well-being of the community we could remove these, he said, drawing an X over the walnut trees. We could do the whole thing in something solid and lasting, like concrete.

The minister adjusted his glasses. Suleyman looked at him.

I like it, said the minister. Very simple. Modern.

Excellent. I believe that we have worked out a compromise, said Jonathan. And to make it all go quickly we'll make sure you get the cranes you need, decent equipment, not this crap you've been using. We can figure something out, swap some of the stuff we've been using in New York. Of course the really good machinery is in Dubai now, but we'll figure something out. Gentleman, I respect your concern for your city, its people, and its architecture. It is a pleasure doing business with you.

As the waiter came to serve their entrées, Suleyman picked up the thick envelope and made it disappear. Then he did the same thing with the two boxes.

I am blown away by how delicious this birdshit is, said Jonathan. This is the best birdshit I've ever tasted.

Back at the hotel Jonathan sat on his square balustraded terrace and called his father. He got Steve's voice mail and left a message. Totally worked, he said. They fell for it completely. We got the permits and we saved a lot, and I mean a lot, of money. Then he let a long pause go as if he were hoping that his father would pick up the phone. Proud of me, Pop? he said into the air. His words floated over the terrace and rocked on the breeze that sashayed across the river. Into the night of salty, perfumed, and polluted air. Out to sea.

Angel's first day as a crane operator was quite possibly the most exciting day of his life. Maybe not as thrilling as the days each of his kids were born, but those long hours had been filled with anxiety, and today he felt no such fear. Aloft, swinging high above Second Avenue in his primary-colored flying car, he could see every borough. There was no wind and far above the streets there were moments of silence when he believed he was an astronaut and moments when the terrain flattened out around him and he felt like a symbol on a map. Either way, he experienced a new dimension, a new relationship with the landscape and to the world. He could hear his thoughts. He could see farther than he had ever seen, a distance calibrated in miles, counties, a quilted planet that seemed more hospitable than he had ever imagined. He thought he could see a baby smiling on Roosevelt Island. And an old woman dying, comfortable, accepting, taking her time, in Crown Heights. And a family eating dinner in Yonkers. And a man, anywhere, everywhere, beginning his life.

27

Poppy stopped seeing her psychiatrist sometime in March. Their last session had been yet another rehashing of her relationship with Ian, trying to understand it, trying to sort through the memories which besieged her at uncertain hours, bits of glass in a sweet dessert, if by "sweet" one meant "escapist." The doctor had provided several interpretations of Poppy's actions and for her ensuing behavior, especially for the promiscuity and the drug use, and the various forms of denial, only some of which the doctor even knew about. But the sessions had become repetitive, wore Poppy down, until leaving the office and opening the door onto Park Avenue she would be slammed with a sugar low so deep she thought she might collapse on the sidewalk. She stopped going.

The chef, Kiki, having been given instructions that the whole family would be eating together at seven, finished putting the last touches on the oval dining table. Dinner was family style tonight, not plated or passed, a casual evening and a rare occasion on which both Steve and Patrizia would dine with the kids, and Steve's older children would be present as well. The well-nourished clan, seeing the delectable offerings, approached the spread, each in his or her specific manner. Roman ravenous, Felix with a book, Patrizia unhurriedly, Poppy distracted. Jonathan and Miranda were joining tonight, he arriving at his place in a style both entitled and uncomfortable, she sliding into her seat self-consciously. Alix had come too. Steve sat down last, as if a conference were being called to order, figures to be reported, depositions to be read. He closed his eyes momentarily, in a reflexive, unconscious action that could have been interpreted as a private microprayer but which was in fact a response to anticipatory chest pain. He caught a glimpse of Poppy out of the corner of his eye and smiled at her, with just the tiniest curl of his mouth, and she didn't see it, didn't see in that moment his specific love for her. These days she sensed it but felt she had no proof and therefore dismissed the idea that she meant something distinctive, something special, to him. Was it because of his grandeur, his overpowering shadow cast over every interaction? Or was it because what she wanted was too much? She knew he did love her, in his way. He had taken her in, loved her as his own. But now his love for her did not seem to extend outward toward her in the warm embrace she needed. It was as though his love was a feeling that never quite left the depths of him.

Poppy scanned the offerings. It was impossible not to smile, slightly, involuntarily, at the sight of so much bounty, and beauty, the starched white napkins, the glistening plates, the food like a tapestry embroidered on the tablecloth come to life, animated and in 3-D. Poppy took all this in and served herself, answered perfunctory questions about her day, tasted the sweet and savory flavors expertly mingled, but the communal experience made it clearer and clearer that her feelings for this collection of people, compared with the feelings that had been aroused by Ian, were not exactly love. Perhaps for Felix what she felt was love, a gratitude and respect that grew into love. What she felt for Steve was fierce, foreboding, a passionate yearning for love. And what she felt for all of them was kinship, closeness, warmth, even when they were their most selfish, cruel, and cold. Everything about them had formed who she was, and she appreciated it. But her early struggles and losses, her particular mental machinery, these factors prevented her from feeling connected to these people in the deepest part of her heart. Everything about them demanded her attention, defined her existence, and more than anything she pitied them their paltry happiness, their chronic unhappiness, but all the force of her unsatisfied need for love, all her longing, had gone to Ian. What she had felt for Ian was what she now considered to be love. It was impossible to change that.

These thoughts were not conscious for Poppy. They rumbled far beneath the surface of her inner dialogue. But passing the shaved-fennel-and-artichoke side dish to Alix, she caught sight of Alix's watch, a large man's Omega, gold with a brown leather band, that she knew had been Ian's grandfather's and which had been given on permanent loan to Alix for one of her birthdays. The white numberless face marked with thin gold lines reminded Poppy instantly of Ian. Blank yet meaningful, unpretentious, solid, true. Suddenly she remembered who had been the cause of her current suffering, the instrument of her grief. She had not thought of him, consciously, specifically, for days. But now, seeing that timeless face, so familiar and so close to her, she experienced an unexpected wave of love for him.

But where was he? Why had he left her? How could he have done such a thing? she thought, reproachfully, as if their parting had taken place only moments and not months ago. She wanted to ask Alix about him, and yet she knew that there was no possible response that could please her. And Alix wouldn't know to soften any blow because Poppy had concealed everything from her. Perhaps Ian had told Alix, but

Poppy didn't think so; he had made such a point of keeping their relationship a secret. She imagined Alix leaning over to her and whispering that Ian missed her desperately and wanted to see her. But then the real Alix pursed her lips and looked down at her forkful of wilted greens, unimpressed. Roman was explaining something about Minecraft to Miranda, who listened semipolitely. Jonathan was trying to get Steve to discuss a transaction while Steve ate silently and breathed with increasing deliberateness. He seemed to wince at Jonathan's business suggestions, lowering his lids patronizingly, impatiently, but in such a way as to defy any accusation that he was not being entirely open to the ideas. Suddenly a painful thought occurred to Poppy: What if Ian had never loved her?

And, recounting events in her mind, she felt that there existed confirmation of this sickening thought in her every memory: in his hidden courtship, his devotion to his work, and even in his decision to cut her off completely, as if to avoid the very idea of her.

He should have never told me that he loved me, she thought. If I'd only known that I hadn't mattered to him I wouldn't be in so much agony now.

It had never crossed her mind before that his love for her had been a lie and now convincing herself of his indifference she came close to despair. Her struggle had seemed miserable up to this moment. Now it was agitating, excruciating, terrifying. She ate her soufflé with an aggressive cheerfulness, practically flirting with everyone at the table at one point or another. She waved the sparkling dessert spoon in the air as she spoke. She giggled desperately, almost defiantly, at Roman's only mildly humorous remarks. She spilled cappuccino on the table. She understood nothing, felt nothing, loved nothing one moment, and then found herself wanting to provoke a scene. Before she could act on the unfortunate impulse, dinner had ended. Back in her room she located some texts that he had sent her long ago. Reading them over and over and over, she calmed down.

She's still part of the family; it's where her body lives. Its brutality, its coldness, feel essential to her. But in her heart she lives someplace else, someplace with him, someplace bordering on the unreal it seems so warm. Tropical in its lushness, enveloping. The slick and lanky palm leaves dangle down. The mad sun, feverish, melts against the water.

April 1 and the fools rushed into one another's arms, squealing, some teary, sharing the news of where they would be going to college. Poppy watched and complimented and commiserated with people she had known since kindergarten, kids whose faces she remembered from when they were still unformed, shining, sweet and silly monkeys' heads, children with whom she had refined the characteristics of curiosity and social aptitude that had enabled her to attend this school in the first place, boys who'd pressed against her at dances, girls who had viciously excluded her from parties and gleefully posted the pictures on Instagram, young adults who had debated mock congressional bills with her and who had explained over lunch in the cafeteria or while watching R-rated movies in their families' media rooms more than she wanted to know about music and television and Internet porn. These were her peers and she felt a compatriot's closeness to them, to their dreams and destinies, but she could not understand their deep, unquestioning, and devout desire to go to college. And they could not understand her refusal. Wasn't this what she had worked for? Hadn't she been a top student, give or take a few scandalous missteps? Didn't she want to be set free? To mingle and daydream in echoing lecture halls? To attend off-campus parties? To speculate in the wee hours of the morning about what kind of work would possibly be left for her generation when it was belched out into the world, and to share the confusions of an uncertain future from the comfort of a wood-paneled, squishy-couched, leafy-viewed dorm room?

Poppy could see their point. She also recognized that some of them would continue their studies in a serious, genuinely academic, or even scholarly way and would go on to truly contribute to society, but for the most part she felt like a lapsed member of some highly ritualized sect, a sinner in the face of tithes or punishing ordeals or the very idea of the elect. She could no longer get on board, play the game, believe in the system, even if there was no other system. This put her in the awkward position of having to feign excitement or disappointment as her classmates told her where they would, or would not, be undertaking their higher education, as if she were a Native American listening politely to a Puritan explain a recent experience of awakening. Her position was also awkward because she had come to school a little drunk. And with several pills in her bloodstream. And with the feeling that today might be the day when she started mixing drinks in the Seniors' Lounge or ran down the sixth-floor hallway naked or smeared herself with paint in the art studio and then swung from the basketball hoop in the gym. It was going to be a long day.

During study hall a big group of seniors decided to go out for a celebration, but Poppy spent the time in the library. She looked wretchedly elegant with her thin wrists sticking out of her long sweater sleeves and her now-cheekbone-length bangs fringing her big eyes. One other person, a junior, was reading in the library too, a boy who'd come in tenth grade and whom she'd never gotten to know, a cute, shy, stoner type who wore hoodies and seemed like he might be interesting if he weren't younger than she was and so weirdly quiet. He raised his head slightly from his book and spoke without looking directly at Poppy. Why aren't you out with the rest of them? he said.

Not looking up at all from her book she answered, Because I'm learning. I am actually interested in the classes I'm taking. This is the homework and so I'm doing it.

Cool, he said.

She lifted her eyes from the page to see him. He was too big for the chair he was sitting in and his legs stuck out like a promontory, thick and strong, in their beat-up jeans. He smiled the tiniest microscopic smile with one corner of his mouth. His hood shadowed his face. He dug his fingers into the pocket of his sweatshirt and took out a pill. He slid it across the table to her.

Oh, thanks, but I have plenty of those, she said, going back to her book.

Doubt you have this one. Brand-new. Exceptional. Guarantee it'll make the story even better.

She eyed the round disk with a slash across its middle, a compacted powder of possibility.

No thanks, she said.

C'mon, he said. It's a present. Take it whenever you want.

An hour later they were unexpectedly close friends and their hunger had motivated them to stagger out into the cold spring air in search of nourishment. By noon they'd had pounds of sugar and salt in various disguises and they sat on a brownstone stoop studying the stringy abstract shadows cast by trees against the side of a postwar white brick building. A chilly breeze blew down the street. Poppy's mouth was dry. The city encircling them had sun and oxygen but seemed devoid of some essential element and there was nothing Poppy could do to feel necessary, needed, as if her progress mattered to anyone in any of the thousands of buildings that spiraled out from where she sat. The world fell away from her in volcanic chunks, as if an earthquake were in the process of decluttering the universe, breaking off pieces of New York all around her while she sat, her head on this boy's shoulder, staring vacantly into the trunk of a tree. The travelers marching along the sidewalk moved erratically, seemed to walk up a steep hill, slid like marbles down a marble chute, flew by like the black-and-white characters that sailed past Dorothy's window during the tornado in *The Wizard of Oz*. Consciously she knew that they were walking at a normal pace with an average speed on a flat surface, but she could feel their panic, and their movements appeared to her like a front, and she could see two worlds happening at once: the everyday scene on a side street in Manhattan and also the hallucinatory revolution that registered in her brain. In the moment it seemed to her that every moment existed this way, that this was reality, or a glimpse of it, this multiplicity of viewpoints, interpretations, experiences. As information entered her mind one variable at a time, color, distance, timing, perspective, and her brain reconstructed it along separate pathways to make meaning, she felt as though she were witnessing the process in action, the whole coded miscellany shattered to smithereens and then resurrected by the cells and synapses that each worked separately to create a whole. It was beautiful.

We should hide, the boy in the hoodie said to her. She thought his name might be Jasper, but she wasn't sure. She would just think of him as Jasper.

Why?

Because they'll find us, Jasper said.

Okay, said Poppy.

Where do you want to hide? asked Jasper.

I don't know. Where do you think? How about here?

Here? We can't hide here, he said.

Why not?

He laughed a short, instinctive, smug laugh. Because we're already here, he said.

Okay, said Poppy. Where then?

My house is kinda nearby.

Can we hide there?

Yes, we can hide there, he said.

A spotlight pooled around Ian as the lighting designer played around from the middle of the audience and Ian and one of the producers talked about the show. They were sitting onstage, in a temporary version of the 1980s set, on a Jennifer Convertibles–type leatherette couch in front of a smoky-glass coffee table. A huge boxy television set sat like a vintage black spaceship slightly off center stage. A female dancer stepped nimbly down from the TV and left it alone, one corner illuminated by the outermost rim of the nimbus of white light that held Ian in its center. Ian was handling a legal pad and gesturing with a pen in his fingers. He told the producer that they were rearranging the order of songs. Now the show opened with "And She Was," a lyrical number in which Jane Eyre was introduced. "And She Was" would be Jane's theme. Next, "Slippery People" as her awful aunt and nasty cousin entered the story. The numbers "Life During Wartime" and "Wild Wild Life" would cover Jane's boarding-school experience. "Once in a Lifetime" was Jane and Rochester's theme. "Girlfriend Is Better" would be Bertha's, Rochester's wife's, theme. "Psycho Killer" was the climactic curtain of act 1, when Jane glimpses Bertha. "Once in a Lifetime" would reprise at the top of act 2, at Jane and Rochester's wedding. "Road to Nowhere," when Jane leaves. "Heaven" for the time Jane spends with the missionary St. John and his sisters. "Making Flippy Floppy" as Jane is struggling with whether or not to marry St. John. "Burning Down the House," of course, when Bertha burns down Thornfield. And "This Must Be the Place" for Jane's return to Rochester. Reprise of "Burning Down the House" for the finale.

The investor nodded his head. He kept nodding for a few seconds.

So, no "Take Me to the River"? the producer said.

Well, you know, Ian said, shifting on the couch, that's not really a Talking Heads song. It's Al Green. It's a nightmare to get the rights. Also, it doesn't really fit into the story.

You had it in there before.

Yeah, I know we did, because you wanted it so much so we found a place, but I'm telling you it never worked. I hope you're okay with that.

The producer nodded his head again. It's my favorite Talking Heads song, he said.

It's not really their song.

They recorded it.

True.

The lighting designer began trying something else, and now Ian and the producer sat in darkness. Without the glow of the spotlight Ian's face looked shadowed and lined. To the producer he appeared to be a hardworking, exhausted director, but Ian knew that he was well past running on fumes, had only caffeine and Ambien and other pharmaceuticals in his veins, and nothing pumping in his heart but guilt and remorse and a terrible feeling like a bad memory, as if every night in his dreams he killed someone, buried them in a field, tried to escape, waited in some lonely farmhouse, and was eventually caught and made to dig up the body. He woke up shaking and terrified in the morning. Only work kept him alive. He was trying to work himself back to life. The producer said:

I invested in the show because of that song.

Because of "Take Me to the River"? That's the only reason? I hadn't realized that.

It was in the workshop version, wasn't it?

No, no, it wasn't.

Wow, I remember it being in there. You see, I know I'm only one of several producers . . .

Twelve, at last count.

And I know I'm not the lead producer . . .

That's correct.

But that song really means a lot to me.

I understand.

The producer patted his suit pocket as if he were checking for a pack of cigarettes. The fine Italian wool of his jacket rippled in smooth, elegant curves. He blinked as he took out his glossy black leather, extremely thin wallet. Ian noted that it was really just a card case. The producer opened the slim case and took out a card. It was an old driver's license. He held it up for Ian to see. Can we get a light over here? he shouted into the darkness.

A spotlight appeared.

This, said the producer, is my driver's license from college. When I first started driving, you know what I played in the car?

"Take Me to the River."

Yes, over and over. It is the happiest memory of my life. That's the time in my life when I figured out who I was going to be. When I met my first wife. When I became myself. Driving, rolling along, windows down, listening to that song. That and "Thunder Road." My two favorite songs.

"Thunder Road" might fit better into the show. Unfortunately, it's not Talking Heads.

The producer smiled as he slid back his card. I know, he said. You can put away the light, he called out.

Back in the darkness he explained, So you can understand why this means so much to me.

I do.

So you'll try to work it into the show?

We'll think about it, all of us. But this isn't an apartment renovation or a custom automobile interior. It isn't just some luxury product.

Ian knew he should stop himself but he was too tired.

The producer raised his eyebrows and inhaled.

But you know that, Ian recovered.

Yes, he said. I know that. But we're talking about entertainment here. It's supposed to please the audience.

It's a creative endeavor.

It doesn't exist without the audience.

Well, let's call it a collaboration then, among the artists, the work of art, and the audience.

Okay, I like that. Collaboration.

The producer stood up. The light was back on him, this time a purplish glow like a techno aura. So, you'll think about it? he said.

Yes, Ian said, thinking that he, Ian, had never figured out who he was going to be. Did that happen? Did people do that?

Yes, he repeated. Absolutely.

In the theater after everyone leaves, the darkness is a deep shade of red. Maybe it's from the red velvet seats. Maybe the glint of gold paint on the swirling ornamentation of the boxes and balconies gives off a reddish glow. There's a smell of diffused sweat and old fabrics and wood, musky like incense. The silence is oppressive—the musicians, the actors, the dancers, all gone—and you can almost hear a whispering echo of their voices but then you realize you can't and that's when the lack of noise becomes a sound unto itself. Ian sits fifth row center in the dark with his feet up on the seat in front of him, just the way he sat that first time Poppy showed up for her internship. He goes straight in his mind to Poppy as soon as the lights are down. He imagines her sleeping, sprawled, her arms flung up around her head. Just a kid. He would like to wake her up, talk to her, ask her how she is, have a conversation. He doesn't really talk to anyone anymore except for the people involved in the show. Or no one outside that circle talks to him. He has noticed a distant coldness from Jonathan, and from Miranda and Patrizia too when he last saw them. Even Alix has been preoccupied, too busy. Perhaps he was imagining the chill from Patrizia and Miranda and Alix but he knows that Jonathan has cut him off, knows that Jonathan was the one who found out, from the housekeeper who'd become suspicious and shown him the receipts, signed by Ian, Poppy's mementos. He knows that Jonathan told Steve. And he doesn't blame him. He also doesn't actually miss him. But he misses Poppy. He thinks about Poppy, would like to see her and make sure she is okay. He worries about her, feels absurd and egotistical for worrying, as if his absence means anything to her, then realizes it probably does, and then senses a new relationship forming to her, and he allows himself to care and wonder. She's probably out tonight with friends, he thinks, the others will be drinking although, since Poppy doesn't like to drink, she'll be having fun in a respectably debauched teenage way. Nothing too dangerous. Nothing too scary. But still he worries about her and wants her to be happy, suspects that she is not. I am not happy, he thinks. And I can't be, he realizes, if she is not happy. I can never have that anymore, any happiness without her happiness. He thinks he is beginning to see some future for himself. He thinks he can safely say that there is someone in the world whom he cares more about than himself. Now he feels that he and Poppy are inseparable, in the sense that his life seems bound up with hers, that he is living his life for her. Not to be with her, but to care for her. He realizes that he is more alone than ever now, that he has left his old self behind, and that he is going, in some way, to put her life ahead of his. He doesn't know how exactly this will happen. But that's what he sees in the darkness of the theater, beyond the present, beyond the moment, past the stage. Into the hot white lights and directly through them, back out into the world.

The same distance separates the director and the teenage girl from the other people in their worlds. Both isolated, alone, tragic characters on an amphitheater stage, enacting some doomed, dishonorable story for the audience, as innocent as sacrificial goats, unaware of what the gods, DNA, destiny, the universal drive toward death, have in store for them. Ian feels himself gaining insight, reflecting, understanding. But he cannot yet fully grasp the fear he touches when he approaches the truth of what has happened. Is it a purely scientific problem or a moral one? An accident of nature or an intentional, ironic twist of fate?

That his mind keeps circling, circling around the problem, tells us something about him, tells him something about himself. He will never give her up, never abandon her. His absurd perseverance has in it valor, humanity, some grace.

She finds it a little strange that no one is home, but Jasper shrugs and says, Why? It's the middle of the day. They're at work. As if it should be obvious to her. She understands that it should be. It's a small place. Dark carpeting. One wall of the living room is painted a charcoal and the other walls are covered with bookshelves. Objects everywhere, on tables, cabinets, a jumble of decors, only the disorderly logic of things accumulated and nowhere to put them. He leads her directly to his room and shuts the door. Then he locks it. She is still adjusting, looking around at his electronics, his books, the bed. It doesn't register that he has locked the door. Then he fires up his enormous computer, it's huge, some massive gaming console, and unzips his sweatshirt. A sound like a missile whooshing overhead and on the screen appear images of people doing things she has never seen or heard of before. Violent, deranged things. At first, it's incomprehensible, and then, suddenly, from every satellite in space comes radiating toward her an unadulterated fear. She does not exist except as fear. She has known pain and regret and other innumerable miseries but she has never felt this exclusive fear.

Hey, she manages to speak up, Jasper, whoa.

Jasper? he says.

That's when she remembers that she has given him the name Jasper, that she doesn't even know his real name.

As he pulls down the shades he says: I don't know who the fuck Jasper is, but there's no Jasper here.

It was a mistake, a sickening error, and she was living it while in her mind existing someplace else. She could be in two places and no one had ever noticed; this fact had been concealed from her until now. She was playing dead. Or maybe she was dead. Her body was in the shaded room but her being was in Felix's room, where it had been the other day, chatting with him about his latest philosophical excursions. Her limbs were contorted and her flesh abused, but her thoughts were with Felix, sweet Felix. He is telling her about Marcus Aurelius. I love ancient Rome, he's saying, and he describes for her Marcus Aurelius's *Meditations*. And now Felix seems to have transported both of them to the Forum, to the Colosseum, orangey-pink light slanting through classical arches. Listen to this, he says, taking the small book in his small hands. I don't totally understand it but it sounds so beautiful, it's something Marcus Aurelius says in the middle of the book. I think you'll like it. And he reads: "You may break your heart, but men will still go on as before." I do like it, Poppy says, out loud, because Not-Jasper is making her say those words, telling her exactly what to say, but what she means is that she likes the line Felix is reading to her. I do like those words, she says in her mind again without saying anything out loud, and I'm glad that you don't understand them, sweet Felix, but I get it. Believe me, I do.

The shame she feels when she gets home is a dark void, and she has the sensation that a chain reaction of decay is being worked out through her, a hideous visitation, a possession by a not-living version of herself. Her hair falls in her face, her head downcast. She tries to sneak in without anyone noticing her and leave no footprint, glide conspiratorially to her room. People should know this, she thinks, that this can happen, this horror. That someone can be alive and die. Being alive is not really a matter of breathing or pumping blood or even thinking. It is an unknown. There is so much that is unknown. You can be alive and exist in a void and therefore not really be alive. That's when she sees Neva, walking back to her room. From where? Roman's room? Felix's? Steve's study? She's fully clothed although it's very late, really the early hours of the morning. In her simple clothes and stoic bearing she conveys some sublime combination of cerebral, womanly, and strong. She looks Poppy directly in the eyes. She does not look away.

Neva stood like a sculpture, rigorous, pure, steely, confident, yet also fragile, full of secrets, slightly surreal. She did not need to do anything but look at Poppy, and Poppy fell wordlessly into her arms. Poppy cried. They did not talk. Neva just held Poppy while Poppy cried and then Neva helped her get into her bed. Neva did not suggest that Poppy wash her face or change her clothes. Neva did not ask Poppy to explain herself. She just guided her, like a spirit made of nothing but awareness, a beam of heightened awareness, guided her to sleep. The last thing Poppy felt before she allowed herself to sink into oblivion was Neva's hand brushing her arm as it covered her with a blanket. A simple hand. A radiant move. A vitality.

You may break your heart, but men will still go on as before.

28

A T 8:15 in the morning the restaurant at the Mark Hotel was not quite full. Many of the tables, most of the round ones encircled by deep wooden chairs upholstered in dusky-pink velvet, had been occupied, but in the rear of the room a table with a view of everybody dining, a rectangular table near a wall with a settee on one side, the side which faced outward toward the encompassing lookout, still sat empty. The vapor of coffee, into which mingled the aromas of green juices and scrambled egg whites and dry-cleaning fluid and fragranced toiletries, slightly stung the eyes. The room was noisily quiet, murmuring. Businessmen and -women discussed agendas and ate breakfast, hands lifted muffins, feet kept nervous time under the tables, fingers adjusted cell phones on the thick linen tablecloths, or touched suit pockets to check if they were vibrating. Brisk waiters shuttled among the patrons and served them more coffee, more fresh fruit, more soy milk. As soon as a new visitor entered the arena the assembled stirred, almost imperceptibly: eyes swiveled, napkins fell, reading glasses were put on, removed, and replaced again. Calculations, instructions, commissions, were altered based on who had mounted which chair at which table. Plans were formulated and revised, with a seeming certainty of purpose but in fact with only the appearance of understanding and, owing to the rising murmur, the surrounding tension, and the chemical scent wafting underneath the smell of food, people actually had little idea what they were saying or agreeing to.

At 8:17 Jonathan waited in the lobby of his father's building for the elevator doors to open and disgorge Steve.

The burnished-brass walls parted and Steve looked out over the scene with his big, expressionless, sleepy eyes, and Jonathan's chiseled but smirking face, childlike for a moment with anticipation and a hint of hope, was the first thing that struck his vision. Steve nodded good morning and kept walking, past the gilded mirrors, across the shining marble floor, as Jonathan swung in line behind him and the two of them exited out onto the street, made a right, and walked to Fifth.

Jonathan felt bold, resolute, with the irritating cheerfulness and assurance which radiate from someone who is anticipating a good fortune that they do not deserve. It seemed as if his dreams were coming true this morning: Steve had allowed him to accompany him to his sacred breakfast meeting at the Mark. Jonathan was truly going to take part. He had been briefed beforehand on some of the crucial matters. He was going into battle like a soldier being groomed for leadership, his rightful position. Moreover, he was being treated as a senior officer to one of the most fearsome of generals.

The morning was clear and crisp. The sidewalk beneath his feet felt solid, bedrock, and he strode swiftly alongside if ever so slightly behind his father the several blocks to the restaurant. In the fresh morning air, the sounds of taxis whistling by, singing like bullets, answered by the dull roar of black SUVs lumbering past, like cannon fire, gave Jonathan the impression that he really was entering battle, and this thrilled him. Although in reality any proximity to an actual battlefield would have been the last thing he would desire.

They turned on Seventy-Seventh Street, ties lifting in the wind, and nearing Madison Avenue they entered the hotel. Steve, striding in like the regular he was, nodded to the men at the front doors, nodded again to the maître d', and kept walking purposefully to the low settee, his settee. Snaking his way through the tables he scanned the room as if assessing the dead and wounded left behind on the battlefield.

A good crowd, he said, glancing around.

Busy today, said Jonathan, as if he always came here with Steve.

The papers, said Steve, to a waiter, as he approached his table, and the waiter scurried off to get the *Journal*, the *Times*, and other international financial publications. Steve had already read them all on his tablet, he'd been up since five, but he liked the authoritative look of the stack of papers on his table.

There were two people seated across from the settee, facing the wall. Steve and Jonathan walked around them and sat down as waiters pulled the table out, momentarily disconcerting and displacing the seated man and woman. They stood up awkwardly, holding napkins, and then rearranged themselves back in their chairs after the waiters had repositioned the table and Steve had been poured his coffee. Introductions were made. The woman chewed her food animatedly, eyebrows lifting, napkin in hand as she touched the corner of her smiling lips, listening to her associate speak deferentially to Steve. Steve kept his eyes half closed, slurped his coffee, set his cup down. The associate pulled on his cuffs when he'd finished speaking. The woman was about to enter the fray when Steve lifted his cup again and took another slurp. Everyone was silent, leaving the great man to his caffeine, saliva, thoughts.

Having pondered for a while, Steve began to speak. He murmured slowly, mindfully, and although he appeared to be answering their request he was in fact asking them for a favor or, more accurately, an exchange. Something to do with not having to add a public plaza to an office tower if he gave them what they wanted, which seemed to be the installation of a particular chain of stores in the building's retail space. The woman furrowed her brow and the man tugged at his cuff as they explained that they didn't have the power to revoke the public plaza mandate. Steve inhaled, slurped, swallowed, pondered. When he opened his mouth again it was with regret. Without the extra space for retail that he would derive from the absence of the plaza, he couldn't promise them a location in the building. He assumed a look of profound apology, a helpless, beseeching expression that came over his face seemingly at will. The woman, accepting defeat while at the same time maintaining her power to fawn, shut her eyes and, inclining her head, sighed deeply, showing through these pantomimes how she was able to appreciate and understand the great man's words.

We'll see what we can figure out, her associate said, looking questioningly at the woman.

Good, said Steve, abruptly, already standing up and pushing himself out of the settee, waiters rushing over belatedly to help with the operation. I'll be back in a few minutes and you'll tell me what you've come up with.

Jonathan looked on as his father made his way to another table across the room. It was a table for four and it had one empty seat. A waiter materialized to pull that chair out so Steve could commandeer his body onto the pink velvet. Simultaneously, another waiter appeared with a pot of hot coffee and filled the cup at Steve's place. As Jonathan witnessed this maneuver—the man and the woman at the table twisted in their seats, also observing Steve at work—Jonathan's perspective seemed to float to the top of the room, to hover amid the ceiling fixtures and gaze down upon the restaurant with its many tables and see that at each one of them, perhaps fifteen in all, there was a vacant seat.

From this lofty height each white-tableclothed table appeared like a big hooped skirt, a belle at a ball waiting for her partner. Flatware gleamed like jewelry. The china reflected the rosy velvet of the chairs and the amber lights that lined the walls like dewy skin reflecting the whirl of a party. This was a dance, a ritual, as orchestrated and as military as a nineteenth-century ball. Waiters' heads swam among the tables like moving hands reaching out for ladies' gloves. And amid the swirl, Steve moved methodically from dancer to dancer. Every table was his.

When Jonathan realized that each vacant seat was meant for Steve, that each table represented another breakfast meeting for the great man, he felt first proud, then surprised, then rejected. Proud that his father wielded enough power to fill the restaurant for his 8:30 breakfast meetings, surprised that he, Jonathan, had not been informed of this, and rejected as he understood that it must work this way every morning, that his father must have held multiple simultaneous meetings at this restaurant for years, without Jonathan knowing. It was trivial, in the scheme of things, and yet Jonathan felt betrayed. There had been so many other betrayals, so many slights and ignominies, patronizing, belittling remarks and demeaning speeches, but Jonathan took this singular display of power, this flaunting of his father's generous aggression and hidden life, as if he, Jonathan, were a jilted lover discovering that he had been cheated on with everybody at the party.

He stood up and left the retail couple to work out their proposal over a second basket of fresh morning pastries. He strode over to the table at which his father was now seated and, pulling up the unused chair from a nearby grouping, insinuated himself into the conversation. He followed his father from table to table, witnessing negotiations, promises made and broken, feigned loyalties, outright lies, all in the space of an hour. He saw that one of Steve's favorite tactics was to provoke someone into being angry with him and then to apologize and fall on his sword, take the blame, go so far as to take himself out of the running for a project, and then, in parting, at the moment of utmost trust, tell his opponent: Just whatever you do, don't do X. X being, as Jonathan well knew, precisely what Steve wanted done. It seemed to work every time. This was like accompanying a grand master on his chess rounds. The exhilaration of being on the winning side, again and again, made Jonathan nearly forget his earlier feelings of rejection and betrayal. This was experience, this destroying of one feeling and replacing it with another, this endless, violent churn of emotion.

Back at the table with the settee, the man with the cuffs and the woman with the elastic face both stood up when Steve and Jonathan returned, having learned their lesson, that it behooved them to get out of the way when the waiters pulled out the table to let Steve, his luxurious gray jacket rippling in the breeze of his oversize, lumbering, yet somehow refined movements, and Jonathan, his trimmer form less commanding, both resume their places on the settee.

So, said Steve, as soon as the waiter had finished pouring

what must have been his seventeenth cup of coffee, what do you have to tell us?

Jonathan felt flattered hearing the word "us."

Actually, said Steve, calling over the waiters to repeat the elaborate exiting process and beginning to rise, I'm going to let you present your ideas to my son. I'm putting him in charge of this entire project.

The whole development? asked Jonathan, barely concealing his pride and astonishment. It was an enormous expansion of the downtown of a major city, and Jonathan had not even been allowed to see the plans. He had been off in Europe and the Near East, not permitted to work too close to home, where Steve liked to run the show.

Yes, said Steve. You're running it. Now I'm going to go use the men's room.

He threw his napkin down as he left and a corner of it landed in his coffee.

A car waited outside the hotel to take them to the company offices in Rockefeller Center. Jonathan began reporting on the discussion he had had while Steve had been gone. Steve interrupted him before he'd gotten far.

That's a bullshit deal. I'll never give them space in the building. Not in that building or any other building in the complex. They're a losing organization, not high end enough for what we're putting in there.

What about the arrangement they made to get the council to revoke the public plaza mandate?

That's good. I'll take that.

How are you going to keep that but not let them in the building?

Steve closed his eyes and shook his head. He leaned back against the leather.

I'll explain to them that I'm doing it for their own good. I'll explain that we'll find them a more suitable space somewhere else.

Got it. Understood.

It doesn't matter if you get it.

What do you mean? I thought I was running the project.

Steve looked out the window: You're not.

Why not?

You're too busy with international.

Why can't I do something closer to home? Miranda is sick of my traveling. I'm sick of it. The jet lag, the bad pillows, the sickening food.

Take your own pillow with you.

I'm exaggerating. The pillows are fine.

Outside the car stores streamed past, in their windows mannequins animated in a series of random incomprehensible poses, like the contortions of prey, seemingly sophisticated arrangements of limbs, awkward bodies caught midmovement, unnatural, expressionless.

But really, just tell me, honestly, why can't I run this thing?

Steve waited a moment to answer, seemed to be ruminating, dismissing ideas. Then he said:

It's for your own good.

That's when Jonathan decided to call Warren and Wolf and to take seriously their proposal for the tri-state-area hotels. Until now, Jonathan had limited his unauthorized dealings with them to the international sphere, his territory. He was ready to talk to them about domestic projects. They could start today.

Already in the car he is gliding, gliding toward the tragic, the enacting of feelings too enormous to contain. He is already ruined; Steve ruined him long ago. But now he is determined, unconsciously, to be a part of his own destruction. He thinks he can bring Steve down without hurting himself. This is his rage. This is his ignorance. This is his minor tragedy.

※

POPPY WALKS TO school in a state of psychedelic dissociation. What has happened to her has split her off from herself. She feels as if she has no memories, but the truth is that she is so consumed by the feelings attached to her memories that she is living inside a memory, a hallucinatory trance. This is even without the drugs. Emotions wash over her and she can't place them or name them or connect them with their original source, but if she could she would feel her mother's voice, dark candied-violet burnt sugar, slide down her own throat, would feel Ian's touch, light green new leaves waving gently like babies' hands, lifting and then dropping her hair in the breeze, would feel Felix's wise happy presence, his pink salty smile guileless and rakish at the same time, forcing her own mouth to curve in a smile.

This inner chaos is entirely invisible from the outside. From the outside she is a tall languid self-possessed New York City high-school girl, poised and confident, not chasing, instinctively elegant, tender and wild, walking to school, taking her time, owning the world.

At a corner she stops for a red light. Her gaze is caught in the glowing red orb. She sees the layers of other colors in the electrified red, blues and yellows, hints of purple and green. It is a Rothko red. As she stares it glows more brightly, orange-red, and seems to lift right off of the traffic light, out of it, floating toward her, suspended in air. It emits a high note like a cosmic dial tone. It voices a frequency she has never heard before. It is singing. Singing to her, to infinity. For a moment, she knows she is loved. By whom? By her mother? By Ian, by Felix, by Neva, by Steve? She loves them; whatever doubts she has had about her love for them disappear and she loves them. She loves Alix, Miranda, Roman, yes, even Jonathan! She loves the kids at school, the people on this block, the man in the taxi turning the corner, the city! She loves everyone in this city, forgives everyone, except someone whom she cannot remember.

Whoever that is will not disturb her now. The city itself is her only home and she loves it, belongs to it, is entirely grateful to it, will love it forever. The red orb hangs in the air. It emits a celestial sound. She loves this madness, knows it is madness, doesn't care.

PART THREE

The River Neva

Human feeling is like the mighty rivers that bless the earth: it does not wait for beauty—it flows with resistless force and brings beauty with it.

—GEORGE ELIOT, *Adam Bede*

29

A LL DAY AND NIGHT he fell, an endless fall. That is the
way Vulcan, the god of fire, fell when he was flung off
Mount Olympus. For Angel it was swift. At least it appeared
swift to others. For him time may have slowed, perhaps he
saw into each unfinished floor of the building as he descended,
looking into the future inhabitants of the apartments, getting
a glimpse of ghostly lives as his form and thoughts cascaded,
his limbs outstretched, body twisted. The way down could be
fast or slow.

Against the blue sky he looked like a hand falling, limbs and
head splayed in different directions, four fingers and a thumb.

It was sunny and there was a spring wind. Angel moved his
machinery, and the crane collapsed. One action had nothing
to do with other. As it was later discovered, there had been
a switch in equipment, inspection bribes, sketchy mechanics hired over the Internet, a bad weld in the crane's turn-
table (a critical component that lets the upper part of the rig
swivel). The top of the crane including the cab split off and

fell more than twenty stories. Angel was the only one in the cab at that moment. The crane had been jumped a few days before and "inspected." Two construction workers were seriously injured, one rushed to the hospital and died of cardiac arrest. The penthouse of the building was demolished. On the ground it looked like the aftermath of a carnival and a battle: smoke, carnage, random dots of bright primary colors among the gray. Water spewed from the building in plumes. The crane had broken into three pieces and fallen in the middle of the street and was on fire. The flames blossomed red and orange and pale blue and then rippled invisible in the sunlight. As if the very heat and meaning of the wreckage were so profoundly terrible as to be rendered beyond the human eye.

The lawsuits spread like a fire too, a conflagration at the center of which stood Steve, because while it wasn't technically his crane company, the building was his development and there were close connections between the crane company and his empire. Not the least of these was the fact that a higher-quality crane had been rerouted to Turkey for a project in Istanbul only days before construction had started on this New York project, the lower-quality machinery having been transferred here on Jonathan's orders, with Steve's implicit approval, Steve having handed over these details, and the entire Istanbul job, to Jonathan. Steve's face grew gaunt in the days and weeks after the collapse, after Angel's funeral and the questioning, the press and the public outcry. There were accusations against him, against the workers themselves, and of course against the crane company, with the head of it accusing the workers of pulling the crane up too high, as a way of fighting back against charges later proved accurate but for which the owner was never held accountable: the bribery, the cheap mechanics, the faulty welding. But before all of that was determined there were the victims and their families and there was Steve with his lawyers, Steve with his torment, Steve up late in his office with Neva, and the subject was death.

Purple-gray shadows speeding across the mountains. Clouds accumulating, gathering, for a calamity. A house could fall from a crack registered miles away. A flame could travel from the dry leaves in the forest and snake like an electrical wire sending unpredictable sparks in the air. A mechanical failure could be caused by nature, human error, bad luck, bad decisions. Most often: a bad feeling that everyone refused to acknowledge the existence of, could not see or understand because they were not aware. A fire could begin long before anyone noticed.

Construction is a dangerous business, he said. There will be fatalities.

But Angel, said Neva. Angel.

The air in the room was sweet and sour and blew in through an open window, the odor of the city and the perfume of the park. Steve grew silent and speculative. He never worried anymore about Patrizia finding them in his office. Whatever she might suspect she would be wrong. He only cared now about saving everything. And his belief was that Neva could help him.

Angel, she said again.

I know, he said.

I know you know, she said.

She feels Angel's fall, sudden, a swift blow. And at the same time she experiences it in slow motion, a succession of descents, orbiting, the way she remembers her slow journey ribboning down the mountain, through the countryside, to the city, across the ocean. She sees his fall as she sees her fall. The dropping from a great height. The gulf between high and low. The lack of balance, only teetering, a plunge. By the time she imagines Angel's fall she has developed a different relationship to her past and she can no longer clearly remember the skinny dog, the fire pit. What she remembers is distance, angles, the lurch in her stomach with each new degree of falling, each depth of understanding how far she has come, how far it is possible to fall, the draining of strength from her shoulders, her chest, her legs, as she realizes that she is never going back, that she had been sent on this journey on purpose, never to return. Somehow she has regained strength. But she is still prey to the terror, the intoxicating, engulfing fear of descent, the awareness of the pinnacle and its relation to the pit. When she thinks of Angel or her younger self she thinks she can see a pair of clawing hands stretch up to the highest peak and pull Angel down, pull her down, like the hands of a lover.

It wasn't long before Warren and Wolf paid a visit. Neva happened to be there, ushered them into the study, and observed. They had documents linking Steve directly to the collapse: to the orders to switch cranes, to the unlicensed mechanics hired over the Internet, and therefore the faulty welding. It would be very difficult to untangle this mess. Steve sighed deeply, heaved almost, and paced the room. Warren and Wolf watched him. Neva stood off to the side, pressing her back against a bookshelf, feeling the sturdy security of the books and their bindings.

Steve looked up from the documents.

What is it that you want from me?

Warren spoke first: We were unhappy about the hotel situation. The way you handled it. Our boss was upset.

Well, we can't have that, Steve said.

Warren smiled. Wolf did not.

I'm glad you agree, said Warren.

I mean he'll have to get over it, Steve said. He should try meditation.

Now neither of them smiled.

Let's not be glib, Mr. Zane.

I'm deeply serious.

So are we.

He should try channeling his anger into something else because I will not be his victim and his punching bag.

There was a tense silence.

We want you to let us back. In hotels, in malls, in the places we want to be. It will be contained and controlled, but we want access to your property without retribution. You can have a piece.

Don't be disgusting, Steve said.

He looked away. His face in heavy folds, drapery on a statue, his jacket hanging. His stature undiminished but his power lessened, softened, stone beaten back by water, by wind.

Wolf spoke for the first time in this encounter. This is what greases the wheels of industry today, he said. This is the way of the world.

That's not the truth, Steve rumbled, shuffling papers on his desk.

You can believe in whatever truth you want to believe in, said Warren, but he's right. This is the only way.

No, it isn't, Steve said.

Don't fool yourself, Wolf said.

I am not a fool! Steve bellowed.

There was a long silence.

It's just an expression, Warren said, startled.

Wolf was unruffled. We have the power now, he explained. Don't make yourself crazy.

Steve glanced across the room at Neva, her back to the wall. A tear slid down her face. So this is what is behind everything, her eyes said. She was like a crying statue, looking on at the suffering of the world and seeing all of it, through it, behind the workings and machinery to the very skeleton and cells into the horror of the slavery and sacrifice she had endured, and so many others were enduring. There was beauty, she vaguely remembered it, but right now all she saw was the horror. She was surprised by her own surprise. It made her realize that she had hoped there was a place free from suffering, a world built on hard work and honesty and life. She might believe that again but she did not right now. All she could see now was that even Steve's world was founded on this awful truth. Is there no end to this? she thought. And in her chest she felt a hollow heaviness, a contradiction, a pain, and also gratitude that she could still feel pain. I am a river, she reminded herself. I can carry this, she said in her mind. I am looking at the truth and I can hold it. I am Neva. I am a river. I am strong. I carry children. I am Neva and I am witnessing the truth.

They sat for a long time without speaking. Wolf and Warren had left and Neva walked slightly toward Steve. He stumbled forward. They sat down, both facing the window.

There will never be another chance like that again, he said. But it wasn't a real chance.

Neva put her hand to his face and made him turn to her.

And what now? she said.

Steve didn't answer.

They'll be after you whatever you do.

Let them come.

We could say yes and then trap them somehow, turn them in again.

They can destroy me with those documents.

Nothing can destroy you.

They'll do it now or later. I should prepare. Save the family, and you.

Please don't give up. We can fight this.

He held her hand.

The best we can do is wait for another chance, he said.

I thought you said that another chance like this would never come.

I meant for me. Maybe there will be a chance for you.

It was only then that it occurred to him: How had they gotten those documents? Who could possibly have given them access?

Someone knocked. Neva stood up, wiped her face, straightened her skirt, and opened the door. It was Jonathan. He was holding some papers for his father to sign.

Not now, said Neva.

Jonathan recalled the first time he had seen her. The airstrip, lush trees, the British countryside.

These are important.

He isn't feeling well, she said.

Well, then I should see him.

He says he can't see anyone.

What about you?

She wasn't sure what to say. She stood in the doorway. He studied her.

And from the other side of the door:

She isn't anyone, Steve yelled.

30

A WOMAN TOOK their jackets and Alix snooped after her, looking into the enormous closet, a room really, lined with hooks. On the hooks were baseball caps layered three or more deep. All teams, all colors, a preponderance of black caps. A billionaire's mudroom. He could wear a different cap every day. Alix pictured him grabbing a fresh cap as he sauntered out of his townhouse, into a waiting car or perhaps for a stroll with one of his dogs a couple of blocks away in Central Park, his unlined face shaded beneath the brim. Or did he have someone else pick out his hat for him? She had been in so many houses like this, but she never entirely understood the inhabitants or felt a part of this world. She preferred apartment dwelling, and little help. She was a hermit, in a way, and too many objects and servants made her uncomfortable.

She followed Ian from the ground floor up a curving staircase, swept along by the flow of people. Ian rushed ahead; he'd meant to be there earlier but she had been late to meet him at the theater, and he wanted to get to the performers upstairs to run over a few things. Alix felt nervous on his behalf. These fancy benefits in private homes. Special previews for the heavy donors. Creating buzz, building interest, giving an inside peek. An easy audience, but still. Everything had to go smoothly, perfectly. Or what? What would actually happen, she wondered. Would the god of disappointed benefactors spoil the show? Would tomatoes rain down from the 1940s French light fixtures? What was at stake, really? Was she sensible to question the value of these events, or was she being haughty? Did she not understand because she had never had to work for a living? But she did work, she had been working on her monograph on medieval art for fifteen years, and she lived modestly, could afford a room for baseball caps but chose not to have one. Did this make her better? Or was she a phony? Should she live in a double-wide house and collect art? Someone had to support artists. Of course she did support artists. Hadn't she supported Ian for years until he could support himself? Didn't she give? In fact, hadn't she paid to attend this fund-raiser? Of course she had. The rich people needed the artists and the artists needed the rich people. They were all connected. No one was pure. Everyone was complicit. Some fortunes were built on a crime, but most weren't. Money was neither good nor evil; only people were.

The champagne was excellent. Her thoughts were bubbling. Her vision the teensiest bit pixilated. Was that a Picasso? Why yes it was. And over there, did she recognize a de Kooning? So many powerful images in one room it felt a bit like a boxing ring. She was punched from every side by muscular, perspective-wrenching paintings, manly agonies assaulting her wherever she turned. This was like being in a poorly hung museum. Too many masterpieces on one floor. She decided to keep heading upstairs.

In the library more-contemporary works mingled with objects and books. A Guston drawing, a Marden print, an Agnes Martin, yes! A woman artist, finally. She could be happy here. A Lisa Yuskavage painting. Well, now, she might just sit down. As she entered the room farther she noticed that in the corner sat a woman reading, wearing a long Fortuny silk gown, looking not the least bit overdressed or out of place. She sported significant jewelry on her bare arms and around her neck, interesting, complicated, yet elegant arrangements of metals and stones. Her face, on closer inspection, was shockingly asymmetrical. She was sexy and unsexy. It turned out, after she and Alix had struck up a conversation, that she was also the woman of the house, the billionaire's wife. Alix vaguely recognized her, an actress in a former life and now a mother, a philanthropist, a supporter of the arts. But not musicals. She detested musicals. That's why she was hiding out in the library. Zinging piano music leaped and kicked its way up the stairs, seeming to illustrate her point. Alix confessed that she didn't much care for musicals either, but that she was there to cheer on a friend. She said goodbye to the woman, Genevieve was her name, and went back to the parlor floor for the presentation.

It was a beautiful night so they decided to walk downtown, all the way home. It could have been so pleasant, but it wasn't. Alix had had too much to drink and Ian was distracted, unintentionally provoking her with his lack of interest.

You know I realized something tonight, she said.

What was that?

I don't like musicals.

Ah. Thanks. My life's work.

Oh please, you're taking this personally?

No, no, of course not.

I just realized that I don't respond to that kind of theater, that's all.

I get it. Thank you.

Isn't it a little interesting? Aren't you the least bit curious how someone could not like something you like?

They ambled along Fifth Avenue, past stores as imposing

and massive as Greek temples, painted gods and goddesses posing in the windows.

People have different tastes.

Yes, but I'd think you'd want to understand those tastes.

You know, Alix, some of us have to make a living.

Of course! I know that. You think I don't understand that?

No. I don't. But don't take it personally.

Well, you're wrong. I understand it perfectly. We all have to make a living, even if we don't have to make money. Everyone has to make a life.

That's what I mean . . .

What?

You don't get it.

Should we have this out? Finally? This unspoken conversation that's been simmering between us all these years? Because if you resent me for my family circumstances you should know by now that they've been pretty fucking miserable.

I don't resent—

Yes, you do! You're jealous.

Ian laughed. No, no, I'm not.

You wouldn't even know if you were, that's how little insight you have.

So who's resentful? Sounds like you think I don't understand you, don't appreciate your pain.

That about sums it up. Yes. She kept going: And you have such naïve views about money anyway, as if you don't benefit from the rich as much as anyone. As if money isn't what we make of it.

She continued: Morality is the real issue. Humanity.

Yes, she said, if an immoral person has access to great wealth they can misuse it, but it's not inevitable. And if an immoral person without money wants to act out their problems, then they can do a lot of damage with very little money, believe me.

Are you finished? he asked.

Yes, she was calming down.

So we're equally disappointed in each other, he said. A perfect match.

Her head was hurting, her feet were hurting. She wished she could take off her heels and walk barefoot on the sidewalk.

He wanted to tell her about Poppy, almost told her about Poppy, needed to show her that his pain, his guilt, his unhappiness, his predicament, were so much worse than she knew. But then he let it go. Some of it was cowardice; he didn't want to get into morality or humanity right now, maybe not ever, with her, on the subject of Poppy. Some of it was pity for her, for Alix. Some of it was friendly love and some of it was the distance that comes from growing, gradually, apart.

A perfect match, she repeated.

The white and screaming lights from a gargantuan storefront lit up her dry, brittle, shoulder-length hair. A demented and drooping halo. What had happened? She had been his best friend for so long. Was it just the secret between them now creating an abyss? No, he thought, it wasn't just that. She was right. It was true. He had taken her horribly for granted. The rest of the walk they discussed trivial matters. They had exhausted this topic of conversation.

31

TODAY WHAT FASCINATES Felix is the history of the Zane family, about which he has been told nothing. When Poppy falls onto his bed, sleepy, hair in her face, looking a complicated combination of crazy and serene, she asks him to tell her what he is researching online.

Our distinguished forefather: "Ebenezer Zane was an American pioneer, road builder, and land speculator."

You're sure we're related to him? I don't think so.

It makes sense. He was in real estate.

Everyone is in real estate.

Poppy, is that true?

Just go on, keep reading.

With his brothers Silas and Jonathan—Jonathan!—he headed west and established Fort Henry in 1769. "During the Revolutionary War, Zane and his brothers defended Fort Henry against two Native American attacks."

Interesting.

He had a sister!

No way.

Her name was Elizabeth. They called her Betty. "She was celebrated for her courage during the second siege in September 1782 when she left the fort to retrieve a much needed keg of gunpowder and sprinted safely under a hail of gunfire."

Just like me, said Poppy. An American heroine.

Then he built some other stuff. A town in Ohio was named after him. He died of jaundice in 1811.

Our ancestor.

So you believe me?

No.

You're so annoying today. So negative.

Wow, if you think I'm more annoying and negative than usual I must be really bad.

Not bad, just unhappy. I think, said Felix.

Who made you the most understanding person in the world?

Ebenezer Zane.

Well, I didn't get those genes. And anyway he sounds like a militaristic land grabber to me.

I think it's really cool to have a family lineage that goes back to the American Revolution. If you don't think so that's your loss.

Brother, I'm nothing but loss.

Poppy, don't be so bleak. It's not all grim.

You keep researching Ebenezer and our distinguished ancestors. You do that. I'm going to go back to my room to keep crying. Or maybe I'll do it outside.

Poppy . . .

No really, I shouldn't be bothering you.

I like having you here. Even when you're a dark cloud.

She kisses him on the head and says as she leaves the room:

Excuse me, I have to go rain.

It's there, in that moment, that she sees that she has gone away, been transported, is watching herself as if she were onstage. The sounds ripple from her mouth in waves she cannot comprehend. Her gestures are theatrical, otherworldly, seen under the light of a glowing moon, clouds racing across its surface, casting strobelike shadows on the player. Who is this girl so desperately unhappy, so transparent, so at odds with the world? This performance captures an essential, universal sadness, and it is too painful for her to watch.

She manages to toss some items into a bag and get herself out the door. She would have died if she hadn't gotten out of the apartment. The spring air punches her in the face in a good way, she feels like a cartoon character, thwacked, with a blast of sweet smells and breezy nonchalance. But then she notices the chill, it is late afternoon, a cool day near the end of May, and she is pissed that she didn't bring a jacket. Her arms are bare and cold. Her jeans have a rip. She walks downtown, half thoughtlessly, half intentionally, not knowing how such a mental state is possible but it appears that it is. She knows where she is going, but she doesn't allow herself to really know. Such is her disorganized, post-traumatic-stress-disordered brain filled with the colors of the budding branches all soft and pastel and curving and bending, surging and dipping, like gentle fireworks, blurry, in slow motion, frozen in midair. The world is an explosion of pink and white, lavender and yellow, and she walks under the archway of trees along the park side of the street for several blocks until she turns eastward and heads in the direction of Not-Jasper's apartment. He has been providing her with a steady supply of that pill he gave her the first time they met. And even though he sickens her, she hates him, he is evil, she cannot forget those little, well, actually they aren't so little, pills. And now he hasn't been in school for a few days, hasn't returned her texts, and so she has been going kind of crazy. She thinks she remembers what building he lives in, something east of Second Avenue, a forgettable old structure squeezed in between two postwar buildings, a buzzer, a tiny elevator. She recalls the aroma of takeout Asian fusion and exterminator fluid that filled the cramped space as they rode up together. Now she waits outside while no one answers the intercom. She hunches over her phone and texts again, fingers whizzing over the letters, while simultaneously leaning against the buzzer. Normally she would not be so rude as to let the whiny honk of the intercom drone on but she figures his parents—Does he really even have parents? she wonders—are probably not home and he doesn't deserve decent treatment anyway. He deserves to go to jail but she doesn't know how to make that happen, is too ashamed to tell anyone what occurred, too enthralled by the pills, too messed up at this point to think clearly about consequences, values, safety, love . . .

His legs appear first, running down the stairs. Of course he wouldn't take the elevator when he was alone, he's too big for it. His torso shows up next and then he comes forward, disjointed by all the panes of thick glass in the double doors of the building. He arrives in pieces, fragments of a classical sculpture, only this one wearing a hoodie and sneakers, jeans, a wool hat. His eyes wary, narrow, stoned, angry.

Hey. What are you doing here?

The heavy glass door swings shut slowly behind him. He doesn't invite her in. They talk on the low stone steps of the building.

Why haven't you been in school?

He pushes his hands into his pockets, looks to the side.

I got kicked out.

What? It's almost the end of the year. I thought that was basically impossible.

Well, I managed to pull it off. It helps if you're on financial aid.

She pushes her hair behind her ear and shivers a little in the dusky shadows of the unexpectedly pretty trees that line the street.

Okay, whatever, I don't even care why they kicked you out. But why haven't you answered my texts?

I've been busy.

Busy? Are you kidding?

No, I'm not kidding. What do you want from me?

You know exactly what I want from you.

He steps down to the sidewalk and leads her to the side of the building. They walk to a darker spot, in the dimmest shadows, near a dripping air conditioner that sticks out of a first-floor window, held in by duct tape and rusted metal bars.

I'm out. I don't have any more.

She closes her eyes and lifts her eyebrows in mock astonishment and real displeasure.

Nice. You get me into those and now you don't have any more. Thank you.

He does a more contemptuous version of rolling his eyes.

You know I could tell someone what you did, she says.

It's too late. You blew that one. And anyway, I've already been expelled for something else. What are you going to do?

I should send you to jail, you asshole. Tears in her eyes now.

He digs his hands farther into his pockets. He blows air out slowly, very slowly, she can't believe how long it goes on.

He turns his head to the side again and says, I can take you to the guys who have it. I don't have any money to get it myself but I'll take you to them. He looks at her, his forehead creasing like a matinee idol's over his unreadable eyes, and says: If you want. Then he looks away.

That sounds creepy, she says. Where are they?

He shrugs.

It's a subway ride.
How long a subway ride?
Does it matter?

She gathers along the way that it is indeed a long ride. When the subway lifts up, elevating on its thin outdoor track, high above the streets, levitating, it feels like to her, and she looks out over the city vast and leviathan, the tangled, cluttered, seamless stretch of buildings and streets like the oceanic debris scattered across a whale's back, the blinking lights arriving like stars drowning in the sea, the whale beneath it all sloping and drifting, the city an animal afloat on the water, half submerged, a dark living rock, she thinks she should exit, get away, turn back. Why didn't she just give him some money and tell him to go by himself? Because she thought he wouldn't return with the stuff? Because she was afraid he would rip her off? How crazy is that? He is more than a thief, more than a liar, she has put herself in peril and thrown her lot in with a bad guy, worse than a lunatic, an exploiter, a user, an amoral force. But the necessary strength to escape does not emerge. She finds herself fixed to the plastic seat, face pointed toward the view, the lights that looked like drowning stars now glinting like fires burning on a plain, the last pale haze of day having settled into early night. No, this is insanity, she tells herself. I am not watching myself on a stage. There is no moonlight. There is no magic that will save me; I am going to have to save myself. I do not want to ferry myself toward some false shore of safety, some story that I once believed in but now know better. She thinks of Felix, of Ian, of Steve. Steve, she once thought he would make her whole. Ian, she once loved him, can't find that emotion anymore, only ache. Felix, sweet Felix, she hopes he never feels anything like this. All of the people she has thrown her dreams onto speed past in the darkening window, reflections of the stories in her head. Then she remembers Neva, and the strong presence—an emanation, a beam of light in her brain—gives her a rush of hope. The next stop she manages to haul her body upward and clutches her bag as she stands to move toward the doors. But his hand is on her skin. It encircles her arm above her wrist. A dread coagulates around her heart. The sallow lights come on inside the subway car, which is practically empty. He tightens his grip.

I don't think so, he says.

32

I N THE AFTERNOON Ian received a text from Jonathan about getting together that night at a club on the Lower East Side. Late. Ian felt a queasy relief reading the message backstage, glad that the rift between them was healing, and at the same time wary of what Jonathan's motive might be, what ingenious aggression and subtle torture he might have in store. Standing amid half-clad dancers and warming-up singers, actors scanning lines, flirting, exchanging their daily gossip of past triumphs and indignities, Ian instantly responded that he would meet Jonathan and was ready for whatever debauchery ensued. The club was an after-hours nightspot called the Purse. Salacious acts were performed for an audience of mega-celebrities, minor celebrities, international billionaires, and locals with nine-figure balance sheets accompanied by models and sports figures and the occasional artist. The club opened at 11:00 p.m.; the show started at 1:00 a.m. Guests were advised to arrive by midnight.

Ian entered Essex Street with a light rain falling. Dark storefronts stood locked with corrugated metal blocking their entry. Lamplight skittered from newly formed puddles to the side mirrors of parked cars. Long-legged women crossed the sidewalk in front of him teetering from shadow to shadow. At the end of a block he turned right into an alley and walked down an aisle of wet pavement, lightly strewn garbage, random windows pouring vague, sooty light down from above. He glanced back behind him at the street and the pale neon in the distance marking more-ordinary pastimes. Then he walked up some low wooden stairs and pushed open a door and entered.

A seething crowd had gathered within. As if the vast structure had been erected around them to contain the hunger and yearning of this motley assemblage, like a meeting place of worshippers on an isolated prairie, waiting for their designated minister to appear. A zinc bar behind which bottles glowed with elixirs and from which drinks ushered forth in antique glasses frothing, bubbles gyrating, pale melon-colored concoctions tilting in front of dark-green-painted walls, lifted by ringed fingers attached to bodies seated on tattered velvet banquettes.

He made his way past the bar through the first crowds to an area of tables set for dining in front of a low stage, curtained and lit with footlights. Handsome men in rippling silk shirts fetched bottles and racks of glasses steaming from the kitchen, platters of hot utensils. Waitresses slid in between the tables placing candles and programs of the night's festivities. They wore stained pink silk bustiers and garish blue-and-yellow stockings, red-and-gold leather high-heeled shoes, and they drifted through the dusty haze like strings of colored holiday lights come to life, fairy-tale apparitions, both charming and decadent, lewd. He had given his name to the maître d' and was being seated at a table near the stage.

Watching him across the clouds of smoky light in the yellow atmosphere was Jonathan.

He caught Ian's eye and wound his way among the tables

and pulled out a chair. He carried a premium whiskey and set it down. He lifted the glass and drank before he spoke. Then he said to a waiter, He's drinking too. Same thing.

Music played. A band in the pit, riffing a slow, grinding Dixieland melody mixed with an alternative moan, a groaning from an organ, and an electric fiddle.

Ian and Jonathan clinked glasses.

I'm glad you called. Here's to your impending fatherhood. Congrats, said Ian.

Jonathan downed his drink and thanked him. You should see Miranda. She is fucking glowing.

That's nice, Ian mustered.

Yeah, fatherhood, he said, looking into Ian's eyes for a moment and then at the stage.

Yes, well, I wouldn't know much about it.

Maybe you should, said Jonathan, still looking away.

Ian knew that Steve had told him everything.

And after a tense silence:

Am I here to be judged? said Ian, noticing the shot of whiskey kicking in. Because I feel like shit—actually much worse than that—already. You couldn't possibly say anything to me that makes me feel more guilt ridden and sick than I already do. But in case you've forgotten I didn't know about any of it at the time. And it's your father who doesn't want me to have anything to do with her. So don't go assassinating my character.

Hey, said Jonathan. Fine.

A long silence between them filled by the first part of the show, circus performers in vaudevillian burlesque, avant-garde strippers, explicit tableaux, an MC in a G-string with a staccato voice that ricocheted from every corner of the space like gunfire. Colored lights filtered the action and bathed it in oranges and violets, wild orchids, and techno greens. Dancers kicked, comedians mugged. The first of several intermissions came. Ian gathered the courage to ask Jonathan about Poppy.

How is she doing?

Jonathan's face acquired a look of concern and brotherly knowledge. She seems good, he said. Almost finished with high school. We weren't sure she'd really make it, he went on, downing another shot, but it looks like she'll get the diploma, he said.

How about her state of mind? Ian ventured.

I'm not so expert in that area, Jonathan answered, smiling broadly and looking down, the creases around his mouth angular and sexy, knowing and oblivious. As you may have noticed, he continued. But she seems okay to me. Looks gorgeous as always, a little skinny maybe, I guess. A little goth these days but nothing too scary. She's quieter, thank God.

Quieter?

Yeah. Not always broadcasting her opinions and criticisms. Keeps to herself. In her room a lot. And gone a lot, I hear from Patrizia. Out at night, you know, the normal high-school sullen act.

Sullen? That doesn't really sound like her.

What is this? Paternal concern? Jonathan lifted his hand and raised his eyebrows to get a waitress's attention.

Ian felt an anger swirling amid his inebriation. A new cocktail. The mixology of emotions.

Yes, he said, maybe it is.

The lights went off. Abruptly. The curtain rose. Another round of parading bodies, a bawdy sketch involving a dancing bear and a girl grinding an organ, a cowboy entering and shooting the bear. Blood, damage, the wailing girl. A psycho western. The bear gets up, bloodied, and keeps dancing. It never falls. The entire cast emerges, carrying pistols, the group whips and lunges in a suggestive and macabre choreography. The crowd has advanced from ceremonial to ecstatic.

Beside Ian and Jonathan sit two overflowing tables, one filled with Russians, the other a group of Indians, Ian thinks. Mostly men in fine suits, a few women in sheer dresses made of silk tissue, fiery sequins, threaded nothingness. They are all whooping and crying out, grinning, gesturing, their faces composed in shadowy oil-painted portraits, hung at varying levels in this moving gallery of dusty light. When the curtain falls again the patriarch at the table of Indians and the patriarch at the table of Russians are engaged in some kind of unnatural ancient ritual. There stand against the wall in a great glass display case bottles of the world's most expensive champagnes. Salmanazars, jeroboams, containing liters and liters of liquid worth tens of thousands, more.

First the Russian ordered one of the most expensive bottles. The lights went up, flashing. A drumroll. Waiters carried the bottle and glasses on a silver tray. Spectators stood. The Indians at the table bowed to the Russian, as he uncorked the bottle and let it flow freely to the outstretched flutes, spilling over diamond-braceleted wrists, foaming over the tablecloth, dripping down men's chins. This continued. The Indian purchased the next-most-expensive bottle. Again: the lights, the music, the drumroll, the silver platter. Now the Indian patriarch uncorked the bottle and walked the outer perimeter of the table, pouring the liquid directly into his supplicants' mouths. It rolled down their faces like tears. Candles sputtered on the linen. Guttural swallows and raucous swoons. The Russians applauded. The Russian patriarch summoned the maître d' and whispered to him. The maître d' rushed through a door. Moments later, the proprietor came out, a well-groomed man in his thirties, and shook the hand of the Russian, congratulating him on purchasing the most expensive bottle in the establishment: $70,000. Lights flashed in strobing exultation. The band unleashed a wail and the drummer ripped. The entire staff emerged, following the bottle, which was too large for a platter, which was carried by three shirtless waiters like a body, sacrificial, their bare muscular arms stretched upward, over the heads of patrons, stiffly straight, Egyptian, carved in stone. The curtain rose, dancers flung themselves around the stage, the men offered the bottle to the Russian, and he gestured for them to shake it, all three of them, with himself at the helm. They shook the bottle. They continued to shake. And then he uncorked it and it burst open and the spume curved like a geyser and bathed the heads of his progeny in a waterfall of froth, like some monster disgorging an ocean, a swallowed kingdom thrown up into the sky, pluming, falling down in an aurora borealis of raining excess. The Indian—or where was he from? Ian couldn't tell anymore, his mind was a cave and he wandered through it with a lantern and torch, searching for a point of light to guide him—the patriarch from the other table, took off his jacket. Took off his tie. Stepped away from his chair and walked over to the Russian. He bowed to him and knelt down before him. The Russian lifted the bottle and poured the last drops of liquid onto the head of the kneeling and proudly defeated man. The game was over.

Walking home, leaving the scene of such supernatural decadence, he is grateful for the normal shrieking of revelers out on the streets and the sharp horns that ring out now and then in the hot night air. He welcomes their piercing, cutting through his thoughts. As if against his will he sees the horrors of his evening, and his thoughts travel instantly to Poppy. How can she grow in a world like this? It is impossible for him not to worry about her. It felt necessary to consider her present, and even more her future: how would she possibly make her way? If he considered these ideas too deeply he felt ashamed, as if he even had any right to care about her, and tormented by his ignorance and irresponsibility.

Four in the morning and Ian veers unthinkingly when he enters the lobby and finds himself in front of the elevator that leads to Alix's side of the building. He presses the button for her floor. Why he's there at that hour she doesn't know, he doesn't know, but she grants him succor, lets him slump on her couch, offers tea.

By 4:40 he had told her everything. A long rambling confession and then a series of questions and answers. She got up and refilled her mug. A weak navy light out the windows. What are you thinking? he said. She didn't reply. She finished her tea and left the cup on the counter. She went into the bathroom and turned on the water. Steam began to mist up the mirror. She closed the door and took off her clothes and stepped into the hot water, as hot as she could bear it. He was knocking on the door, saying, What is happening? What are you doing?

I'm taking a shower, she called out.

Why? he said.

Because after what you've told me I need to take a very long, very hot shower.

While he sat on the couch he remembered Poppy sitting on his couch. So fragile and so alive.

———

They talked as the day rose. He tried to remember every detail of his relationship with Poppy, his motivations, his feelings, what she'd said, what they'd seen. He was back to telling Alix about his adventures, only this wasn't any adventure; it was some compressed version of a lifetime, a journey, an ascent, a descent, a horror, a moral awakening. Sometimes she asked him questions about his relationship with Poppy that were impossible to answer. I didn't know myself then, he explained. But I love her differently now, this he could say truthfully. Alix had her own opinions. How he must have known, subconsciously, who Poppy was. Alix was hurt. Ian tried to keep the conversation calm but his heart was not calm. Neither was hers.

No past. No present. The future the only thing that mattered. Poppy's future. There was no future for him except hers. Love is not romantic. It is savage, dramatic, mundane, unfair. The purest love he'd felt was this love. He was in pain but it was not suffering. It was the grief of real love. He listened to Alix talking but in his heart he spoke to Poppy: I love you. I'm so sorry. I will do everything I can for you. I will find a way to take care of you.

He thought about the picture Poppy had slashed and put in the plastic Baggie and thought that he should have kept the shreds and tried to keep her, keep in contact with her, but he didn't know how. He voiced her name out loud in his mind.

When Alix was finished talking he said, I'm sorry.
   It's okay, Alix said. You didn't know.
   Should I leave?

Where will you go?

To the theater. I have a tech rehearsal. We open next week.

I wish this were a rehearsal and we could change the story, Alix said. I wish I could change all of it: no me, no Diana. That you'd never met Diana but that there was a Poppy for you—at least a decade older, of course—and it was all okay.

He didn't say anything. He looked at her tensed face, the softest lines around her mouth, her dry hair, her familiar eyes.

You mean you wish that you never existed? This never existed? Our friendship?

Then you wouldn't have met Diana.

I might have.

But I introduced you, she was my aunt, I got you into her class. And you became close to her by hanging around with me.

He leaned his head back.

Alix, that's called life. This could have happened a million ways. It's not your fault. You're the last person whose fault this is.

That's all true. But I still feel guilty.

Don't. Hate me but don't hate yourself.

That would be a change.

Please, try.

I don't think I can manage it. I actually hate myself more now than ever. And you, I hate you too, she said looking up quickly from downcast eyes. I hate both of us. I hate us both so much that I want to die, she whispered.

He was quiet for a while.

Don't say that, he said.

I can't change.

We have to.

How do we change? she said.

I don't know, he said.

I think you do, she said. I think maybe you already have.

After he left she stood for a long time in the kitchen. Boiling water, watching the flame, pouring the tea, breathing the steam. A ceremony. Fire and water. The elements. She was like a creature emerging from hibernation, hungry for the simple things. It was a blue spring day, sun piercing the window, reaching out to her. Why was she even drinking hot tea? Because she was cold, always cold. Even on this summer morning of shocking yet everyday beauty—the trees on the roof terrace of the building across the street swaying, touching the cerulean like paintbrushes making loveliness come alive—she wanted fire, steam, heat. Would she always, always feel cold? Ian's love for Poppy, illicit, unnatural, hit her as a betrayal. A chill in her bones like a wind rattling the frame of her being. An unlit candle behind her eyes. She turned on the oven thinking that she might cook something but knowing perfectly well that she would not.

A minor vibration. An invitation. A valve. The oven waiting. Her watching. Watching herself, mortified.

33

PATRIZIA RECEIVED the call from Poppy while at the reproductive endocrinologist's office. She was having some blood work done. Checking hormones. She answered the phone with one hand while the other stuck out to the side, arm straight on the armrest, tourniquet tightened, bright red filling the tube like fresh paint being poured. She listened only half attentively, part of her watching the nature program playing on the far wall across the room, baby penguins, baby elephants, baby lions, a part of her focusing on her breath to take her mind off of the puncture, part of her noticing the slight bump in the abdomen of the nurse and wondering if the nurse was pregnant and then part of her managing her jealousy, her sinking hopes, her calculation of how old the nurse must be—probably thirty tops—and then silently wishing her luck while not knowing, really, if the nurse was actually pregnant. All this transpired while she listened to Poppy haltingly explain that she would be spending the night, and probably the weekend, at her friend's house and that's where she'd been yesterday and she was so sorry she hadn't called but only e-mailed earlier to explain.

Which friend? Patrizia asked, with vigor. She was trying

to assume a more disciplinarian demeanor after having completely overlooked last night's indiscretion.

Jas . . . Jasmine, Poppy said. Jasmine Carpenter.

Carpenter? Who's that?

She's new this year. She's been over to the house but I don't think you've met her.

Where does she live?

In Brooklyn. Far.

What neighborhood? Patrizia asked, rolling her sleeve back down.

Yeah, she's new, Poppy said. She's brilliant. A math genius. I've got to go. I have a class.

Poppy, I asked you what neighborhood.

Patrizia was ushered into a dimly lit examination room. As the door closed and she prepared to undress from the waist down and put her feet in the stirrups for a sonogram, she said: Text me later with Jasmine's number. Steve will want to know where you are. Poppy, will you please remember to do that?

They'd already made Poppy end the call and taken back her phone.

She forgets how she got here. Already the elevated subway ride, the burning fires on the plains, are less than a memory, have receded into irretrievable negative space. She forgets how she got from the station to this corpse of a house, its innards in ruins, wires falling, swinging from the ceiling, boards loose, a black mold metastasizing along the wall. That the world goes on in a place like this is incomprehensible. Then it isn't. It is more than possible. Now she knows a new pain, can't tell if it is a return of many old pains or something actually new, but it seems new, a never-before-experienced desire to die purely as a way out.

If Steve were here he would see his empire—so crafted, so controlled—attacked at its most damaging and personally hurtful point. A sleek animal shot in its soft eye.

A man reaches out in the dark and takes hold of her hair and grabs her as if she were on a leash. He walks her into the middle of the black space and swings her down on a damp mat. Several bodies have materialized in the room. One kneels behind her with his knees pressing on her hair and tightening around her head. Another's eyes dart and swim in the gloom like round white fish as he grabs one arm and a leg. Another looms, towering, and spits out that they are not going to do anything to her now, as if this were not doing anything. She screams until someone covers her mouth. She bites the hand. It flies off for a moment and in that instant they smash something against her tongue, far back, toward her throat, cover her lips again, and tell her to swallow. The men's voices have been rising and rising in crude excitement until they seemed not human but beings made of lava, corrugated metal, and dried blood. An unruly race of degenerates. Clubs dangling off their joints instead of limbs. Wretched wolves as big as ragged bears but not animal, instead mechanical. Their movements as if programmed by the sickest hack. Wild robots, abducted from the living, stripped of feeling and turned against life.

To enter into the deepest fears, to enter the house of the dead, is not really a matter of confrontation. It is a matter of holding on, grasping slippery walls in the dark, waving arms in the blackness, stumbling, finding a fallen wire, a thread of meaning. Surrounding that thread is an emptiness stretching outward, and upward, in every direction.

In that emptiness is the place beyond fear, beyond hope, where the last thought tries to rise and goes to die. Its charred and broken feathers whisper down.

34

STEVE HAS ALWAYS been the first one to wake, if he sleeps at all. This morning he hoists himself up, a beast rising, lumbers to the bathroom, his legs spindly in proportion to his massive torso, folds of Roman emperor flesh cascading as he moves. As he gets ready he is still half asleep, dreaming, he was dreaming about Poppy, days when she was little and he would wake up early with her. She might even have had the distinction in those days, over ten years ago, of getting up before him. He would peek into her room, find her playing, watch her unnoticed, wonder at the intricate games and the fantastical drawings. Was she working through the loss? Would she ever be okay? He asked these questions because he had loved his sister, and now his niece-turned-daughter, wildly, uncharacteristically, in a way that made no sense to him but which he could not deny. Poppy's long little-girl hair fell to the floor as she sat and sang. Eventually she noticed him, did not stop singing, and they went to the kitchen together.

In those days he might make the two of them breakfast. In those days he would lift her up onto the counter, her night-gown puffing out around her knees as she elevated, sailed, in his arms.

He finishes dressing. Patrizia is still asleep. The boys are asleep. Neva's door is closed. He knots his tie as he roams the hallways, finds himself in front of Poppy's door. It is ajar. He imagines if he pushes it open he might find her sitting on the floor, singing. Or stretched out on the bed, drawing. One light turned on in the dim room. Her thoughtful face intent, her big eyes narrowed, concentrating. Her little-girl self preserved, not ghostly but immortal.

At the same time as the door swings open from his push, several images flash across his mind. Her cherry-red nose on the plane back from London when he told her she could not come to work for him yet. Her name printed in the documents he had had Ian sign that day in his office. Memories of attempting to protect her. Had they been misguided? More controlling than loving? He didn't know. Couldn't know. Those questions lay outside the bounds of his personality.

The room was empty.

Although the questions lay outside his ability to ask them, they did exist, somewhere, in his unconscious, in his deepest recesses of feeling, in his body.

The bed had not been slept in.

She might have slept at a friend's.

But this had been a school night.

Of course she was practically finished with school, no college to go to next year; he brushed aside his disappointment.

The room was empty. It felt especially empty.

What was that sensation? A nausea, an ache in his shoulders, a wave of sickening remorse.

It was wrong that the room was empty. Wrong that she was gone.

The nausea blossomed as he rode down in the elevator. It bloomed up from his stomach to his chest, his neck, throughout his head, growing in lurches and grotesque fast-motion spurts of evolution, becoming different species of plant, of toxic flower. The ride down seemed uncomfortably long. As the flowers twisted and wrapped around his skull he noticed that the dull throbbing ache in his shoulders had become a verifiable anguish, a shooting prismatic cutting as if from a sharp diamond, a mineral slicing. He grabbed his head with his hand, as if he were trying to extract the guilt, the pain, by removing his face. He had done what he had thought was right but it was not enough. Or perhaps it had not been right. And he knew, instinctively, that he had pushed her away. Farther than away, he suspected. Somewhere he did not want to consider. He felt the sick logic of his life click into place. His hand fell limp at his side as the elevator doors opened, and he walked, much to his surprise, several steps.

Seized by a feeling, a question, and an answer all at once: "It's so cold. What am I doing? This is it." A reflection in the shape of a candle glanced off a mirror. The candle's flame elongated, flared brighter than ever, lit up everything, shrunk, grew dim, and then returned to the hard silver of the mirror. A heavy door slowly swung shut, cutting off the warm wind and leaving only an air-conditioned chill.

Steve died in the lobby in the doorman's arms. By the time the ambulance arrived it was over. While it happened, Neva was dropping off the boys. Patrizia was back in an examination room, dressing. Jonathan, Miranda, and Alix rushed to the hospital, meeting Patrizia and Neva there, but they were all too late.

Later, back at the apartment, everyone assembled except Poppy. No one could find her. The school had no record of Poppy's arrival that morning. Patrizia's assistant was trying all the numbers listed in the school directory. She couldn't find a Jasmine Carpenter in Brooklyn. Maybe Patrizia had misheard the name. Poppy wasn't picking up or answering texts. In the hectic disorganization of death, shock, grief, and stupor, a slow-moving confusion dictated the tone of events, settled on everything like a blowing ash. Individuals enacted their roles with no understanding of their meaning. People's concern for Poppy surfaced and then sank, repeatedly, throughout the day. Amid all the upheaval and arrangements her absence was not forgotten, but overlooked.

No one knew that Steve had thought of her, would have been thinking of her had he been alive.

A haze clouded the proceedings although the day was sunny. Objects that stood out took on absurd significance, all out of proportion to their actual importance. On the way to pick up the boys from school, Neva felt she could see every leaf distinctly on every tree. The metal clip in Patrizia's hair threw off bullets of sunlight as she hurried a bit ahead of Neva on the sidewalk. Patrizia had come with her, to tell the boys herself, sitting them on a park bench not far from school, hugging them and then nodding to Neva to help her get them home. Back in the apartment, Neva noticed Felix's pants, crumpled on the floor of his room, and she thought the folded forlorn softness was a dog and she would never forget it, imprinted on her brain like a real memory. A blue dog, whimpering, on the rug. As she held Felix, and rocked him, she looked at the dog. Patrizia was contending with Roman, who had locked himself in the bathroom.

———

Sitting next to Felix on his bed, Neva felt the glide of wheels beneath her. She would go on. She kept a constant vigil in her mind to go on. Nothing felt final, only endless.

I'm going to miss Dad, said Felix.

Of course, said Patrizia, who had just walked into the room, taking his hand.

We all will, said Neva. And we will never forget him.

Felix lay his head down in Neva's lap.

Remnants blew through her mind. The singed debris that drifts on the wind after a ruinous catastrophe. She stood in memory in his study that was empty now. Where once she'd watched him handling the sharp glass trophies, the deal totems, on his desk, holding them lightly in his enormous hand. Where she'd placed her fingers on his back when he'd stood with his hands on his knees, coughing, with weeping eyes. The amber light pierced her memory. My heart, my heart. Her eyes did not weep.

Miranda walked slowly down a hallway to use the restroom. Her ballooning belly preceded her, covered in a thin black tunic that fluttered around her thighs. The hot breeze through an open window, insisting on summer. Jonathan, uncharacteristically gallant, asked her every now and then if she needed anything. His face was pinched, and for the first time in his life he looked confused, thought Alix. He kept walking from the living room to the library to the kitchen, wandering around the huge apartment, pressing numbers into his phone and hanging up, checking messages which she didn't entirely believe existed. He could not inhabit the world without their father. She could, but Jonathan would flounder.

She stepped out onto a balcony to get some air, to breathe in the city fumes, to check her messages, and realized that she had not told Ian. He deserved to know.

When she heard his voice she started crying.

It's a nightmare, she said, as she explained. We're all in the apartment together for some reason. Really a nightmare.

It must be, he said.

I hate to admit it, but I wish you were here with me.

I wish that too.

Apparently, Dad left instructions in a safe in his study. He wants to be cremated. I keep picturing his ashes blowing around and rising up into a gigantic gray version of him telling us that we're doing this all wrong. He scared me.

I know. He could be scary.

She kept crying.

He was even scarier in my mind though. Why was that?

People are not just who they are. They are histories, feelings, mistakes, what we imagine them to be.

Thank you for saying that and not just saying he was a monster.

They were quiet. Cars honked from below. Ian said:

Can I ask: How is Poppy handling it?

Poppy isn't here, Alix said, wiping her face with a tissue-thin scarf, sliding it up underneath her sunglasses.

Isn't there? Where is she?

We can't reach her. She was at a friend's house and isn't picking up or answering.

Well, who's out there looking for her?

Patrizia's assistant is on it.

On it? What the hell is she doing?

She's making calls.

Has she called the police?

Ian, don't get hysterical. You're like an overprotective father.

No, you guys are crazy. You've abandoned her. As usual.

Hey, that's not fair. We're a medicated, barely functioning disaster here. Just trying to make it through this.

That's what you always say.

Fuck you. My father just died.

Maybe it will force you to grow up. Where is Neva? Is she with the boys? Can you put her on? Put her on.

Alix got Neva and Ian explained how to trace Poppy's cell phone. He knew it had a locator app. They traced it to some-place in New Jersey. The phone had been on a winding itiner-ary, from way out in Queens, to Brooklyn, to Staten Island, and the last spot they could locate was in New Jersey. He told her they should call the police.

You do that, Neva said. And I'll go myself.

What? he said. That's not a good idea.

She quietly ended the call.

She did not want to alarm Patrizia, Felix, or Roman. She calmly explained that she had news from Poppy and that she would go and collect her. Felix lifted his head, bleary. He said: Yes, please, get Poppy. Patrizia asked: How will you do that? And then turned her attention to something else, and Neva left the apartment and went to the garage. She knew the attendant.

She held the keys and sat in the driver's seat. She said out loud: I will never forget you. She started the car.

———

Would you save her if you could? Go back to the worst moment and rescue the foundling you, the orphan, the girl? Of course you would. For you, to know and to act are the same thing. For you to go on, to continue, means to save her and, by saving her, save yourself, save them all. For you the whole world exists on top of that mountain, clouds turning, fire sparking, voices low. Go back to that moment and the clouds reverse their course, the fire quiets, the voices stop.

It begins with a child.

35

O N T H E H I G H W A Y she had not gone far when she started thinking about what might have happened to Poppy. There was no point in not imagining the worst. The problem of Poppy was an extension of the worst, as it unfurled, leaden, gray, like the highway itself. Cars pulled ahead, fell behind— mostly behind because she was speeding—some colorful, like occasional toys scattered along the road, odd moments of macabre joy on the journey. The joy did not take away the pain, and the pain did not take away the joy. There was some comfort in that. Some.

Along the sides of the highway the green trees blur and it always seems that there is something hidden behind the screen of color, some magnificent estate, some gleaming sculpture in a garden, some last idyllic tree behind the trees. Its bright fruit glistens. Its leaves dangle down. The rushing of the green gives the illusion that there is another world, and maybe there is, but as soon as you stop the car and get out to look for it the rushing ends, the trees separate, and you cannot find this garden.

The traffic gathered and slowed as she approached the bridge. Cars drifted like dead bodies on a river. The bridge loomed, at once majestic and ordinary. The water below, as she crossed the bridge, flowed molten and ferocious, forging on, implacable. Stalled in traffic she checked the GPS for directions to the spot in New Jersey, the gray circle where the app had last located Poppy. Neva knew that Poppy would not be there anymore, but she would probably not be far away. She would find her.

How are you going to do that? a voice in her head asked.

The same way I have done everything.

How is that?

By not worrying about myself.

You're very brave.

No, I'm not. I'm just determined.

Or out of your mind.

No, I'm in my mind. Very deeply in my mind.

She followed the line on the little screen. Watched it curve and turn and imitated its movements with her hands on the wheel. First she encountered tall apartment buildings, some houses. Factories, machinery. An endless road. Was this the Pulaski Skyway or the New Jersey Turnpike? She hadn't driven in so long. Angel had always done the driving. She could feel his presence as if he were in the seat beside her. Angel's daughter had asked to visit Neva and the boys. Her mother was too distraught to play with her anymore. Neva and Felix had entertained her with games and a walk in the park. She'd ridden the carousel. Saddled up on the orange pony with a turquoise bow in her hair, the bobbing and circling an outsize distraction, a celebration. She'd visited the sea lions, watched their bulging shadows as they leaped. She'd wondered at their muscular, flexible necks. Felix had taken her by the hand and they had marched, happy soldiers, underneath the turning clock with the bronze animals.

They say all roads lead to Rome, but on the globe today do all roads lead here, to this hotel with the smeared glass fish tank in the wall, the back room, the hidden business of buying people? Jonathan made it possible for Warren and Wolf to use some of the Zane properties without Steve knowing, at least for a little while. He probably would have found out, but Jonathan was willing to take the risk, to risk everything. Steve had set this in motion, that was how Jonathan looked at it, and perhaps he was right. But neither Steve nor Jonathan understood how complete the circle came, how perfectly circular was this globe. Neither of them saw Poppy sitting in the van that pulled up at the hotel, saw her get out with the others, saw her huddled in the back room, her fate the same abandonment, the same shipwreck, as the others', all oceans pouring into this dirty fish tank.

It's here, in the hotel, that you can see even more clearly what is going to happen, that you can feel the vibration, the distant rumblings, of the fall of the House of Steve. They can't see it clearly, don't really know it is happening, are not able to witness it, can't feel distinctly the trembling, or hear the avalanche.

Clouds race across the mountainside. In the fields, stalks whip back and forth. In the bright glade, animals rush by, darting out from their places. A bat, disoriented, flies through the window of the mansion in the daylight. Flaps frantically in the rafters. Wraps itself in a curtain, entangled, thrashes and whines. Knocks over a lamp from a desk. A bulb breaks. A hot wire touches paper. A flame alights.

She is dismissed from the hotel. Only a few girls needed today. She rides back in the van and weeps without letting anyone see because she knows now that her fate is unimportant. This is the depth of despair and the height of wisdom. But she feels neither despair nor wisdom, just a hollowing out of her hopes, whatever hopes she had left.

Through her teary reflection she sees the gritty unspectacular landscape of stores and multiplexes, restaurants and gas stations. Perhaps this is no different from what the world would look like after an apocalypse. She remembers someone telling her that she was already living postapocalypse, and she remembers remembering that thought and agreeing with it at a later time, but all of that seems like another life, as if she were only now actually, truly experiencing the end of the world. Maybe this is what the end of the world felt like? A continual rediscovery that it was ending.

Poppy had the dullest sense that at one time she would have found this idea humorous. Here, she found it sad, and she had no way to distract herself from the sadness. She realized that she used to pick and choose what she saw but now she saw all of it. The sweeping waste, the orphaned towns. They rolled through her reflection, rolled right over her, inside her, ruminating, brooding. They seemed to be the only things that wouldn't leave her, wouldn't leave her alone. It was as if her body had become a computer and the external world streamed across her skin, a three-dimensional screen in the shape of a young woman, bearing a constant flood of images that did not reflect her thoughts and feelings but replaced them. If she'd had the strength she could have seen herself as a beautiful machine, still capable of thought and feeling, ready to run like some fantasy action hero in a movie across this landscape of devastation and exact some justice. But she did not have the strength, not now. She was a screen in the shape of a person and she had been hacked.

Neva was back on a highway now, a smaller one, as she followed the green line deeper into the state. When she approached the point at which the map met her actual location an eerie familiarity announced itself in her sternum, a malignant fear. Not the thrumming of anxiety or the gaping canyon of panic but a radiating, internal bleeding. It reached her shoulders, ran down her arms, circulated through her system as she recognized fast-food restaurants and generic names of plazas, big box stores and local businesses. The geometry of this intersection blinded her for an instant. It went white, like a flash, as if she were recalling a mental picture she had taken.

This could be any place, she said to herself. Everywhere looks like this. The sign of the multiplex, the font of the hardware store. The pun in the name of the sandwich shop. The pizza parlor with its oily yellow gloom. It was all so unmemorable that no one would have remembered it unless it was truly a memory. But she had to admit: she had never been here. She had never seen this particular strip mall through the windows of a van. But she had seen places similar, too similar. She was

close. She could feel it. She figured they might have tossed
the phone out a window or into a garbage can around here,
on their way someplace in the area. She knew, unfortunately,
how people like this behaved. She kept going past the flashing
point on the screen and drove farther. She pulled into several
anonymous plazas and pulled out. She kept going. She kept
going.

She pulled off the highway into yet another parking lot. She
stepped out of the car and stood against it while she looked
around. A hot summer wind brushed her dark, wavy, slightly
spiky shoulder-length hair and her simple black clothes, but
her angular purity remained untouched by the air. Her memories attacked, tumultuous, swarming, but her body gathered
strength, finding its power. Her mind scanning, eyes narrowed, heart flooded with feelings. Then she saw it. It was
a nail salon. In the window was a sign. It didn't say STRESS
REDUCTION like the one she remembered from her past.
Instead it said: STIMULUS PLAN.

She walked to the gas station on the far side of the movie theater. She made a brief transaction and then walked back to
the salon. She was carrying a can in one hand and had slipped
something into her pocket. Her eyes squinted into the shapes
of tiny beautiful green fish arcing slightly in the sun. She
strode into the salon and what happened next was a bolt of
mythic lightning, a series of fierce shudders that illuminated
the day, broke through the darkness covering the ordinary
world. An awakening in vivid bursts of light. In the front of
the salon sat a woman behind a desk and beyond her little
tables and chairs for manicures and along one side of the room
a row of huge padded lounge chairs with basins at their feet

for pedicures. To the left of the entrance was a wall covered in nail polishes, rows of reds, pinks, nudes, oranges, blues, corals, greens, novelty colors, sparkles, shimmers, glossy topcoats. Neva heard the door close behind her. The woman at the desk raised her head to ask if she had an appointment, but Neva didn't answer, she kept walking past the three or four women getting manicures. One in a sweater saying she was always chilly even in summer. There was one along the wall in a sundress getting a pedicure, calling out that she was always hot wasn't that funny. Others skimmed magazines. Faces looked up at her from their work, from their leisure. She brushed past an area for drying toes and fingers on top of which rested stacks of magazines that slid off and tumbled as she past. The woman from the front desk, her pretty black bangs staying stiffly straight, rushed after Neva as she headed to the back of the salon. She knew there would be a maze of treatment rooms. A bathroom. And then a narrow door, like the door to a broom closet, this one the entry to another world. She opened it and continued and the light was dimmer now and she walked down some stairs and then she started to hear screaming from behind her, from the woman with the stiff bangs. Once she started screaming Neva turned around and yelled at her to get everyone out, get everyone upstairs out. Neva kept going and back here was a darker hive of rooms, and noises came from behind closed doors. A door opened and Neva pushed past a man with no clothes, scrawny, his hair lank. There was more screaming now but she could not really hear it, she was flinging open doors and telling people to leave. No one appeared to be in charge but she knew someone would come and that's when the body rose from a metal stool and came toward her, a woman not with a black cap of hair but with a slicing voice. Neva pushed her into a small room and locked the door from outside and the woman banged and banged on the door and screamed that she had her phone and was calling the police. Neva looked quickly at each girl. She had never looked away from anything but now she looked away as soon as she identified that they were not Poppy. Until there, curled like a cat in a corner of a room, a ragged figure. Drugged. Awaiting use. Neva thanked the universe, which she felt did not deserve gratitude, but she thanked it anyway. She grabbed Poppy and pulled her up off the floor and pushed her out of the room and said, Do not look back. Keep going. Get out. Poppy stumbled and her bruised legs wobbled in a pair of tiny shorts and her arms were akimbo and she continued moving up the stairs. Go! Neva screamed. Poppy turned around. I said go, said Neva, just keep going. There was a stream of them leaving like the stunned and frightened passengers on a wreck. The woman with the stiff hair pushed her way back downstairs. Neva opened the can she had been carrying. She lifted the lid and started pouring gasoline over furniture, onto the walls, into the old stained carpeting. She motioned for the woman from the desk to get the older woman out of the room, to take her away, now or never. A fat man, bulging, not strong but large, grabbed Neva from behind but she elbowed him away and covered him with gas. The woman with the bangs had taken the woman with the slicing voice. They were gone. Neva ran up the stairs and lit a match. The last thing she saw was the face of the man, aghast, dripping, oily, a face detached from a painting of a mythic battle or rape, a shining head, screaming, reddened, running past her up the narrow stairs, fleeing into the salon. She threw the match down the steps and it landed on the dark carpet. The flames skittered and snaked and found one another and erupted in a frenzy, an inhuman, crackling mob.

What Poppy remembers as she runs up the stairs: the assault in the black room. Worse than she had experienced it at the time. At the time, the brain detached, protected, dissociated. As she runs up the stairs and her legs hurt she feels the deep bite of a mouth on her thigh. She feels the stiff grip of a hand around her neck. She feels the burn of the pills. The salty stabbing in her mouth. The metallic taste of liquid down her throat. The knees grip her head. The wild robots lunge and howl. The bite, the grip, the stab. This is what she remembers on the stairs.

It's there, running up the stairs, that she finally knows what has happened to her. She sees that her life has been deranged. She sees that it has always been deranged, but that she had not previously understood how mad, and had never realized how it was not she who had been insane but her circumstances. And now those circumstances, of birth, of environment, of place, of love, had caused a craziness to infiltrate her too. For her the madness of her everyday life had been mundane until recently when it had taken on the quality of death. Of an afterlife existing within this life. The insanity had been hidden for so long by money, by structure, by society, by walls. No one had seemed to notice. The lack of awareness seemed to her at this moment like a wall of steel that had hidden from view the obvious truths. Maybe someone had once told her to run away, but how could she have run away from everything she knew? Everything she loved? There had always been people in her life, all her life, who had been crazier than she, loving her, distracting her, enjoying her because of what they described as her wit, her inspiring intelligence, her superb, indefatigable sense of style. And it had been love, but not the love she had needed.

She doesn't know precisely when the image of despair became burned in her brain but it was at some point on the stairs. It's the image of her mother, rising, tubes dangling from every orifice, fighting off the wild robots in the dark room. Death against death. A battle to the end. As she runs up the stairs Poppy is running toward that image. She isn't afraid. She is running, reaching toward that image. Then it vanishes. Even death disintegrates before her eyes. The vanishing of that image is the image of despair.

For her it was when she reached the parking lot, that ugly expanse, cars randomly assembled, the slow reverse of a vehicle backing up and gently turning and driving away, that she had cried. She'd wept without caring if anyone saw her because she was crying tears of release. Not happiness. Not joy. Not yet. Simply tears of release.

Around her, the scene of the strip mall, the signs, the letters on the signs, their significant fonts each representing a type of promise, and the cars, one by one pulling away as if by a tide, or standing still, left on the beach, all around her the scene melted into a vision of nature. And as she stood there she turned around and with her mind she let a great gray arcing shield of water rise up, crest, foaming white horses running away, and crash down on the stores, the cars, the parking lot.

She would have to do this many times over the course of her life, many thousands of times, before the scene was wiped away.

———

When Poppy stops turning she sees that the wave in her mind is, outside of her mind, a fire. A real fire. Neva shoves her in the car and drives away.

The fire burned for thirty hours. No one seemed to know who started it. By the time the firefighters arrived almost everyone had left the scene. It had begun in the basement. They thought they had it under control but then the floor collapsed. The local papers contradicted one another on the exact timing of the fire, but they all agreed that no one was hurt.

36

H E HAD OWED them a lot of money and so he had offered
her to them, not directly, not in a way that she could
prove, but that's what he'd done. And they had taken her.
Why wouldn't they? They had dropped her off at the hotel in
case she had been needed. When she hadn't been—needed—
they had driven her in the van to the spa and had been waiting for the drugs to take full effect. She had not yet been used.
Not in the way they had intended. She had been able to identify them in pictures but they were never found. At least the
other girls had gotten away.

It's always the middle of the night. Buried underground and
then clawing her way out. Dirt in her mouth, the distinct grit,
the taste of wet soil. In the nightmare she is trying to speak
but the earth blocks her words. Dry fragments, insects, crawling to the back of her throat. She coughs up a spray of particu-
late world. She vomits mud.

She gets up in her sleep and walks to the window. She pushes
away the drapes and puts her palms on the glass. She is stand-

ing in a T-shirt and loose pants, facing the city, hands splayed against the night. Felix is watching from the doorway, the low light from the hall outlining his boy frame. What is it? he says. Why are you screaming?

She turns around. She can feel the mud sliding down her chin, her neck, sticking to her nightgown.

Why are you opening the window?

She widens her mouth but cannot speak.

It was a long time before she could speak to anybody. Especially to Ian. In dreams he stroked her hair, and then disintegrated into night. She cried for Steve. She cried for everyone.

Once in those nights of underground dreams she had left the apartment, walked along the quiet streets, and gone to the park. She lay on the grass like a beggar or a dog and listened to the end-of-summer birds as the sun was rising. They argued and debated like philosophers who had no better place to be. She had no place else to be. She felt the cold ground. She scratched through the vivid-green grass and dug up a black clump. She put it in her mouth. It tasted like the dirt in her dreams, but slightly sweet. She felt the sharp blades of grass pressing against her T-shirt. She kicked off her sneakers and pushed her bare feet against the dewy hill. She rolled back and forth, back and forth, over the wet grass, attempting to press herself back into the earth.

When she finally agreed to see Ian he explained. He had decided the night when he had told Alix everything, the night before Steve died, that he would tell her. Tell her all of it, in spite of Steve, in spite of what he'd made Ian sign. Papers did not matter. Only she mattered, he explained. She was his child.

She had already had to comprehend so much that this new knowledge was simply another blow that she had to absorb. She took it in. She held it. She was horrified, amazed, unbelieving. He explained that it was the reason he had ended it between them, and had he known what would happen to her as a result he would never have done it that way. He would have told her that first night he had known. He would go back and change everything if he could. He would spend the rest of his life making it up to her.

The rest of his life. Was that a long time? Or not that long? Time had taken on a new meaning. Time was eternity, perceived in little bits. The rest of their lives was a long time and it was nothing.

You're a survivor, he said to her across the table.

A survivor? She said she didn't feel that she'd survived.

You have.

Barely.

You will.

Please.

I will do anything.

There isn't anything for you to do.

There must be something I can do.

Like what? Give me back my youth? My sanity? My self?

The steam from her tea had stopped rising. Her hands wrapped around the cold cup. She tried to look at him for moments at a time but her eyes would drift, or dart, to the side, looking at the spot where the wall met the window, or focusing on the back of someone's nodding head. She felt a burden, a pressure to explain herself to him. At the same time, she felt it was impossible to explain herself. This only added to her feeling of desperation, of futility.

You say you would do anything for me, will do anything, but there is nothing you can do to protect me. It's too late. Everything is gone.

Please don't say that, he said.

Why not?

It isn't true.

Yes, it is.

You have your whole life ahead of you.

Is that a joke or just a cliché? She looked into the cold tea and then up at him.

It's neither. I mean it.

You used to be funnier.

They sat in a nearly empty café. She hadn't wanted to go to his apartment, or have him over.

Maybe I will be again someday. Funny, he said.

You act like things change.

Things do change. People can change. I've changed.

So have I, I guess. But I don't think I can change back, she said.

You can change into something else.

She blew into her teacup, pointlessly. She felt another wave of pressure, a demand to ease his pain. But it was time to discard that kind of unnecessary responsibility. She experimented with telling the truth.

I can't help you feel better about all of this, she said.

I know.

Her hair had grown longer. She wore a long loose sweater that covered her wrists, almost reached to her fingertips.

Her bony fingers curled around the cup. She looked into the orange liquid.

I'm not sure that I can ever see you again.

I hope that isn't true. But I understand.

The edges of her mouth wrinkled and drew a smile and frown simultaneously. It was a line of pure feeling, not happy or sad but living in the full emotion of the moment. It was form, not style, a form of strength.

She stood up. The scrape of her chair.

Where are you going?

I'm leaving now.

Please don't, he said. Please don't leave yet.

I'm leaving. I'm leaving you.

As she walked out the door her eyes squinted, darted, clenched. She caught sight of shadows on glass, the reflection of her coat, letters running backward, a sparkling wave of rhythmic chaos. The mumbled sounds of the restaurant rose in her consciousness and then quieted. Out on the street the reassuring traffic and random pedestrians calmed her nerves.

Ian watched her walk away as if she were a hidden piece of his heart that had taken shape outside of him and been hurled back with a violent force. Which of course she was.

She was gone and in her place was his love for her. The love of a parent. He let her go.

37

NEVA SAID GOODBYE to the family and traveled for a few months. Felix missed her terribly. He wrote to her, long, richly detailed letters. He insisted on writing by hand, not e-mails, and he spent forever choosing the stationery, addressing the envelopes, picking stamps. It was a healthy distraction from the collapse that was taking place around him. His world broke apart in chunks, a glacier cleaving. Zane Enterprises, with which he had never much concerned himself, became a headline, an accident from which to look away. Whatever pride he had taken in his father's business had altered into not shame but bewilderment, confusion, and concern. On the hall table there were always stacks of large envelopes from law firms. His mother threw away whole tablefuls of documents in disgust or rage or irresponsibility, he could not tell. Maybe they were not important documents. It was impossible to determine which ones mattered and which did not. He was aware that his father had died leaving a trail, a highway of litigation. He was aware that the company had to let people go, had to move offices. He was aware that things had not ended well. As always, he took a philosophical approach. He knew that in the scheme of things even the collapse of a company, a dynasty, an empire, would be washed away by time. But that did not change the feeling in his chest of a door opening and closing, swinging, unhinged, banging as the wind picked up, and creaking in the night. A mournful movement that was the beating of his heart.

No one knew exactly when Neva was returning so it was a surprise when Poppy saw her in an art supply store on Second Avenue, downtown. Neva had the same angular aspect, the same hair like ink, the same green eyes. Poppy had started taking drawing classes. She was purchasing paper, charcoal. Neva was looking at a display of colored markers. She explained that she was buying some for a little girl she knew. Actually, they were for Angel's daughter.

Neva and Poppy kept talking and they walked west together, for a long time.

What am I going to do? asked Poppy. What are we going to do?

What are we? said Neva.

They walked onto a pier. It stuck out into the river like a branch into the air. They stood on the end of the branch, dangling above the water.

Can't you tell me anything? Anything that will help?

I don't know that I can, said Neva.

Can't you try? Can't you tell me that you will always be here for me or that I will be okay or that you will never forget me?

Neva said nothing. Then she said: I can't promise any of that. Anyway, you're too old now for my promises. You make your own.

They both looked out over the water.

Why are you being so cruel now, of all times?

I'm not being cruel; I'm just being honest with you. I've always been honest with you.

Is that all?

It's enough. And it's what we have.

Poppy licked the tears on her lips.

What about hope?

What about it?

Can't we have that too?

I didn't say you couldn't.

But you said all we have is honesty.

Hope is not dishonest. Hope is nothing but honest. It's very strong. Yes, I think you should have hope.

Well, what can you say that will help me have it? Because I don't anymore. I've lost it. I can't find it.

You'll find it when you no longer expect it to give you exactly what you want, or even close to what you want. You'll have it when you see that hope is patience, waiting, time.

That doesn't really sound like hope.

Are you sure you aren't asking for false hope?

Maybe, she said, squinting, searching. I think maybe I'm just asking for love.

Neva turned to her.

That you have. You have all my love. You have it for as long as I exist, and you can remember it for as long as you do.

Poppy couldn't tell the difference between the water in her eyes and the water behind Neva's head.

So if I have love I have hope?

If you have love you have hope.

What about love conquering all. Poppy smiled. Is that true?

No, that's not true.

So what conquers all?

Nature, said Neva. Her hair blew out behind her like the black feathers of a bird.

Nature conquers all? said Poppy.

Yes, said Neva. Nature conquers all.

They stood hugging on the pier. You could see them standing and they looked like one person, their hair blowing around together in the wind.

EPILOGUE

IN THE CITY'S PARKS the trees stood holding the late-summer light, glowing with it, giant natural lanterns. Scattered blankets spread out over the lawns, covered with people, the afternoon flowing out from them in a soft current. Children walked by bodies of water and stuck their hands in the wet rushing. A kite jerked in the wind, spermatozoically. In the air was the contentment of people inside a mystery that they did not need to understand. The kite rose frantically higher, then softly fell.

The House of Steve fell not softly but with theatrics, like the final scenes of a complicated saga. Investments were unwound, properties sold off, debt restructured. A certain slide in social standing was endured as part of the loss of financial power. Some friends disappeared. Some advisers shrugged and stopped returning phone calls. Others flew in to assess the rot, pick the bones, and save some meat. Not everything was lost. Through the secular miracle of world markets, bonds, banks, rehypothecation, mortgages wrapped in credit wrapped in words, funds were salvaged, some real estate retained. Damage was done and yet the individuals survived. Even the worst of them, Jonathan, never went to jail. This was, like one of the conundrums Felix puzzled over, unbelievable. And yet it was true.

As it turned out, Patrizia had discovered in the examination room that she was pregnant with Steve's child. She never had a chance to tell him. But it was what she had longed for and in spite of the shock of Steve's death she carried the baby to term. She named him Stefano. Roman ignored the infant but Felix enjoyed him, its wobbly head, its alien eyes. Felix grew up quickly as a result of the birth of this sibling, and came into his own, found music and a sense of purpose. He learned how to make guitars. He painstakingly bent and molded the wood. He began composing electronic symphonies. He chose a new name for himself: Phoenix. He wrote a wildly ambitious orchestral piece and dedicated it to his late father.

One of the movements of his symphony is inspired by Hanshan's Red Pine Poem 253:

> *Children, I implore you,*
> *Get out of the burning house now.*
> *Three carts await outside*
> *To save you from a homeless life.*
> *Relax in the village square*
> *Before the sky, everything's empty.*
> *No direction is better or worse,*
> *East just as good as West.*
> *Those who know the meaning of this*
> *Are free to go where they want.*

————

Poppy often finds herself hearing this music, these words, in her head.

Alix fell in love, truly, for the first time. She had run into Genevieve a few days after the benefit for Ian's show, and eventually Genevieve left her husband. She moved out of the townhouse with the room of baseball caps—her children were grown and had left home—and into Alix's apartment. Alix finished the monograph on medieval art she had been thinking about her entire adult life. It was published. She saw much less of Ian. But she was a devoted aunt to her niece, Miranda and Jonathan's daughter, the precocious and surprisingly unspoiled Greta. Alix took Greta to the Metropolitan, the way she had taken Poppy, and the two of them sat on the steps licking ice cream, Greta's buckled shoes planted firmly on the worn stair.

Alix doesn't remember, sitting on the steps with Greta, the time she had met Poppy on the same steps, the chilly air messing Poppy's hair around, Poppy's forehead furrowing into a series of unspeakably pretty commas. What Alix knows is a kind of comfort with Greta—who looks much like Poppy did as a child, although whenever this is mentioned Alix says she doesn't see it—and with this child she feels an ease far removed from competition or tension, a second chance, a playful love.

Perhaps Greta was fortunate that Jonathan had lost nearly everything after Steve died. Short-selling, poor investments, the real estate slump in certain emerging markets. But Steve had saved him from total ruin, had put certain trusts and executors in place, ensuring that the benefits of various loopholes and tax advantages would soften any blow. Nevertheless, Jonathan's circumstances were reduced. And the company was destroyed, he would have said. Creative destruction, others might have countered. His losses tempered him and forced him to become slightly less selfish, less vicious. It wasn't so much the money as the social recalibration. At one point he had to ask Patrizia for financial assistance, which pleased her and irritated her in equal measure. He sought her attention at a family gathering, cornering her in a quiet room, while Stefano and Greta were on their way to Mars, packing lipstick, trucks, candy, and socks in a shopping bag. They were off. It was raining on Mars. They didn't have an umbrella.

Ian's show stole the season. The critics rhapsodized, audiences spread infectious word of mouth, a cult following developed, and even Angus, usually so spiteful and patronizing, praised it in a lengthy piece. It captured the moment. It made sense of the times. And it moved people. Night after night they experienced emotions coursing through their bodies. Hot reds and cold blues, cool greens and warming yellows, traveled down their arms, through their torsos, burst out the tops of their heads. It wasn't just sensation, it was feeling, and it was thought. The consolations of art could be found in a simple candle on a stage, a voice rising up, the communal catharsis of the gathering. Ian watched from the back of the theater as the players gave themselves over to the music, to the story, to the human beings watching them. Together the actors and the audience rose up, ripped outside of time, elevated themselves like beams of light, and, like flames, set the house on fire.

He talks to Poppy at night when he is alone. For now, that has to be all right. He doesn't expect her to care. He keeps talking. He whispers, he cries, he won't forget.

She does care, she does wonder, although she wishes she did not. She begins to care about herself again, to wonder about her self. She begins to put herself back together, saying her own name over and over.

The love they have is an attempt to express the inexpressible. There is no word for it.

Eventually, Poppy was able to forgive Ian and have a relationship with him. It was not exactly a father-daughter relationship. He had not raised her and she had known another father, Steve, whom she would always think of as her father. But Ian knew her and their connection grew and deepened when she finally allowed it. He helped her when she decided to apply to college. He listened to her weigh her options, complain about deadlines, talk through her essay, and resolve her plans. He did not pressure her. He did not advise her. He only listened. He listened and reflected, and communication moved between them like satellite intelligence reaching back and forth across oceans. They were relieved to discover who they were supposed to be to each other, and in time they moved forward. They moved on.

You have to keep going, he told her without saying it. He told her by showing her, by continuing to try. He let her know she would always have him, that he would always be there for her to talk to. You'll see, his actions said, I am here for you.

Poppy and Ian and Phoenix walk together in a park, near Poppy's apartment. They make an odd kind of family but it is an arrangement that works. Poppy and Phoenix loop their arms around each other's backs, Phoenix has grown, Ian ambles a few feet to the side. The distance between them is like the distance between letters, between words in a sentence. Irregular but with a logic. Relaxed and elegant in its simplicity. It makes sense, this empty space. It makes meaning.

Their shadows stretch out in the late-afternoon light as if for miles, like a wake running behind them.

When she leans on the railing and looks down into the Hudson River, Neva sees an emptiness which contains everything: the mountains she came from, this city she has made home, and the other rivers she visits when she travels. She goes back to visit Russia. She stares into the River Neva and sees the Hudson.

The river is always moving on, always emptying itself out. In this emptiness is the washing away of meaning to find the deeper meanings, the stillness, the unburning fires at the bottom of the river. She looks for them, catches glimpses, colors, glints of red and orange rushing past, turning blue, then black, into eddies, swirls, clear and cold.

———————

And like a river Neva moves on, flows forward, continues. She carries children. She carries Angel's daughter in her arms. She helps their family. She moves on from Patrizia and Stefano because Patrizia decides to do it differently this time, to spend more time with the baby. But Neva will never lack for children to carry. She finds a girl, back in Russia, on T. Street, and she saves her. She saves others, from Russia and from other countries. She works with people around the world, hoping to build a highway of freedom. She gives her life to the movement. She is a movement.

Neva walks along the Hudson River. She sees a vibrant violent calamity of light rain down on the water, smashing into it, sending electric radiance into the air. She keeps walking. She goes on. She feels her heart move outward like an army of roses, marching, ablaze, on fire. She runs with the strength of feeling. She rushes with the meaning of emptiness. She flows with resistless force. And she carries beauty with her.